Feng Shui
Love™

Feng Shui Love™

A NOVEL BY

Joni Davis
&
Lisa Hyatt

palari
Publishing

PUBLISHED BY PALARI BOOKS

A DIVISION OF

PALARI PUBLISHING LLP

Copyright 2009, 2010 by Joni Davis & Lisa Hyatt
ISBN 9781928662242

Library of Congress Cataloging-in-Publication Data

Davis, Joni.
  Feng shui love / by Joni Davis & Lisa Hyatt.
    p. cm.
  ISBN 978-1-928662-24-2 (trade pbk.)
  1. Feng shui--Fiction. I. Hyatt, Lisa. II. Title.
  PS3604.A966F46 2009
  813'.6--dc22

                              2009039552

Cover by W. Lauraine Davis

Published by Palari Books, a division of:
Palari Publishing LLP
Richmond, VA 23220

For More Palari Titles visit:
www.palaribooks.com

For Joan Bird,
our first editor and number one fan.

Acknowledgements

Thanks to the people who believed in us and the magic of
Feng Shui Love:

Robert Squillante and Jon Beckner, our personal Feng Shui Loves.
Thank you for all of your love and support.

Dave Smitherman, our publisher. Thank you for all of your
knowledge, guidance and patience, but most of all for not dropping us
when we sent you the wrong file.

Lauraine Davis, Artist Extraordinaire. Thank you for being our most
entertaining critic and creating the best book cover in history.

Sharon Baldacci, our good friend and mentor.
Thank you for all of your advice.

Our editing and design team: Arlene Robinson, Ben Miller, Wes Foxwell,
Lizzy Kolodner, Skylar Dempsey, Ted Randler, Lauren Rinker, Jared Rowan,
and Kacy Smitherman. Thank you for your tireless input.

Our junior consultants: Catherine Squillante, Kyle Beckner,
Julia Squillante, Lily Goodman, Karsen Beckner and Nick Squillante.

We also want to thank our support system: the Hyatt Family,
the Rickman Family, Ellen Quinn, John Milesky, Fred Tribuzzo, Betty Deluke,
Mary Anne Sparks, Pamela Armstrong, Kelly Madures, Tracy Ryan,
Cissy Skipper, James Johannes, Susan Budowski, Kathleen Long,
Alice Leone, Jane King, Susie Greenstreet, Carolyn Ilch, Donna Stallings,
Fran Rackley, Tammy Stevens, Kelly Goode, Sherry Ballard, Bennett Fidlow,
Kirk Schroder, Ian Titley, Heather Brown, Susan Hughes,
and the too numerous to name but very fabulous NetJets Family.

We would also like to thank the nice people at the Fairmont,
Nordstrom, Starbucks, and Kate Spade New York.

Chapter 1

You know how when you read your horoscope over breakfast and it says *Check your wiper blades,* and you think *how disappointing,* because you really wanted to know if the new guy who works down the hall has soul mate potential? But then on the way to work your wiper blade flies off, and you look around suspiciously for the camera? Well, that was how my life unraveled on Flight 767 to Barbados.

Richard and I were en route to a romantic island resort for our second honeymoon when I came across my March horoscope in *InStyle* magazine: *This month you'll see the true character of someone close to you, and it's not a pretty sight. Things look up when travel opportunities arrive at the end of the month, and money finds you too.*

I promptly read this aloud to Richard, who didn't even look up from the brief he was reading.

"Richard," I nudged his arm, "Did you hear me?" Realizing there was only a week left in March, I figured it was imminent. "What on earth do you think I'll find out?"

"I can't imagine," he replied nonchalantly. "But at least you'll have money and a nice trip to look forward to."

We both laughed, snuggled into one another, and I dismissed the horoscope as a message for some other poor Pisces. *But maybe their trip will be somewhere nice,* I remember thinking. *Maybe Italy.*

After landing, off we went from the airport to our hotel,

where we made love like alley cats in heat. Believe me, that hadn't happened in a *long* time. Of course we'd always had sex, but in an obligatory sort of way most of the time. Not unexpected after fourteen years of marriage, I guess. I was certain Richard felt that way too.

A couple of weeks ago, I'd heard him ask one of his friends, "How many times can a person still be awed by the Grand Canyon if they see it every day for fourteen years? Even the most avid canyon fans will eventually resort to mentally balancing their checkbook on the burro ride down."

To which I chimed in from the kitchen, "Well, there *is* more than one way to ride a burro, Richard."

So far, the trip was off to a magnificent start. . .phase two of our lives together. I called it this because the last decade and a half—phase one—had been all about Richard. First, putting him through law school, then getting him established, until finally he made partner last year. Phase two was my turn. A family. Oh, he'd always *said* he wanted a family, but the timing was never right in his book. So when I turned thirty-eight this year, I gave him a serious "state of our union" address. And Richard finally agreed that we should start on baby-making right away. Hence, the trip!

While we lay there in satisfaction, he gazed at me, stroking the length of my arm. "God, you're still gorgeous," he said. "Look at you, still as hot as any twenty-year-old. How about I call room service, order my little princess some strawberry waffles?"

"Why Richard, you haven't called me that in years," I said, admiring his athletic frame.

"Well, I haven't felt like this in years. It's like I'm falling in love with you all over again." He sat up and took my hand in his, "Lil, I know I've taken you for granted, but it's all about us now. And starting our family."

"Oh, Richard." I squeezed his cheeks with my hand, forcing him to keep his eyes on me. I blinked away the sudden tears.

"What if we can't. . . I mean, we haven't used birth control in over a year."

"Lily. . ." Richard grabbed my hand. "Don't do this to yourself. There's no reason we shouldn't be able to have a child. Women have babies well into their forties. If nothing happens soon, we'll check my sperm count. It could be me. Maybe I'm shooting blanks!" With this, he started to tickle me.

"Richard! This is serious," I said, retreating from his reach.

"So am I. Now that I've made partner, we'll have fewer distractions." He pulled me back into his arms. "Now, less talking and more fun stuff that makes babies." He rolled over on me, covering me with kisses.

Although I couldn't resist worrying about the possibility that I was barren and would never have a baby, I gave in. "What about my waffles?" I said through his kisses. He said something about us working up an appetite first.

In retrospect, I wonder why those red flags aren't visible to the human eye. It would be quite useful if they literally popped up on top of the offender's head. That way, even if you didn't know what it meant at the time, you'd know to start looking for what it could possibly mean in the immediate future, much like the check engine light in your car.

Those first two days were indeed a second honeymoon. We were like one of those obscure perfume ads on TV, you know the ones where the couple just rolls around in billowing white sheets, all sweat and passionate kisses. And day three started innocently enough as well, with Richard and me enjoying the blue waters of the Caribbean. We were engaging in child-like play, doing dolphin dives through the waves, when my bathing suit strap snapped. I rushed back to the room to change into a cute little pink number that promised to take inches from your hips and miraculously add them to your breasts (yes, we know it's scientifically impossible, yet we've all bought one, now haven't we?), when I heard Richard's cell phone ringing.

Knowing he'd been waiting for a call from opposing counsel regarding a million-dollar deal he was negotiating, I grabbed the phone and tried to get his attention from the balcony. As I waved my arms to Richard below, expecting to hear the sexy voice of his senior partner Mr. Schroder, I was surprised to hear instead the sultry voice of Lee Ann Byers, Richard's ex-Hooters Girl-turned-legal assistant. We'd met at several firm functions, but never quite warmed up to one another. I guess it was because she could never quite shake that Hooters Girl image. Oh, she tried dressing the part, but she just never quite pulled it off. You know those women who just seem to try a little too hard—they always wear a little too much makeup, always have a little too much hair, and always show a little too much cleavage. That was Lee Ann.

Now on the other end of the line, she sounded a little too much like Edie on *Desperate Housewives* and a lot less like the professional legal assistant she was supposed to be. I picked up a nearby pen, poised to take a message. I didn't dare jot down any of the vile accusations she was spewing forth about my husband. My head was spinning, trying to decipher the absurdities pouring into my ear. All the while, something in the hollow of my stomach churned and flipped. At lightning speed, she recounted all of the sordid details of a three-year affair she claimed to have had with my husband. My God, the woman should have been an auctioneer. In exactly forty-seven seconds I learned more about her than I had about Princess Diana in an hour documentary on the Discovery Channel.

She was rambling on about how she'd been living in their love nest, had recently traveled with him on business, and was now carrying my husband's child. She demanded to speak to Richard, saying she would not be put on the back burner, that she would not be used and tossed away like some old tissue. My head was still trying to catch up: *Did she say she was carrying his child?*

Somewhere during this real-life *Jerry Springer* episode on which I'd magically become a guest, Richard appeared. Noticing my ashen face, he asked me what was wrong; had someone died? I managed to hand him the phone while I looked across the couch half-expecting to actually see Jerry. Feeling my life unravel like a ball of yarn, I was only able to catch pieces of Richard's conversation: *it's over, not mine,* something about *his wife*—wait, that's me. What did he say about me? I couldn't believe what I was hearing. My Richard really *had* been having an affair with his legal assistant. I mean, it was insulting enough that this scenario was so cliché, like doctors and their nurses, or dentists and their hygienists. Now *my* Richard had become a stereotype with his legal assistant. Maybe that was the tagline of this Springer episode: *Stereotypical Baby Daddies.*

I kept waiting for the commercial break, when Jerry graciously offers his guests refresher makeup and snacks. God knows I could've used a little concealer and a diet soda, but there was nothing offered except for my bastard husband's philandering-deer-in-the-headlights look while he stood there with the phone pressed against his ear. When his cell phone finally clicked shut, I had a million questions I wanted to ask and a million obscenities I wanted to scream, but all I could seem to utter was a sound akin to that of a mouse whose leg had just been snapped in a mousetrap lever. At that moment, I think I would have taken the mouse-leg scenario over my own.

I closed my eyes and convinced myself I would wake from the horrible dream at any minute. And Richard would be by my side, ordering my waffles with strawberries and whipped cream just as he had the previous two mornings.

Sadly, that was not the case. As I opened one eye and looked at Richard, he explained that although he'd been involved with Lee Ann a while back, he was absolutely certain there was no way she was carrying his child. He spoke with what seemed like genuine sincerity, and had I not just seen the "Seven Signs of a Sociopath" episode on *Dr. Phil* the week before, I might have actually bought it.

It was at that moment I realized I didn't know this man at all, and that I'd spent the last fourteen years of my life with a fictional character named Richard Chamberlayne, and unfortunately not the actor. Although it did seem that my Richard was definitely a better contender for an Oscar nomination.

After several hours of crying, arguing and sorting through the entire demented mess, I packed my things and headed for the door. Richard begged me not to go, but with a final dramatic turn, I fixed him with a scorched-earth glare and said, "The worst part of this whole sordid ordeal, *Dick*, is that you actually let me think that horoscope was for some other poor Pisces when all along, you knew it was for me!" And with that, I slammed the door and forced myself to wonder where my mysterious source of money would come from, and where I might be traveling to at the end of the month. Anything to avoid thinking about the ruin of my life.

Chapter 2

A four-hour boarding ordeal and three cute umbrella drinks later, the reality of the situation began to settle in. I started to cry. Uncontrollably. Onto a honeymoon couple sitting next to me. The new bride tried to console me while I recounted the surreal events of the last three days. The new groom leafed lazily through a copy of *InStyle* by the window. *Wait, that's the magazine,* I thought, grabbing it out of his hands and frantically flipping through it while the two looked at me like I was nuts.

"See? Right there. Pisces," I sobbed, pointing to the horoscope. To which New Bride replied, "Me, too."

At this point, I have no explanation for my actions other than temporary insanity. I leaped across her and grabbed New Groom by the shirt collar. "So, what's she going to find out about *you*, buddy boy? Huh? Sleep with her bridesmaid? Just fess up now and save this nice girl a decade and a half of heartache!"

New Groom slumped in his seat and covered his crotch while I barreled on, berating the poor guy for several minutes. I was mildly aware of someone pulling on me, but I pressed on, hurling insults at New Groom while I repeatedly produced the cold, hard evidence: this month's Pisces horoscope. When showing it to him was no longer enough, I shoved it in his face, poking him in the eye and knocking an iced tea off his tray and into his lap. New Bride and the passengers seated in rows twelve through seventeen gawked at me in horror. Thank goodness he wasn't confrontational at all, but simply recognized me as the heartbroken lunatic I'd become and graciously chose not to press charges upon landing.

When I stepped off the plane at Dulles Airport, the chill of early spring in DC smacked my face, sobering me up and reminding me that my days in paradise were definitely over. On the taxi ride home, I observed the sprinkling of pink and white dogwood and cherry trees lining the streets, promising warmer days ahead. The sight of their happy, mocking blossoms made me want to toilet-paper them. I wondered what Richard was doing. No doubt trying to find his way home with no credit cards or money, since I lifted his wallet on my way off the island. I needed a head start, to get away from him for time alone to think.

As the taxi pulled in front of our posh Georgetown brownstone, nostalgia washed over me, remembering the day Richard first brought me here. He was fresh out of law school with a fat job offer in his pocket when he put the key in the lock and showed me our future. It was everything I wanted: high ceilings, crown moldings, and columns separating the living room and dining area. He practically skipped; he was so excited as he guided me through the newly renovated and thoroughly modern kitchen, the master bedroom with a sitting area and fireplace, and the extra bedrooms for our future kids. He had been absolutely giddy. And so had I.

As I stand before it now, I hate it. I hate him. I supported him and our dream through all those lean years, until he became the big-shot attorney he always wanted to be. Wait. Was that really our dream or just his? What happened to my dreams? I wanted to be a singer, the next Bonnie Raitt!

Tears stream down my face again, as I feel someone's hand on my arm. Startled, I jerk away, thinking Richard somehow beat me home. But it's just the nice little cab driver patiently waiting for me to pay the fare. I pull out Richard's wallet and pay him with cash, adding a fat tip. He smiles, and then gives me an un-expected hug, telling me everything will be all right. I, on the other hand, have serious doubts. He gives me a thumbs-up as he opens his door to get in. Then he yells over the roof for me to re-member that everything happens for a reason. I watch him pull away, motor sputtering, puffy black clouds of smoke trailing in his wake. Not unlike my marriage.

After fifteen minutes of sitting on the stoop, I'm finally able to move, and I open the door. The floor is littered with three days of mail, and the place has an eerie quality, like someone died. I cautiously enter and drop my bags by the door. Needing at least one thing to be normal, I start to sort through the mail. And there it is. About a third of the way through the stack is a bright, cobalt-blue envelope addressed to Lily Chamberlayne. *American Financial* is printed on the return address label, and through the plastic window I see, *Pay to the Order*.

I flash back to the horoscope and shake my head smugly.

I pick it up and wander into the living room, where I pour myself a glass of pinot noir and collapse onto the couch. I hold up the blue envelope and try to guess the amount before opening it. Six months earlier, Richard had transferred a rather sizable chunk of his firm's assets to this stock and put it in my name. He said it was for tax purposes, completely legal, just breaking up the bulk of his assets or something to that effect, and I didn't need to worry about the details.

"Ten thousand," I say aloud before tearing into it. My eyes widen when I see that it's actually thirty thousand! The accom-panying letter says something about a recent stock split and div-idends, and some other financial mumbo jumbo. I'll have to decipher it later. Right now, I'm too emotionally drained from having watched my marriage implode and collapse like the dem-olition of a mid-city high-rise. I suddenly have a vision of men in hardhats stationed around our room in Barbados. When Richard walks in, a portly one gives the word to blast over his walkie-talkie. I instinctively jerk, remembering the scene. There should be a requirement to post a notice before your marriage is blown to smithereens. At the very least, someone should have placed one of those wooden barricades outside our hotel room door. I feel myself tearing up again at the thought.

No. I am not going to cry anymore. What's done is done.

I reach over and turn on the radio, scrolling through the stations to find something that will brighten my mood. Smooth jazz would usually do the trick, but it reminds me too much of Richard, and I'm afraid in my current state that I might go all Tony Soprano with a fireplace poker on our expensive stereo. So I keep scrolling until I hear a familiar Bon Jovi song. I crank it up and sing along, "*You give love a bad name.*" My foot starts tapping to the beat, and next thing I know, I'm out of my chair and dancing around the living room. I grab the remote off the coffee table and use it as a microphone while I continue to belt out the lyrics with Jon. I prance from one end of the imaginary stage to the other, rallying the audience to clap their hands.

I finish the song with a high jump onto the couch, punching my fist in the air in time with the final drumbeats, then end with a dramatic bow, thanking the good people of DC for coming out and cautioning them to please drive home safely.

I wonder if people realize when they're losing their sanity, or if it just goes. Just like that. In a blaze of Bon Jovi.

Winded, I collapse into my favorite chair as an old Blondie song comes on. That was fun. I haven't had a chance to sing in so long, I forgot the burst of energy it sends running through my veins like a lightning bolt. Why don't I listen to this station more often? It reminds me of my days with Brook Bellevue, my best friend from seventh grade through college. Oh, the fun times we used to have club-hopping and going to concerts in the eighties. And any time I had a singing gig, there was Brook, right up front cheering me on.

I start tapping on the coffee table to the beat while thinking about those days when I dreamed I'd be the next Bonnie Raitt. Of course Richard ended that. "No wife of mine will be singing in seedy bars!" When I protested, citing my passion for singing, he suggested I sing at weddings. That was wholesome in his eyes, a nice little hobby for me while he was on his golf outings, which I now realize were probably hound-dogging expeditions for some younger version of Lee Ann. That bastard. Plus, wedding singers just don't have the same audience.

I glance at my wedding photo on the mantle and remember how boring our wedding singer was. When I think about it now, I liked the crowds in seedy bars. There were all sorts of characters that you just don't find at the country club. But I had just landed the job as Mrs. Richard Chamberlayne, and Richard's dream became my dream. My role was to support him as he became a successful attorney, for which I received a promise of two kids and a golden retriever in the yard. So, right out of college, I gave up singing—even at weddings—and got a job with a waste management company selling Dumpsters. Don't laugh; I made good money. Men will buy anything you're selling when you show up on a construction site in a skirt and heels. The sales skills I learned in that job provided us with a nice lifestyle while Richard was in law school, and later during his climb up the law firm ladder.

Brook and I grew apart during those first years of my marriage. She was never too crazy about him, and he was less than thrilled with her. He used to call her my crazy groupie friend, and Brook just called him Dick. Back then I hated it, but it's definitely starting to grow on me now. In fact, it was downright comfortable when I used it back in the hotel room.

Word to the wise, ladies, if your best friend doesn't like your new man, leave him. That's another one of those pesky "check engine lights." Don't ever discount your girlfriends' opinions. After all, who knows you better?

As for Brook, our relationship gradually dwindled to a couple of calls per year and obligatory cards on Christmas and birthdays. I miss her. She was the one person who could make me laugh until my stomach hurt when we were together. My God, I don't even remember the last time I had a good laugh. I need to call her, even to hear her say "I told you so." Because she certainly did.

As I rub the arms of my favorite chair, I can't help but remember when we got it. It's actually a chair-and-a-half chaise lounge that feels like you're sitting in a cloud. It's a lovely shade of mauve that Richard always referred to as pink. He never let me forget what a concession he made to have his buddies over to watch football in a pink chair. I think about how many times he and I sat in this chair together over the years, watching TV, and realize that our chaise lounging definitely diminished in our later years together. I guess that's why he turned to Lee Ann. I wonder if his ex-Hooters baby mama ever sat on my lovely mauve chair. I suddenly leap off as I envision Lee Ann in leopard skin lingerie perched on all fours on my favorite chair. I hope she gains a ton of weight with this pregnancy and never loses it! And I hope those big double-D breasts she's so proud of sag to the floor after childbirth.

Okay, enough with the negative thoughts; it's killing my Bon Jovi buzz.

I grab my phone, scroll through until I find Brook's number, and dial. When she finally answers, I can barely hear her muffled voice on the other end of the line through what sounds like a rendition of Loverboy's "Turn Me Loose."

"Hello? Brook, is that you?" I yell into the phone.

"Brook Bellevue here," she shouts over the noise. God, it's good to hear her voice.

"Brook, it's Lily," I shout back.

"Lily! My God it's been forever! Wait. Hold on, I can't hear you." The sounds of Loverboy get louder, and then a clanking sound like a door banging shut before Brook comes back on the line. "Okay, I can hear you now."

"Was that a Loverboy song?" I ask while refilling my wineglass.

"Worse, it was Loverboy live," she woefully informs me.

"You're kidding, are they still together?" I chuckle and take a sip of wine, remembering an Aerosmith concert we attended in high school. Brook finagled backstage passes from a couple of roadies by telling them her aunt was in the hospital with Legionnaire's disease, and it would mean so much to her if she could just have an autograph before she passed away. It worked. . .until one of the guys in the band started asking questions about how she got it and what the symptoms were. When Brook told him she thought her aunt got it in a hotel while on vacation, the guy freaked out and started ranting about how much time they spend in hotels and the amount of risk they must be exposed to. It was like watching an elephant run amok at the circus. Managers were trying to calm him down and someone was trying to give him a pill. The backstage area was cleared out, and the party was over.

Once outside, a magazine writer asked Brook what she'd said to set him off, and she told him that next time she'd just have her aunt lose a leg in a shark attack instead. She and the writer ended up talking for hours, and Brook's career was born. After that, we'd worm our way backstage at every show that came to town. We became known as groupies-light, because we didn't do drugs or sleep with band members. We'd just hang out, socialize, and direct them to the nearest liquor store or strip club, kind of like a rock star concierge. In return, Brook got an interview. She wrote reviews for local newspapers and magazines all through college. Afterward, she moved to New York and landed a job at a music channel as a real rock-and-roll journalist.

"Lily! You still there?"

"Sorry, Brook, I was just thinking about the time we went to Aerosmith back in the eighties. But back to Loverboy. Are they still together?"

"Unfortunately, yes. About 300 collective pounds heavier, but still together. I'm on assignment."

"What are you doing working with them?"

"Drew the short stick, I guess. Enough of me, you sound funny. Everything okay with Dick in DC?"

She always could read me as clearly as she could her *Rolling Stone*. And suddenly I'm tearing up again, and when I open my mouth, I can only manage a strange squeak. Why does that always happen when you're trying to be cool?

"Lil, what happened?" she asks. When I don't answer right away, she says, "I know tricky Dick couldn't have died, because you would've said something right away and not gone on about Loverboy first, like I would have if I were calling to tell you that Dick had died."

I have to laugh, which makes my nose run. I give her the condensed version of Richard and the baby-mama drama. She doesn't even say I told you so, which is another reason I love her.

"What an ass!" she says. "What are you going to do?"

"I don't know. I need time away from him to think."

"Well then, come to New York and stay with me!"

I quickly mull this over and decide that might be exactly what I need right now. "Are you sure? I don't want to impose."

"Are you kidding? I need you here. I just broke up with my own bastard, Mitch Ellis. He's vice president of programming at the music channel. Seems Mitch decided to replace me with a newer, younger model, but failed to mention it until I walked in on them in his office playing Clinton White House games at his desk."

"Oh Brook, I'm so sorry," I say, silently cursing all men.

"Yeah, me too, but only because it resulted in an unfortunate incident involving a lot of screaming, glasses breaking, and the much needed removal of a bad hairpiece from his head. Needless to say, I was immediately demoted and transferred to their sister station *80's Today*, where I'm forced to hunt down and keep tabs on the if-they-ain't-dead-they're-touring set.

"Well, it doesn't sound too bad, the eighties were fun."

"Yeah, *in* the eighties. Try listening to Loverboy at the Mautuck County Fair in the new millennium." Voices mingle together in the background, then she says, "Hey Lil, I've got to run. Loverboy's about to do their encore of "Lovin' Every Minute of It" and trust me when I say that you would *so* not be. I'll be back in New York in a day or two, so call me with your arrival time. I can't wait to see you."

"Me, too, and thanks, Brook." I click off feeling much lighter. The thought of spending time with Brook again makes me smile. I crank up the music once more, thinking how much fun New York will be. Thankful that the wine has finally numbed my senses enough to relax, I drift off to sleep with the old Flock of Seagulls song lyrics playing in my head.

I ran so far away. . .

$\mathcal{C}$hapter 3

I f only the alcohol buzz had lasted. After a fitful night, I wake at 5:00 a.m. with a pounding headache. I check my messages. Six from Richard, each sounding more humble and desperate than the last. He won't be able to make it back to DC until tomorrow, seeing how I stole his wallet. Good. I can take my time packing and get out of here by early afternoon. Since Brook won't be home yet, I decide to take a train up to Philadelphia and stay with my parents for a day or two before heading to New York.

I dread having to tell my mother that her cherished son-in-law is a cheating bastard. My father and little brother are both attorneys, so Mom was thrilled when I brought Richard home. I climb the stairs to the bedroom to start packing, and just as I'm wondering how to break the news, the phone rings. Caller ID says it's her. What is she doing up at this hour? I bet Richard got to her first. I reluctantly answer.

"Hi, Mom," I say.

"Oh darling, Richard called. He's worried sick about you. Where are you?"

"I'm at home, and shouldn't you be saying something more derogatory about Richard? Like, I can't believe that lying pig snot of a husband did this to my baby girl? He did tell you what he did, right?" I say, throwing myself on the bed.

"Now sweetie, I know you're hurt, but don't be hasty. He explained his indiscretion, and he knows it was terribly wrong, but

</p>

he swears it was just a few times, and she definitely *could not* be pregnant with his child."

"And how is he so sure? Because he wore a condom every time he fu—"

"Darling!" she shouts, cutting me off. "Don't be vulgar."

"And don't you dare defend him!" I jump to my feet and start to pace. "What he did was unforgivable. Put Dad on the phone." I know Dad will take my side.

"He's not here, but he's worried sick about you, dear! He retained Marty Janice, the best divorce attorney Richard's money can buy, to look out for his baby girl's interests in this sordid ordeal. Personally, I think your father is overreacting."

"No! Maybe he's just reacting like a caring father," I screech.

"Now honey, calm down. What Richard did was unforgettable yes, but eventually you'll be able to find it in your heart to forgive him. Remember, time is a great healer. How about a couple of weeks at a very expensive spa? I could come with you for support," she says with an audible exhale.

"Mom, are you smoking again?" I grab my suitcase from the closet and toss it on the bed.

"It's just one, and it's only because I'm so upset about you and Richard." She exhales again. I can almost smell those skinny little cigarettes through the phone, and of course once again I feel guilty. Mom always makes me feel like it's my fault whenever she smokes. Because she *worries* so much about me. To this day it's like a reminder that if she dies of lung cancer, it will be my fault.

"Mom, I don't think a trip to a spa's going to wipe away all his betrayal. Besides, I'm going to stay with Brook in New York for a while." I grab an armload of clothes from the closet and toss them on a nearby chair.

"Brook? Darling, really? I don't think she's going to give you much support on this. She doesn't even like Richard."

"Well, maybe she's very perceptive." I sort through the

clothes, discarding on the floor what's not going to make the trip.

"Just think about the spa. We could go to Sedona. They have the most glorious sunsets. Justin, my feng shui consultant, says they also have wonderful energy-clearing workshops."

She continues to rattle on and on about the effects of positive and negative energy. Usually when she's on a tirade, I have no idea what she's talking about, and this time is no different. I walk into the bathroom and tap my phone on the granite countertop.

"What was that dear? I think we have a bad connection."

"No, Mom. Listen. I'm going to New York. I was going to stop by and see you and Dad on my way, but if you're just going to try to push me back with Richard—"

"Okay dear, no pushing, I promise. Please come by. You can see the new koi pond we had put in. It's very good feng shui." Apparently Mom has traded in her obsession with faux finishing for feng shui, which has something to do with moving your furniture around to bring good luck instead of changing the finish from natural to warm umber.

"Mom, my marriage just blew up in my face, do you really think I care about koi?" I ask as I swipe all of my makeup from the bathroom counter into a cosmetics case.

"For the love of my ass"—her trademark phrase since I was in the fifth grade—"I'm trying to be supportive. You said stop talking about Richard, so I stop talking about Richard and change the subject to something benign, and I still get grief." She punctuates this with an even louder smoke-blow.

"I didn't say you couldn't talk about him. I said stop trying to push me back to him. You can say all the mean things you want about him. It might even make me feel better. This is about me, Mom. I'm the injured party here."

"I know that! But you can still look at fish, for crying out loud."

And still, I tell her I'll show up.

❂   ❂   ❂

After an hour of packing, I realize I'm going to need another suitcase. I go downstairs and look at my Barbados luggage still parked in the foyer. I feel like I might vomit. "Ok, be strong," I tell myself as I unzip the largest one. All of my brightly colored Lilly Pulitzer resort wear is tangled and balled up inside. I didn't really take the time to fold before I left the island. I flip the suitcase over and empty everything on the floor. "You clean up this mess, you cheating bastard!"

I chuckle at the thought of what Mom and her feng shui consultant would say about the negative energy of that gesture. My mother, Lauraine, has always been a bit dramatic, which for an easygoing Pisces like me can be draining. She lives her life like some matriarch on a soap opera, hoping that the story line never goes flat. And God forbid she not be in every scene. Dad's law firm is her very own *Boston Legal*, with all the drama of my brother Todd working there, as well as his wife Nancy. I thought we could avoid all that by Richard and me making our own life in DC, but I guess all we did was become new characters on another network.

I carry the empty suitcase back up to the bedroom and start rummaging through dresser drawers for appropriate New York attire. As I open the last drawer, I find myself face to face with our Fairy Tale Wedding photo perched on top. "Idiot!" I shout to the smiling couple, not sure if the slur was meant for Richard or for me. After I criticize my big hair and grab a tube of lipstick to draw horns on Richard's head, I place the picture in his underwear drawer, a subtle reminder of what happens when you can't keep them on.

An image of Richard and Lee Ann starts to seep in and I realize, as exasperating as she is, I do feel like I need my mommy at the moment. When I told her I'd be up on the late-afternoon train, she seemed thrilled. Seeing how Dad was out of town on a big case, it'd just be us girls. And she promised to only speak of Richard in the most insulting ways imaginable. In fact, she said she'd spend the whole day compiling a list, much like the Top Ten on *Letterman*. God love her, my lunatic mother.

I'm disappointed that Dad won't be there though. Technically, he's my stepfather. My real father, Walter, died in Vietnam before I was born. When I was two, my mother married James Stevens and he adopted me, so he's the only dad I've ever known. Even though Todd came along a year later, Dad has always shown a little favoritism toward me. Maybe he was just overcompensating so I wouldn't grow up with a daddy complex and wind up dating married men or dancing in a strip club, but he's always referred to me as his first-born angel. Poor Todd. He's probably the one with a complex. I've never seen a more ambitious guy; straight A's in school, star running back, and now top-billing attorney in Dad's firm. He married his legal assistant, Nancy, two years ago and they continue to work side by side. In fact, they have become quite the legal powerhouse.

I guess I should feel guilty glomming all of Dad's attention growing up, but really I adored it. Besides, Todd might not have been so successful otherwise, and I might have ended up like Lee Ann, pregnant with some married man's baby. I can't help feeling a little envious of my brother's marriage though. They have so much in common.

I wonder, as I fold a few long sleeve t-shirts and add them to the pile, if that's why Richard lost interest in me. I never even asked about his work anymore. All he's heard from me the last few years is baby, baby, baby. "Well, you've got one now, buddy boy," I say while forcefully folding a pair of jeans. Too bad Dad won't be there, he would offer to have both of Richard's legs broken for what he did to his precious daughter. The more I think about the sordid mess, the more I think I'd consider letting him.

While I wander around my beautiful home, packing up stuff for my getaway, it dawns on me: Why am I the one leaving? He should be the one out on the street. There should be some kind of consequence for what he's done, which should involve heavy suffering. Although I guess when I financially ruin him for adultery in our divorce, he'll be suffering plenty. But I want something immediate. Maybe I should just stay here and change the locks. But how will that make me feel better? Then I'd just have to wallow in the broken promise of our future together by seeing all the daily reminders.

Wow, look at that, I'm already thinking about divorce. *But what other option is there?* I think as I zip up all my suitcases. I could go watch a couple of sunsets in Sedona, forgive Richard, then come back to what—a marriage with no trust and every other weekend with Lee Ann's baby? Don't think so. I definitely need to go somewhere that I'll have a support system, somewhere I won't risk running into Lee Ann buying baby formula at the grocery store. So, New York it is.

I see through the window that the cab I arranged for has arrived. Maybe I'll still call a locksmith and have the locks changed before I go. . .a little spite can be healing.

I leave my wedding ring on the hall credenza on top of a stack of mail as a final gesture.

Chapter 4

L ater that evening I arrive in Philly and am whisked away to my parents' perfectly feng shui'd house, as Mom so proudly points out. She recently went on a big redecorating kick and hired Justin, a feng shui expert from New York, in an effort to "restore harmony"—her words—to their home. In her defense, the house itself does appear tranquil; it's the inhabitant's constant hovering that's messing with the harmony. The inhabitant's friends aren't helping either.

She must've taken an ad out in the *Philadelphia Sun* for word of my unfortunate incident to spread so quickly. I barely survive the next two days with Mom's friends, distant relatives, and neighbors dropping in every five minutes to see how I'm doing. I expected to drink wine and trash Richard while watching chick flicks with Mom. Instead, I'm bombarded with casseroles and people speaking in hushed tones while patting my hand. I wasn't depressed when I got here, but now I'm starting to feel like I'm attending a wake.

I start opening and slamming cabinet doors in an effort to release some of my frustration while searching for a wineglass. If I have to hear one more person tell me how sorry they are, I swear I'm going for the knife drawer. I have a vision of myself holding Ziggy, my mom's Giant Schnauzer, at knifepoint while warning everyone to step away from the casserole dish. Don't worry, I'd never hurt poor Ziggy. He's great. I'd only use him as a faux hostage to escape the madness. Believe me, he'd understand. Living full-time with my mother for the last eight years, I'm sure he's cased the knife drawer himself more than once.

On day two, my brother and Nancy drop by with the wonderful news that she's pregnant. Why couldn't my family be in the medical profession instead of the legal one? I could really use unlimited access to a prescription pad right about now. But I put on my game face and join Mom in congratulatory hugs and cheek kisses, while really I want to shove them both in the new koi pond. I wonder if Justin would say that's good feng shui?

Under the circumstances, you'd think they would have kept their news to themselves until I left. As Nancy rambles on about paint colors for the nursery, I smile and offer one of Aunt Betty's oatmeal cookies. Of course she declines, pointing at her expanded waistline and making a grand show of declaring that she knows it's just awful timing, but "Look on the bright side. Now you have a cute little niece or nephew to look forward to. A light at the end of the tunnel, so to speak." She concludes by squeezing my hand for effect, not knowing that the only light she's conjuring up at the end of my tunnel is that of a semi-truck heading straight for me—only she and Richard are riding in the car in front of me.

Okay, not nice, I know. I swear I'm usually not like this. I know she means no harm, really. The only consolation to this blessed news is when I notice Ziggy peering out from under the table with the handle from Nancy's new Prada purse in his mouth. At least someone around here can act out the passive-aggressive tendencies I'm feeling. While everyone else scolds him, I slip him some food under the table.

After dinner, the happy couple finally leaves, and I sit at the table to finish off what's left of Grandma Joan's homemade fudge. It's an old-fashioned melt-in-your-mouth slice of heaven, or a pound of heaven depending on your mood. I'm starting to envision a marketing plan for this stuff when Mom interrupts my thoughts by shoving a small pink heart and a book into my face. I have just enough time to see the title—*Feng Shui Love*—before her barrage ensues. She explains that the heart is made of rose quartz, a crystal that attracts love. I nod while savoring the last of the fudge.

"Honey, you must read this book right away and place the heart in the far right corner of Brook's apartment as soon as you get there." She hands me a cup of tea and proceeds to lecture me with her recently acquired feng shui theory that if things are in the wrong place, negative energy is created that can sabotage every aspect of a person's life. And that something in my town-house back in DC called my "love corner" simply must, must, *must* get some emergency attention.

Acting like a sassy adolescent, I playfully toss the pink heart in the air and catch it in one hand just to annoy her. I smile the fake smile I perfected as a teen and tell her I agree wholeheart-edly that the inappropriate placement of Richard's penis has in-deed created enough negative energy to blow my marriage to kingdom come, but I don't see how rearranging a few nightstands is really going to help at this point. My mother can't see, for the love of her ass, how I can be her daughter at times like this.

The next morning I jump out of bed realizing I'm getting the hell out of here today. On the ride to the train station, Mom keeps pointing out that maybe I could go home, rearrange my love cor-ner, and save my marriage. "Honey, if you go home now, you can spend Easter with Richard. I don't think your dad's going to make it home, so maybe the three of us could spend it with Todd and Nancy."

"Sounds great, Mom, but I don't think I'll be up for celebrating holidays next week, or even this year."

She offers to walk me into the train station, but I practically trip on the curb I'm getting out of the car so fast. After a quick hug, I bolt for the escalator and am settled into my seat within minutes.

Sometime later, I awaken with a jerk and a crick in my neck as the train has just stopped on the tracks for no reason that I can see. Public transportation, you gotta love it. It's been four hours since I left Philly. I could have driven myself and moved faster than this snail's pace.

In the seat to the right of me, a teenage couple is giggling and cuddling. To the left there's a family with a mom, dad, and two kids. I reach into my purse and offer the children a stick of gum. The cute little girl with blonde curls asks if I have any children. I reply no, but I'm going to have a baby niece or nephew soon. That only gives me an image in my mind of being an old-maid aunt. I get teary-eyed again thinking of Richard and all the broken dreams. Seeing my tears, the little girl turns suddenly away and becomes fascinated by the teenaged couple.

I have to stop thinking about this. I rummage through my backpack and find the feng shui book Mom gave me, thinking it will pass the time. I flip to the first "flagged" chapter entitled "The Love Corner." Leave it to Mom to put a red sticky note where she wanted me to go first. It describes in detail how this area of your home can make or break a relationship depending on how it's arranged.

Five chapters later, as the train pulls into the station in New York, I begin to wonder if Mom could be onto something with this stuff. I hate to admit it, but there does seem to be some logic to it. I shove the book back in my bag and decide to reserve judgment until I can finish reading it. However, I am open to blaming the demise of my marriage on something, anything other than the fact that Richard could have found Lee Ann more interesting and desirable than me.

Chapter 5

"P lease tell me I look as young as you do, you skinny blonde bitch," Brook says after she flings the door open. Barefoot and flowing brown hair, wearing a pink fitted t-shirt and low-slung hippie jeans, Brook looks just like she did in college.

"Younger," I say as I fly into her arms for a big bear hug. "At least nine days' worth, ten if it's a leap year." I feel a sudden wave of sadness bubble up. We used to celebrate our birthdays together until I met Richard. How did I let so much time slip away? Oh no, here come the tears again.

When I don't release her right away, she says in true Brook fashion, "All right, I know you're relieved to have escaped your mother, but don't go slobbering in my hair. I have to interview A Flock of Seagulls later tonight."

"Oh my God, you're kidding," I say while finally releasing her. "They can't still be around," She takes my bags and leads me into the sunken living room of the huge apartment she inherited long ago from her aunt.

"Sadly, they are. Damn that bastard rug-head Mitch." She drops my bags on a nearby chair and heads for the kitchen. "At this point in my career, I should be hopping a private jet to Chicago with Bono, not catching a bus to Scranton to watch another relic eighties band hang on to their glory days by a thread."

"It's got to be a little bit fun, right?" I ask as I follow her. "We always had a blast chasing down rockers."

"Yeah, but they weren't *sitting* in them back then." Brook opens and closes kitchen cabinets. "You hungry? I could order Chinese from the corner."

"That sounds great. I'm beat. Don't think I could do a night out tonight." I slump against the kitchen wall.

"So you're going to pass on coming with me to see The Flock?" Brook chides while she grabs two glasses and a bottle of white wine from the fridge.

"As tempting as it sounds. . .and sadly, that should tell you about the state of my social life. I'm going to pass. The last few days with Mom have taken a toll." I follow her into the living room and plop down on an overstuffed loveseat, then prop my feet on the coffee table in front of me.

"No worries, Lil. You just relax and make yourself at home. We'll have plenty of time to paint this town pink when you're feeling better."

"Isn't it red that we're supposed to be painting?" I ask while she pours me a glass of wine.

"It was red when we were twenty. I think the best we can shoot for now is pink. Maybe fuchsia if we're really feeling sassy." She raises her glass to mine and gives it a little clink. I let out a sigh, realizing we're climbing awfully close to forty. I never thought I'd be single and alone at this age. *What's next for me now?* I wonder. I thought my life was all set, and now I'm feeling genuine fear.

Brook grabs her phone to order Chinese. Looking around her apartment, I spot a familiar photo album in a stack by her chair: bright red, labeled *Italy 1986*. I grab it and flip it open in my lap to a picture of our senior class standing on the Spanish Steps in Rome. I never knew it, but Brook is quite the pack rat. I dust off another album, our college scrapbook: big, black-and-gold letters stand out, *RAMS 1990*. There are so many pictures of Brook and me: our first dorm room, spring breaks in Daytona Beach, our first apartment, at our favorite club, Rockitz.

While Brook's on hold she peers at the photos over my shoulder. "My, what big hair you have, Grandma!"

I laugh and point at one of her pictures saying "You planning to fly away with those wings, Miss Breck Girl?"

I continue to turn through the pages. Pictures of band members are pasted in between backstage passes and concert tickets. Then I see it—the one of me with Adam, the drummer from Kickin In. Queasiness begins. I have to set the book aside and take deep breaths.

Brook hangs up the phone and gives me a quizzical look. "You okay? You look a little pale."

"I think I might be sick." Cupping my hands to my mouth, I jump up and look around.

"Down the hall, first door on the left," Brook yells, jumping up and ushering me on. "And for God's sake, don't get any on my new bathmat."

I've never done that before. I mean out of nowhere like that, where one minute you're fine and the next you're blowing your cookies. Now I feel fine again. I guess I'm really not cut out for this high-anxiety stuff. I'm meant to lead a much more tranquil life. My birth sign says so. After making it back from a "clean" hurl—not a drop on the mocha-colored shag bathmat—Brook has replaced my wine with a cup of tea and looks genuinely concerned for my emotional state.

Seeing her brow arched in worry, I start to cry. A lot. In between sniffles I manage to squeak, "This is why I can't get pregnant."

"What are you talking about?" she spouts.

"It's karma, Brook! It always comes back to bite you in the ass when you least expect it. Don't you remember?"

"What?" Brook says, looking confused.

"The picture," I say pointing at the open page in the album. "Remember?"

She moves closer to get a better look while I continue to sniffle and grab the box of tissues. "I've tried to forget." I say blowing my nose loudly. "Every time I pee on the little stick and it doesn't turn pink, this is why." I give a dismissive wave toward the photo album. Brook starts to speak but I cut her off. "My marriage fell apart because my husband knocked up his trashy legal assistant. Meanwhile; I—his wife—have been hiding the same secret about myself!"

Brook looks even more confused. "You cheated on Dick?"

I push the photo album in her face, forcefully tapping Adam's picture. "No! My affair with the married drummer, for Christ's sake!"

She sighs, shaking her head. "Are you still beating yourself up over that? It was a lifetime ago." She puts the book aside. "You are not being punished for that now."

In between sobs I say, "Yes! I am! I am experiencing the bad karma from hurting someone else—"

"Who exactly do you think you hurt? Adam?" She takes a seat on the coffee table in front of me. "That guy was such a hound dog. You're lucky you didn't catch a disease from him."

"What about his wife? I hurt her."

"Are you kidding? Do you honestly think he told her? He was just relieved that you went and got. . ." She lets the thought trail off.

"You can say it. I got rid of it! I—the woman who wants a baby more than anything—had an abortion!" I turn away from her.

She leans forward and squeezes my knee. "Hey, nut job. Listen to me." She pulls my arm so I have to face her. "This is not the same thing as Richard. You were single and only 19 years old! You were naive, drunk, and seduced by the charms of some rebel rocker. Hell, he probably put something in your drink. It was the only one-night stand you had in your entire life. You didn't know he was married. So let it go."

"But what if I can't?"

"Lily, you made your choice, and regardless of what anyone may think, it was the right one for you at the time. Now honestly, don't you feel that way too?"

I grab a tissue and blow my nose, remembering how I agonized over that decision back then. But she's right. When I think about it, even now, I do stand by my choice.

"I do," I finally respond. "But that doesn't change my guilt or karma."

"Your guilt is something that you're going to have to live with. But karma, I'm not sure I believe in." She hands me my tea as she retrieves her wine. "I believe in reality. And I think the reality of you not getting pregnant has more to do with your lying, cheating, Dick of a husband being out of ammunition, having shot it all over town!"

I have to laugh at this.

"Now wipe your nose, and stop with this." She hands me the box of tissues as she moves back to the couch and picks up another old photo album. "We still have a ton of people to make fun of."

"How do you not believe in karma?" I ask while shifting my position to get a better view. "You're a fellow Pisces."

"You know I don't put much stock in that astrology crap. I just live my life." She leans back on the couch and sips her wine.

"But you can't deny how accurate they are sometimes," I say, taking a cautious sip of tea.

She snorts. "You come from a legal bunch. You know if you bend and twist and read between the lines enough, you can make any statement fit the situation."

"No, I don't think so. Sometimes a horoscope's just too dead-on to explain away." I tell her about mine on that infamous flight to Barbados. She shrugs it off as the door buzzer sounds.

"Saved by the bell." She jumps up and heads for the foyer, as I grin at her retreating back. I've never been able to convert her to my way of thinking. I believe in ghosts and signs, she believes in alcohol-induced hallucinations and plain old coincidence. She's always maintained that a daily horoscope could never be relevant for every single Pisces on earth, and I actually agree.

I feel a lot better and the smell of the delivery has sparked my appetite. Brook has always been good medicine. I head to the kitchen to grab some plates and napkins for the Chinese food, but stop when I notice my cell phone in the side pocket of my purse lighting up. The caller ID tells me it's my mother. With a heavy sigh, I answer.

"Hi, Mom, miss me already?"

"Of course, darling, but that's not why I'm calling. It's Richard. He's in the hospital having emergency surgery. Seems his appendix was in jeopardy of rupturing any minute."

My initial reaction is to grab my purse and head for the door. Without even thinking, I'm ready to rush to his side, not giving a second thought as to how he betrayed me. But then logic takes over. "Mom, is this some kind of ploy to get me to see him?"

"For the love of my ass, the man's having surgery. You're his wife. You should be with him."

I watch Brook go about setting out our food. The smell of orange cashew chicken wafts my way. I haven't been able to eat a decent meal in days, and suddenly I'm starving. Am I going to run to my cheating bastard of a husband's bedside for more heartache and drama? Or am I going to sit down to a nice Mongolian buffet with my laidback, supportive friend and relax?

"Mom, I can't, my wonton soup's getting cold. I'm sure Richard's in the hands of a skilled surgeon and half-a-dozen doting nurses. He'll be fine."

I hear her exceedingly audible smoke-blow. "You can't be serious. You really aren't going to see him because of wonton soup?"

"There's also orange chicken and steamed dumplings."

"Are you drunk, sweetheart?"

"Not yet, but I do have it penciled in after dinner."

"Did you at least put the heart in the far right corner at Brook's?"

I roll my eyes. "Not yet," I say with an exasperated sigh.

"Darling, why not? Don't be so selfish. If you're not going to do it for you, at least think of Brook. Since you're sharing a living space, your luck and hers are intertwined."

"Okay, Mom," I say, snatching my purse from the table and fishing around for the pink heart. "Brook, would you please tell my mother, before she has a coronary, that I'm putting the heart in the freaking corner?" I hold the phone out toward her while I walk the heart to the corner.

"She's putting the heart in the corner, Lauraine," Brook yells at the phone, then tears into a spring roll.

"Happy now, Mom?"

"Make sure it's the far right one, darling. What did you do with the other heart?"

"What other heart?" I ask with an eye roll.

"Never mind, darling. Justin said you'll find it when you need it the most."

I'm going to kill her. I hear her sigh.

"You know, I really don't think this New York thing is a good idea. Maybe you should just stay with me until you're ready to go home."

As she says the words, I feel something shift inside my cells. I'm not going home. No cooling-off period is necessary. What's at home for me? I see now that I was in desperate need of a new life, and New York is as good a place as any to start one. Besides, I'll have my best friend back, and what could be better than that?

"Good night, Mom. And tell Richard karma's a bitch." I click off feeling empowered and sit down to eat at the coffee table, where Brook is already halfway through the cashew chicken.

"So what's with the heart?" she asks.

"According to my mother and her feng shui, it will bring love into our lives."

"And you thought your apple fell far away from the tree," Brook chuckles as I give her a *look* through furrowed brow.

Chapter 6

It's been a month since I landed on Brook's doorstep, and the massive amount of exposed skin glowing on the streets below indicates that summer is on its way in Manhattan. I should be having a grand old time wandering the streets of New York, lazing the days away in sidewalk cafés or lounging around the park, people watching. At the very least, I should have gotten up early and headed down to Rockefeller Plaza to stand outside with a corny sign touting my undying love for Matt Lauer, but I've done none of those New York things so far. I've taken to my bed with the clichéd covers pulled tight over my head all four weeks, coming out only for diet soda, potato chips, and tuna melts.

I've become a TV junkie, watching nothing but Lifetime, *Oprah* and *Dr. Phil.* I'm starting to feel like I did in high school when Mom caught me smoking and made me chain-smoke as a punishment until I threw up. It worked, haven't touched one since. Even today, I'm pretty sure my throat would start to convulse if I attempted to kiss a smoker. Unlike cigarettes, I just can't live without my diet soda and daily visit with Dr. Phil. But I decide enough is enough and emerge from my hole today, a new woman. A glimpse of myself in the hall mirror doesn't support the "new" part of that claim, but hey, I've only been operating on this proclamation for 30 seconds.

I hear Brook on the phone while I make my way to the kitchen, brushing last night's potato-chip crumbs from my hair.

She doesn't sound happy. I enter her scene: laptop open, papers strewn everywhere, typing at a furious pace. She keeps repeating a steady stream of *yeses* and *uh-hums* into the headset clamped over her ear. She gives me an eyebrow raise when I breeze by with a wink. As I opt for the coffee instead of the diet soda, she gives me a thumbs-up.

"Okay then, I think I've got it all. Tell him I'll have it on his desk tomorrow morning." She clicks off her headset but leaves it attached to her ear. "Well aren't you a sight for sore eyes? Want me to make you some eggs?" She continues to type.

"Nope, coffee's fine for now. I don't want to jolt my system too quickly by giving it real food yet."

"Does this mean the mourning period's over?" She raises her eyebrows in a hopeful question mark.

"I think so," I say with a definitive head nod while I fill my cup.

"Good, I want you to try speed-dating with me." She leans her chair back with a grin.

"What? But I'm just coming out of mourning," I say, spilling my coffee onto the countertop. "It was only a month ago that I was on my second honeymoon!"

"Come on, I've wanted to try it ever since I heard about it, but didn't know any single friends to drag along with me. But now that you're here. . ."

"But I'm not single." I re-pour my coffee.

"Oh God, you're not going back to Dick, are you?" She makes a pained face and lets her chair fall back on all fours.

"Well, no." I fumble with my coffee mug, adding way more sugar than I usually do, ignoring her relieved sigh. Apparently, my answer isn't convincing enough.

"Thank God I didn't go on and on about what a turd he is," she says. "Then you get back with him, and I'm the turd for saying something. That would've been really awkward. I'm so glad I didn't say anything."

I swat her with a nearby dishtowel. "Okay, I'm not going back to Richard, but I'm not ready to date either. It hasn't been the appropriate amount of time, and I'm still married for Christ's sake."

"And what is the appropriate amount of time to wait when your cheating husband's already picking out strollers with his pregnant girlfriend?"

"I see your point, but I'm vulnerable. What if I just jump from one turd to another?"

"Well, at least you'll be covering fertile ground." She makes a drumbeat on the table. "Oh come on, it'll be fun. Just think of it as a practice run. There's no pressure to date any of them. You're just going along for me. At the very least, we'll have new material to laugh about later over a good glass of wine."

"Well, I guess it could be fun," I relent, and she gives an encouraging head nod. "And we could use some new material," I add. Another head nod from Brook, this one more enthusiastic. I flinch at the thought of what I'm about to agree to. "Okay you win, sign me up."

"Just did. Specifics are waiting in your inbox." She gives a final click on the keyboard, downing the rest of her coffee.

"This isn't going to be like the time you signed us up for that fishing trip in college, is it? You know the one that turned out to be one of those crazy adventure things where you feed sharks from a cage?"

"Of course not." She flips her laptop shut and stands. "They let us swim freely amongst them on this one."

She hurries out of the room, leaving me to wonder what Dr. Phil would say about dating this soon; although, I'd hardly call six-minute chat intervals dating. More like sampling cheese spreads from a deli tray at the supermarket. No one really buys any of that crap. And it will be a nice gauging of my market value as well. Looking in the mirror today is definitely not going to give an accurate reading of my man-magnet potential, seeing how I haven't bathed in days. But a little jaunt around an assortment tray of eligible men could give me a good idea of what I still possess that's working like it should.

After a day spent easing back into life with Starbucks and a stroll through the park, I'm feeling a little more optimistic. Ahh! May in New York City. Certainly makes it easy to feel this way, even though it's hard to ignore all the happy couples walking by holding hands, some pushing baby carriages. I've been reading more of the book that Mom foisted on me, and according to feng shui principles, negative thinking attracts negative energy. I *am* trying to push out all negative thoughts, including my ancient history. I'm even starting to look forward to the whole speed-dating thing. It's been way too long since Brook and I had an adventure together, and I think this will start that old train a-rolling again. Perhaps I've finally made it over some sort of hump. Sure, I'm still mad at Richard, but I don't feel so hurt anymore. Brook's right, I don't need to waste time mourning over him. I'm finally able to see things clearly, and I'm positive I don't want him back.

He has sent dozens of flower bouquets since I left him, which Brook's been doling out to the neighbors. He has called about a hundred times, but now I don't have to scramble to find my phone every time it rings, only to see *his* number flash on the screen. Brook showed me how to download a special ring tone for him, "Love is a Battlefield." She's so thoughtful. Now I can ignore his call without getting up. Just yesterday, he left a message saying he couldn't believe I was here and that I let him go through his surgery alone. I wanted to call back and ask where Lee Ann was, but didn't want to break my streak. I read somewhere that you can break any habit in thirty days if you resist the temptation that long. And I'm determined to break the Richard habit, because no matter how much I miss the security of a relationship, there's nothing left for me there. Even if Richard and I somehow got past his affair, there's no way I could ever accept Lee Ann's baby when that was what I so desperately wanted with him.

Oh my God, I'm nearly forty. . .*I* want a baby!

I pick up the pace heading back to the apartment, as an urgent need for action calls. I'm not sure what kind of action, but I feel like I've got to do something to jumpstart my life in the direction that I want to go. I spot a fountain next to a hotdog cart, and figure that's as good a start as any. I reach into my pocket for a penny. Instead, I pull out a pink heart. I look at it for a moment before realizing this must be the other heart Mom was talking about. What the hell. I kiss it, make my wish and hurl it into the fountain. "Bring me true love," I say aloud, "and hurry!" I turn to see the hotdog man giving me a wink and a thumbs-up. I smile back, but then speed-walk past.

As I arrive back to the apartment and toss my keys on the side table, I'm startled to see something gray darting from the kitchen. I squeal and jump up on the couch cushion, trying to figure out what just darted by. Oh, who am I kidding, I know what it was. I'm in New York City in an old building. What else could it be?

As I step carefully to the next couch cushion, I see a long tail slithering around the bathroom doorway. A shiver goes down my spine at the thought of how big the rat attached to that tail must be. Just as I'm about to crawl out of my own skin, I hear a key in the lock. Oh, thank God, it's Brook! I immediately broad jump across the couch, hurdle over the ottoman (realizing I should've gone out for track and field events in college instead of wasting time with the Photo Club) and prepare to land on Brook's back.

Only it's not Brook. It's a man! And I can't stop myself midleap, so I crash into the stranger, knocking both of us to the floor.

While I scramble to my feet squealing, partly from the rat and partly because I might have just collided with an ax murderer, I try to think rationally. Weapon, weapon, what can I use as a weapon? I grab the nearest thing, which happens to be a half-empty liter bottle of water from the credenza, and point it at him while taking a karate stance.

"No thanks, I'm not really thirsty," he says between chuckles while he rolls over and gets to his feet.

I screech, "I wasn't offering you a drink, you lunatic! I was telling you to stay back." I position myself in front of the door, ready to run.

"Stay back or you'll throw water on me?"

His question holds amusement and familiarity.

"I've been meaning to come by and say hi," he says as he brushes himself off and heads into the living room, his stride casual and unconcerned. "Gosh, Lily, you haven't aged a bit, and still wacky as ever I see." He bends down to rifle through some papers on the coffee table.

I remain in my protective position by the door. "Excuse me, Mr. Stranger Man," I say, snapping the fingers of my free hand. "Have we met?"

"Ouch. The fact that you don't remember me means that I must not have made much of an impression back then." He looks up with a grin but continues to rummage through Brook's files. I take a quick mental jog around my memory banks, but nothing. Maybe it's a trap. Maybe he's one of those clever criminals who appear to know you, when in fact it's just a ruse to get you to let him in.

But wait, he did have a key. "Refresh my memory," I say, and continue to stand guard by the door.

"Will. Will Forrester from Hayden High." He apparently finds what he was looking for as he tucks a folder under his arm and straightens up to face me.

It hits me, the skinny little chemistry nerd from high school. "Oh my God! Will?"

"Well, I think it was actually 'Weenie Will' to you and the

other cheerleaders who used to eat lunch in the quad."

"Oh my God, we did call you that, didn't we?" I finally shut the door and disarm myself by setting the bottle down on the end table. "But that was only because you were so, uh, small back then. Obviously you've had a growth spurt somewhere along the way." Even though he's lost the pimples and added at least a foot, he still hasn't completely shaken his nerdiness I see. I think he's wearing the same Clark Kent glasses he had in high school.

We lean in for an awkward hug, our collarbones pressing together only a brief second. He says, "Yeah, the skinny little geek finally grew into a tall lanky geek. Hey, sorry I scared you when I came in. I thought Brook would've told you I was stopping by."

"I guess she forgot. Plus I was already jumpy from the big rat that darted by just before you came in."

"Big rat? I can't believe a rat would come in here with a cat." He peers down the hall curiously.

"Cat? What cat?" I ask in disbelief.

"Ah, so you haven't seen her yet," he says knowingly.

"There is *no way* there's a cat in here. I've been here for weeks. I would've definitely seen a cat by now."

He smiles. "Not necessarily with GG, the Gray Ghost. She only appears randomly. Most people don't believe she exists because they never see her." He shrugs, adding, "For some reason, she seems to like me. Watch."

Will makes a cat call with a "here kitty, kitty" and sure enough, a big fat gray cat appears in the hallway and saunters our way.

"Told you," he says triumphantly. "I think she's just really grateful because I sprung her from the rescue shelter last year, and brought her to Brook *and* this cushy lifestyle."

"I can't believe it, there's really a cat in here," I say as she gives me a wide berth and wanders over to Will, giving his leg a head-butt. "But I've never seen a food bowl anywhere."

"Yeah, I think she'll only eat in the closet, and the litter box is in Brook's bathroom behind the door." He bends down to pet her, letting out a little sneeze.

"That's weird," I say, while thinking what's really weird is that Will seems to have such intimate knowledge of Brook's apartment, yet she never mentioned him to me.

"Well, I've got to run," he says, giving his watch a glance. "Tell Brook I'll catch up with her later about the benefit." He breezes by with a quick shoulder squeeze then stops by the front door. "I'm really sorry about your husband, Lily. Hang in there. See you later." He gives a little wave before shutting the door behind him.

The cat immediately disappears down the hall while I try to process the idea—no, the *fact* that Brook has a thing going with Weenie Will from chemistry class. Cool, rocker-chick Brook and Weenie Will?

In all fairness, he's not so weenie anymore. He must be at least six-two, with noticeable definition in his arms. But he still seems two pens short of breaking out a pocket protector. Not bad I guess, but definitely not Brook either. No wonder she didn't tell me about him. I can't wait for the interrogation to begin when she gets home.

All that strolling down memory lane has made me hungry, so I head to the kitchen to make a sandwich. The doorbell buzzes. Could Brook be hiding another geek from high school? I chuckle as I circle back and press the speaker by the door. "Who is it?"

"UPS," a voice replies. I buzz him in and envision a cute twenty-something dressed in a tight shirt and brown shorts bounding up the steps two at a time with a box balanced easily between his broad shoulders and bulging biceps. I open the door and step out into the hallway to catch a glimpse of the young Adonis sprinting up the final landing, only to hear the ding of the service elevator at the other end of the hall. The doors open to reveal an overweight, brown-clad fifty-something in desperate need of a bra. He wheels a trolley of three large boxes toward me, huffing and puffing all the way. When he says my name, I'm surprised the boxes aren't for Brook, until I recognize the loopy L in the address label. What on earth is Richard sending me now?

I have the guy drop them off in the living room, and then stare at them for a good ten minutes before finally tearing into the packing tape with a kitchen knife. Clothes, books, and personal papers, all neatly packed in giant zipper bags. I pull out one bag after another of my personal belongings and pile them on the couch. It feels weird going through my things like this, like they belong to someone else who's just passed on. Why did Richard pack up my stuff like this? I guess maybe he's laid me to rest already, that cheating bastard. He's the one who messed everything up, and he's the one who should be going through *his* things, not in neat little plastic bags but in trash bags strewn across the front lawn.

I don't know why this pisses me off, but it does. I mean, is he over me just like that? A few calls, a few flowers, then screw it, he's over me? He should be groveling at my feet right now to take him back. Not that I would, mind you, but a little Prada boot licking should definitely be in order.

I start to unpack in a huff, looking at everything he deemed important to me. . .my jewelry—well, what didn't end up going with me the day I left—my chick flicks, which damn, I could've used the last few weeks, and all of my favorite white t-shirts. He always said they all looked the same, but clearly they aren't. Why do men have such a hard time seeing any difference between a crew neck, a v-neck, and a ribbed Henley, yet bring *them* the wrong screwdriver out of a set of twenty exact replicas, and they give you a look like you have two heads?

While I pull the contents from the final box, I notice a man's sweater lying in the bottom by itself. Why did Richard send me one of his sweaters? So I can snuggle up with it when I'm missing him? Fat chance. I heft it up, preparing to fling it down the hall. *No wait, maybe I'll line GG's litter box with it.*

I hold it up, envisioning it strewn with clumping lumps, and I realize it couldn't be Richard's. It's too big. I give it a whiff, and sure enough, it doesn't smell like his cedar shelves either. Where did this come from, then?

I rummage through the contents of the box again, noticing a theme; a photo album from my youth, a scrapbook or two, some yearbooks, cheerleading trophies, concert tickets.

Oh my God, I remember now. It belonged to Sweater Arms!

Chapter 7

I met Sweater Arms on a class trip to Italy our senior year of high school. Brook and I had talked about it all year, about how we'd find our true loves in Florence or Tuscany—mine being a wealthy vineyard owner, hers the lead singer of a rising rock and roll band— and we'd live out the rest of our lives in wedded dual-country bliss. Brook came pretty close when she met a young musician performing at an outdoor concert in Venice that year. Leonardo De Duffino. Currently known as Leo Duff, humanitarian, world activist, and of course, lead singer of the mega-popular band Duff.

He and Brook were inseparable our last few days there. He wanted her to stay and travel through Europe with him while he was on tour with his band, then he would come to the States with her and try to get his music heard in America. Brook was all for it and I think her hippie mom probably was too, but her dad insisted she get back on that plane or he would personally drag her back by her hair.

Brook's parents were a real-life version of *Dharma and Greg*. I don't know how they are now, but back then, her mom, Riva, was a pot-smoking nonconformist who ran a small art gallery, and her dad, Jerry, was an orthodontist. They met in college, and somehow managed to stay together for twenty years before Riva finally moved out to New Mexico to live in some kind of hippie commune. Her dad moved to Chicago and remarried a schoolteacher with three kids.

Brook was devastated when Leo did finally make it stateside later that year but never called. He instead seemed to have developed a penchant for Playmates and alcohol, and was no longer the down-to-earth rocker who stole her heart in Venice. Like most musicians, he burned out early, had a stint in rehab, and tore through his money faster than a spoiled socialite. He made a major comeback a decade ago by restructuring his band and donating a large portion of his record proceeds to various world plights. He also married a nice Italian girl who didn't feel the need to parade around with two giant silicone cantaloupes attached to her chest. Today he's the most coveted interview in Brook's industry, but her pride keeps her from going after it. I told her she shouldn't let that stop her because he probably doesn't even remember her anyway. If I recall correctly, she threw an olive at me. Or was it an ice cube?

Doesn't matter; the point is true love evaded us that magical summer in Italy, although I can't help but smile now as I drape the old sweater across my shoulders.

Sweater Arms and I first met on the Air Italy flight back home. We were halfway across the ocean when we hit severe turbulence. The plane kept pitching and dropping; people around us were saying prayers and singing hymns. Even the flight attendants were white-faced with fear. Once, the plane tipped so hard a cart full of coffee mugs turned over, sending shrieks throughout the plane and the flight crew scrambling to their seats.

Everyone around us was getting sick. When the woman seated by the window in our row started to projectile vomit, Brook and I made a dash for a vacant row behind us. That's when I found it—a beautiful olive green cashmere sweater with two maroon stripes down the sleeve. There was a break in the stripes near the cuff, where some sort of insignia was stitched. I wrapped the sleeves around my shoulders, and was somehow able to fall asleep. I dreamed the most vivid dream of a man standing behind me, his arms wrapped loosely around my waist. I never saw his face. I just experienced the feel of his soft, sweater-clad arms interlocked with my own; giving me the most intense feeling of happiness and security I've ever felt, before or since. This feeling became my vision of what a perfect relationship would feel like. And I knew right then, those arms belonged to my soul mate.

I awoke to find the sweater had slipped down around my waist and the plane descending calmly into Philadelphia. Brook was doing a crossword puzzle in the aisle seat. I told her about my dream, and vowed to find my "Sweater Arms," as he would be affectionately known from then on. She wished me luck; then pointed out, "Before you start going door to door in search of the Cinderfella who might fit your sweater, you should consider that maybe he was not wearing a sweater at all, but just has really hairy arms."

Ah, to be eighteen again and so full of hope. My soul mate search lasted exactly sixty-four days before I became obsessed with something else; I think it was the spiral perm. Now I wish I'd stuck to the search for ole Sweater Arms. It would've saved me countless hair follicles, not to mention the embarrassment of that rotten-egg smell you'd have for weeks after getting one of those perms. I remember once, on a romantic midnight swim with Kenny Allsdale, the smell was so intense he thought I kept passing gas. As for the sweater, I did have every boyfriend in college try it on at one time or another. But overall, I think I stopped believing in the magic of it.

Then I met Richard, an Ivy League graduate headed to law school from a good Virginia family rich in Old South traditions and manners, with a promising future for some lucky bride. And though he wasn't my type back then, my parents couldn't encourage the relationship enough. Mom especially, was in favor of my settling down and abandoning my singing aspirations. For some reason, she was always more opposed to my singing than Richard.

The first time we went out, I managed to maneuver myself in front of him while we gazed out at the waterfront from the restaurant's patio. When he slipped his arms around my waist that first time, there was none of the magic from my dream, and his sweater was actually kind of scratchy on my skin. But I figured it was time to let go of silly childhood fantasies and start living in reality. So I tossed aside my old soul mate theory and forged ahead with a new dream; wife and eventually mother. As our relationship grew, so did my love for him, even though I never felt what I had dreamed about. By the time we got married I was twenty-four and happy to become his wife. Richard was great; he was a *catch*. So what if he wasn't Sweater Arms?

Note to self: this is called settling. Don't ever do it again!

I hear a key in the lock and look up to see Brook step in carrying a grocery bag and a handful of mail. I can't help but give her my best Cheshire Cat grin from where I'm sitting.

"What?" she asks with a chuckle, and casts curious eyes on the boxes.

"Oh nothing," I say from my spot on the floor. "Didn't know you had a cat."

"You actually saw GG?" She stops to drop the mail on the table.

"Yeah," I say, and continue to rifle through the box.

"Really, where?" Brook carries the grocery bag to the kitchen.

"She came right out," I say, shuffling some items around in the box. "That is, when your boyfriend called her."

She lets out a hearty laugh while she opens and closes a cabinet. "Yeah right, Will and me? Good one." She reappears with a handful of pretzels. "What's all this?" She pops one in her mouth.

"What's all this? What's with *you* dating Weenie Will without telling me?"

"I'm not dating Will. And he's not so weenie anymore, in case you didn't notice."

"I did notice." I hold out my hand for a pretzel. "I also noticed that he seems to have intimate knowledge about your bathroom, not to mention that you have a cat together."

"Believe me, GG doesn't belong to anyone. She merely tolerates me because I feed her. Will rescued her from the shelter exactly ten minutes before her scheduled permanent nap, which would explain her crush on him. But he's allergic, so he brought her here."

"How do you explain his key status, and why have you never mentioned him?" I ask while I drape *the* sweater around my shoulders.

"He just feeds the cat when I'm gone, and I *have* mentioned him. Several times. Remember I told you he solicits funds for a research unit in the oncology wing where he works? That he's planning a big holiday fundraiser?"

"But I didn't know 'Will' was *Weenie* Will."

"I thought I told you when his twin sister died a few years ago that I saw him at the funeral and he lives in New York, and we started running into each other. Any of this ringing a bell?"

"Oh my God," I gasp. "That's right, his sister died of a brain tumor. And I guess it just slipped past me that Will was Weenie Will." I slump back against the couch, remembering his sister.

"Yeah, Wendy was living here and Will was living in San Jose. When she took a turn for the worse, he came here to help. His fiancé starting playing squash to fill the lonely nights back in California, and ended up squashing his heart when she called off their engagement to marry someone she met on the court."

Ouch. At least she wasn't pregnant, I think to myself.

"He sold his company, came here, and now does some kind of computer consulting work and started 'Wendy's Wish,' a privately funded research lab over at the hospital."

"That's so sad," I say, pulling my sweater closer around me.

"It is. Why are you wearing a sweater? It's seventy-five degrees out."

"Oh," I jump to my feet and model-walk past her with it, "do you remember this?" I turn side to side.

"Um, are you referring to the goofy walk or the sweater?"

"The sweater, silly." I hold it out in front of me, then wrap the arms around my neck and pretend to kiss it.

"Oh my God, it's not. . ." she jumps up and grabs it from me. "Sweater Arms!" We both shriek, then she asks, "Where did you get this?"

I nod toward the boxes. "Richard, that rat bastard, sent me a bunch of my stuff. Can you believe the nerve of him? Lee Ann probably helped him." I shudder at the image of her pawing through my things.

"Relax, turbo, I had him send the stuff," Brook says, perching herself on the arm of the couch.

"You *did*?"

"I saw you didn't bring much, and I didn't want you to have to hear once again how sorry he is just to get your summer clothes. Can you believe he actually asked me if I'd convince you to get back with him?" She shakes her head at the thought. "I told him in my most pleasant voice not to worry, that I was already doing everything I could to convince you to get back at him, he just needed to be patient."

I had to laugh, knowing how much it must've irked him to ask her for a favor in the first place. "What did he say?"

"Something to the effect that he was *not* going to lower himself to exchanging childish insults with me. I told him to shove it and just send the stuff."

"Thanks," I say as I give her a hug.

"Okay you nut. Now, how did you still have the sweater?"

"It was in a box of memorabilia. I haven't seen it since before we got married. But I think it's a sign, don't you? That it would turn up now?" I dance around the coffee table with my sweater.

"Yeah. A sign that you're still crazy after all these years."

Chapter 8

The next morning I roll out of bed and trip over a pile of indiscernible stuff. I have *got* to start putting my things away if I'm really going to stay here, which I am. Brook and I discussed it last night, and we agree that it would just be crazy to try to find a place of my own when she has this big apartment all to herself. So it's official; I'm living in New York. Wow, just like *That Girl*. All I need now are some groovy outfits and a journalist boyfriend to wrap around my finger. Imagine that—me with a boyfriend. Not a lover, not a partner, not a significant other; but a boyfriend. How retro! I like it.

My cell phone begins to chirp from the chair across the room. I grab it, noticing it's my mother. "Hi Mom, I was hoping you were my new boyfriend."

"What BOYFRIEND?!" she shrieks through the line.

"Oh, Mom, relax. I was just trying it on for size." I fiddle with my hair in the mirror, catching the Gray Ghost herself in the reflection when she meanders into my room. I turn slowly, careful not to spook her.

"Well, take it off immediately. It doesn't suit you at all." Mom exhales with a cough.

"Neither does your smoking. Does Dad know, by the way?" I ask as I slowly crouch and reach a hand out to GG. She gently head butts it.

"Darling, I don't think your father cares one way or the other," she says through the sound of street traffic.

GG throws herself dramatically on the rug in front of me. For some reason, it reminds me of my mother. "Where are you?" I ask.

"Just a few blocks from you darling, that's why I called. I wanted to invite you to breakfast."

"You are?" I say, jumping to my feet, sending GG scrambling under the bed. "But I just got up, I haven't showered yet, why are you in the city? Richard isn't with you, is he?"

"Of course not. I had to come in to meet Justin, remember my feng shui designer from New York? I told you this darling, usually he comes to me but—"

"Mom! The point?" I interrupt.

"We're picking out the new fabric for my drapes. Why are you so screechy all of a sudden?"

"I'm not screechy," I screech before lowering my voice. "I just didn't know you were coming and made other plans."

"What plans?" she asks with suspicion.

I glance at the clock and wonder if I meet her, how much of my day she'll consume. "I was kind of planning on looking for a job today," I say with a wince.

"What?" She yells over traffic, "Why on earth would you look for a job? Richard has plenty of money, and you're not going to be gone that long."

"Well, Mom, I told you already that Richard and I are over. And he does have plenty of money to pay the hefty alimony that I'm sure I'll be getting, but I kind of need to find something to do with myself. Maybe I'll revive my singing career. . ." I tease.

After a long silence, "Mom, still there?"

"Sit tight, baby. Mama's coming." Dead air follows. I have to laugh. I would try to call her back, but there's no point. She'll be here within thirty minutes with an assortment of quiche and breakfast breads, so I might as well just enjoy the delivery service. I should find some sort of little singing gig though, just to drive Mom and Richard crazy. Ooh, Richard would die if he knew I was using his alimony to support my singing gigs!

When I come out of the shower a few minutes later, GG has emerged again and is sniffing around my dirty clothes pile. I wonder why she's all of sudden taken with me. Maybe she smells Will on my clothes from when we collided. The recollection makes me grimace with humiliation. What a lunatic he must think I am. I chuckle at the thought while I throw on a t-shirt and sweat pants, and then wander into the kitchen to make coffee. I can't wait to tell Mom about Will. I wonder if she'll remember him.

Once the coffee's brewing, I peruse the paper to make sure the world outside is still intact, then flip to my horoscope. *A friend or family member has valuable information for you, so listen up. Workplace dramatics heat up this week; try to stay out of the fray.* Okay, since I don't have a job, no worries about that last part, but I do have friends and family.

I'm pouring coffee when the door buzzer sounds. Oh good, I'm starved. I buzz Mom in and remind her which apartment it is. Maybe this won't be so bad. We'll just have breakfast together, then she'll be on her way, and I'll have the rest of the day to figure out what kind of job I should get. This is kind of exciting; being able to just completely switch gears in the middle of my life. And having the luxury of Richard's money, I can try anything I want.

Mom comes in with a flourish as usual, bringing two paper carryout bags of food and dragging her wrap on the floor behind her. I have to chuckle.

"Oh baby, you look thin. I brought quiche." She gives me a quick kiss on the cheek.

"Good, I'm starved. I made coffee." I dive into one of the bags as Mom abruptly stops. I look up to see her peering around the room with a wrinkle forming between her eyebrows.

"What's wrong?" I ask, wondering if she smells the litter box.

"Oh darling, you can't stay here, the energy's all wrong. Look at all these sharp angles. Very bad feng shui." She ventures farther into the living room, shaking her head.

Best to distract her before she starts rearranging furniture. "So, do you want to eat in here or the kitchen? I'll get some plates." I nod toward the kitchen, hoping to coax her in that direction.

Too late. She's already removed her laminated bagua card from her purse. Thanks to *Feng Shui Love*, I know that's what it's called. It's an octagon-shaped chart that shows the different sectors of your house laid out to the principles of feng shui. I hurry into the kitchen hoping to avoid her lecture again on how moving my stuff around can change my life.

"Is this her desk?" Mom calls out with a hint of disgust.

I peer through the doorway while slathering cream cheese on a sesame bagel. Mom is gesturing wildly toward the dining room, where the dining table has been shoved against the wall and stacked with multiple files, magazines and tapes.

"No wonder Brook never gets anywhere in her job; look at the mess her career corner is in!"

"What's wrong with using the dining table as a desk?" I ask through a bite of bagel. "She clears it off if she's going to have people eat there."

Uh-oh. Mom pushes past me and tosses her big leather tote onto the kitchen table and starts to unpack. I pour her coffee and arrange her quiche on a plate, then settle in at the table with my own while she goes on nonstop about feng shui. I couldn't get a word in even if I wanted to, which believe me, I don't. Years of being her daughter have taught me it's best to just let her race off on her tangents and nod a lot in response. So that's what I do, in between bites of my yummy breakfast. When she's gone I'll have to condense the word-pile into something I can understand. I won't admit it to her, but I am just a little interested in feng shui after reading about it on the train.

As Mom puts it, feng shui is the ancient Chinese system of living in harmony with our natural elements—the Chinese have been doing so for over five thousand years—and supposedly, by creating balance within our environments, we energize the life force or chi that surrounds us, which helps stabilize the yin and yang.

Yeah, that's great Mom. Fascinating, I'll read about it later, I think as I tear into another slice of very good spinach and feta quiche. While I wonder where she got it, she's saying how I should familiarize myself with the bagua, or at least carry one with me; at which point she hands me my very own purse-size laminated copy. Yay.

"Okay, first we need to find your love corner, since that's the area in your life in the most distress at the moment." She grabs her coffee and heads out of the kitchen.

"Find my love corner?" I ask while I spread a slab of butter on a pumpkin muffin. "I hope it's not anything like trying to find your G-spot, because that's still a mythical place to me."

"Darling, please, do I really need to know such things about my daughter?" she calls out. Through the archway I see her standing at the front door, holding up her bagua card and casing the room. "Besides, I have a wonderful instructional booklet and video if you're really curious."

"Mom," I whine, "I'm eating. And I really don't need the mental image."

"You brought it up. Now come here and look at this."

I begrudgingly get up and wander into the living room, finishing off the muffin as I go. She's standing in the middle of the room, pointing madly to the right-side corner. Bookcases line both walls there.

"I knew it. See—right there—this is why Brook can't find a stable, loving relationship." She makes a grand gesture with both arms toward the right side of the room again.

"What are you looking at?" I ask, not noticing anything at all strange among the bookcases. She takes me by the arm and leads me over as if I'm a child who's in trouble for writing on the wall and I'm pretending I don't see it.

"This! Look at all this clutter and old crap." She points to all the books and figurines and stuff that Brook has in the bookcases. Then she pokes around behind the furniture in the vicinity. "My God, is this luggage?" she asks, holding up a duffle bag she found on the floor.

"It's a duffle bag, Mom. I don't know what she uses it for, but yes, I suppose you could call it luggage."

She drops it in the chair as if it were soaked in some kind of contagious virus. "That's why all of her men have baggage." She waltzes around the chair and stops to lean on the bookcase. "And what is all *this* saying about her intentions?" She gestures to the numerous framed photographs of the various men and friends in Brook's life.

I notice a picture of Brook with Mitch Ellis taken at some event. It looks recent. I guess she just forgot to take it down. "Maybe that she likes her friends and harbors no resentment toward some of her exes?" I raise my coffee mug for a sip.

"Wrong. It says she still has connections to these people, and that she's not open to committed love," she says, as she gestures like Vanna White before settling her frame against a bookcase.

"But what if she's still friends with these guys? Is she supposed to burn all of their pictures?"

"No, darling, she can display them somewhere else." She starts taking them down. "Perhaps her friends-and-family sector, but not in her love corner. Which, by the way, is your love corner as well as long as you're staying here."

"But I don't even know most of these people," I say, taking the pictures from her and putting them back. "And besides, we can't just start rearranging Brook's stuff without asking her."

She takes them back down again. "Don't you want Brook to find love, dear?"

"Well, of course I do." I wrestle another picture from her.

"What did your horoscope say today?"

I do *not* like that glint in her eyes. "I. . .don't remember. Something about work."

"Well read it again, because the one I just read in line at the bagel shop said something about a family member having valuable information for you," she says with a wink. She's right. My God. . .and using my own birth sign against me. Are there no boundaries to the lengths she will go?

"All right then, carry on," I say. "But can't you work somewhere else? These are her personal items. You can't just rummage around in them."

Mom lets out a sigh and surveys the room. "Okay, I'll work on the dining room for now. But you and Brook need to read that book I gave you right away."

I won't encourage my dog-with-a-bone mother by telling her I'd already started reading it and was secretly intrigued. "Okay," I say, and head back into the kitchen for another cup of coffee. I guess Brook won't mind Mom cleaning up and clearing out a bit of the clutter. "Just don't do anything too drastic," I yell from the kitchen.

"The only thing drastic will be the change in her life," she yells above the sound of dragging furniture.

Chapter 9

I t's been a month since Brook signed us up for speed-dating, and tonight's finally the night. My stomach has disappeared, replaced by knots while I wait for Brook to come home. Until she reminded me this morning, I had all but forgotten about my promise to go with her.

I've spent the month of May settling into my new city and scouting out my new regular spots. I found a dry cleaner one block over with a nice little Vietnamese lady and a Starbucks around the corner with a hunky twenty-five-year-old. He's become my day-maker as he extends a muscle-bound arm in my direction every morning, offering me a smile and a compliment with my double mocha latte. I've also become a regular at the organic market two blocks up that stocks the biggest artichokes I've ever seen. And when Dad came up for a couple of days, we checked out a bunch of restaurants that are his favorites. Mom couldn't come. She was having the floors redone or something, so it was great to have just some Daddy-and-me time. Although he had seemed distracted, he was very encouraging of my new life here.

"You ready to go?" Brook says as she tosses her backpack onto the kitchen counter.

"You scared me. I didn't even hear you come in."

"Lost in thought, dreaming about your speed-date in shining armor?" she chides.

"You know how skydivers freeze up at the door and have to

be given a little shove—" Before I can finish my sentence, she has me by my waist and is ushering me toward the door.

"Here we go then, remember to keep your eye on the horizon," she says as she drags me through the living room.

I catch a glimpse of our newly feng shui'd dining room as we pass, and I must admit it looks magnificent. The dining table is now back in the center of the room, free of clutter and perfectly decorated with a runner and red candle centerpiece. Mom also rearranged the pictures on the wall and changed out one with something that was hanging in my room. Brook loved what she'd done so much she agreed to let Mom redo whatever she wants. My first thought upon hearing that? *Great. Mom's going to be over weekly to restore harmony to our lives.* As Brook pushes me into the hall and pulls the door shut behind us, I have a sinking feeling that my parachute might not open tonight.

❂   ❂   ❂

When we enter the hip eatery and find the place nearly deserted, I'm more than a little apprehensive. Surely we can't be the only desperate speed-daters in town. Maybe we're just early. Brook gives me a nervous look as we head to the bar. I plop down on the stool while she orders us a glass of wine from the bartender, who looks like a young Val Kilmer.

"I thought you said this was all the rage these days," I say.

"Well, that's what I read," she replies while she checks out sexy Val's backside when he turns to retrieve our glasses.

"He's too young for you," I point out.

"For a relationship, yeah, but not for recreation," she replies with a giggle.

Young Val returns with our wine and sets them down with a smirk, "First time speed-dating?"

Brook makes a lame attempt with, "Sorry, speed what?"

"Oh, don't be embarrassed," he says. "It can be a riot if you just let go and have fun."

Before she can respond, I chime in. "So you've done it before?"

Young Val bursts out laughing. "Hell no! Why would I have to speed-date? Look at me," he says with a slap on his hard abs, then wanders away to tend to patrons at the other end of the bar.

"Are we really that pathetic?" I ask Brook while I try to hide behind my wineglass.

From behind her own glass, she says, "Come on, you're not going to let some punk make us doubt ourselves, are you?"

Out of nowhere, a chirpy little woman in her early forties appears and shoves a form under our noses. "Are you here for the speed-dating?"

We look around nervously, and nod our heads. She introduces herself as Miss Mackie and thrusts two forms at us accompanied by those little two-inch pencils with no erasers and says, "Fill these out and bring them to the billiards room."

While we dutifully fill out our forms, we keep a watch on the door and see several nerdy-looking men in their late thirties or early forties enter and glance around.

"Oh God," I say as they trickle back toward the billiards room, "are those the men we have to spend five minutes with?"

"It's six minutes, and yes it looks that way," Brook says, and downs the rest of her wine. We exchange a look, and then both eye the side door.

"I can't see that far, is there a blasted fire alarm on it?" I ask. She gives a somber nod. Just as we're about to make a plan B, the chirpy Miss Mackie returns to escort us to the billiards room. My guess; this wouldn't have been the first time she's heard the wail of a fire alarm before she gets everyone seated.

As we tentatively take our seats, we notice all the glaring eyes on us. I hate to sound so conceited, but there is no doubt that Brook and I are definitely the best-looking things here. Not that

that's saying much, considering most of the people here seem stuck in some sort of fashion time warp, apparently from assorted decades. Brook and I are at opposite tables, and there are men already seated across from us. Mine isn't awful looking, just incredibly short. Tiny even. I think he could technically qualify as a little person. I'm not sure what the cutoff height is, or if there is even such a thing, I just know that he's on the petite side.

Tiny Man breaks my inner debate by extending his child-sized hand for me to shake. "So what's your name?"

"I'm Lily. Lily Chamberlayne." I reach across to shake, careful not to squeeze his little fingers too hard.

"I'm Sam, Sam Adams. Yeah, I know what you're thinking. I hear it all the time."

Oh thank God, he's going to address the petite issue right up front and is completely fine with it. "Little person is the correct term, right?" I blurt, somewhat proud of myself.

He eyes me with something akin to contempt and sets his beer down deliberately. "I was referring to the beer," he says in a huff.

Oh right, the beer! I'm such an imbecile, maybe he's not an official little person at all. "I'm terribly sorry. I didn't mean to offend you. I just, uh, well, I uh, obviously you're petite." Uh-oh, his expression tells me that "petite" for a man is not as complimentary as it is for a woman.

"Lady, I can assure you, my height has never been an issue before." He narrows his eyes and turns sideways in his chair. Oh God, do we still have to sit here when things have gone terribly wrong, or can we just scurry to the corner and wait for the bell to ring?

Thankfully, Miss Mackie raises a small bell and gives it a little shake. "Okay," she chirps, "let's get started." She dings her little bell again and sets a timer in front of her. Petite Sam glares at me from across the table.

"Okay, obviously we got off to a bit of a bad start," I venture, hoping to somehow salvage this first dip back into the dating pool.

"You called me petite!" he snaps back.

"Well actually, a lot of my girlfriends would love to be called—"

"It's not exactly the same for a guy, you know!"

"Well I certainly didn't mean it in any way as something derogatory. Really." I can feel my face begin to flush, and even I'm annoyed with how lame it sounds. Petite Sam turns away again, polishing off his beer and signaling for a waiter. Oh God, my first time at the plate and I don't just strike out, I have to hit the guy with the bat as well. And hard!

I eavesdrop on Brook's table to see how she's faring, and it doesn't look like things are going much better for her. Paul, as I can read from his nametag, is in the middle of a long dissertation about rabbit ears: the antennae, not the long fuzzy ones apparently. He's explaining the finer points of signal strength versus radio waves, while occasionally wiping the sweat beads from his bare head with a pristine white initialed hankie. He looks to be the original 40-year-old virgin, and my guess would be that he still lives in his mother's basement. Brook is smiling politely and nodding her head a lot. At least she hasn't alienated poor Paul. Of course Petite Sam stopped speaking to me for what seems like hours ago. Who knew five minutes could be so long?

Ding ding!

"Okay, well, it was nice meeting you, Pe—*Sam*." I extend my hand, but he's already scampered away. *Oh well,* I think. *Shake it off.* With an unhealthy amount of anticipation, I wait to see who will be next.

Unfortunately, my hope dwindles quickly as I watch Neal take a seat in front of me. His 1970s lime-green leisure suit doesn't turn me off nearly as much as his continuous snorting—his really loud, obnoxious snorting. I guess it could be a deviated septum or a sinus infection. As the minutes pass painfully, I learn that

Neal is in pharmaceutical sales, which leads me to wonder if he means that in quotes. Could explain the incessant snorting. When I mention that my ex is an attorney, he nervously asks, "A prosecutor?" He then goes on to ask how long I've been divorced. When I say I've only been separated two months, he takes his pencil and actually scratches me off his list right there! Like I would ever go out with him anyway.

I glance over to see how Brook is doing with her second contestant, whose name is Calvert, and overhear him saying he's a widower who sells water purifiers. Oh, and he has five home-schooled children. This time it's Brook's stubby pencil I hear doing the scratching.

Four wines and twelve bad dates later, we finally stumble out of the bar in a fit of laughter. Despite what seems to be representative of the available men out there, I still have hope of finding Sweater Arms. Maybe it's because I'm drunk, or maybe it's because I'm just not giving up. At least not yet.

Chapter 10

The next day, I wake with a hangover. Yet some of the wincing I'm doing is spurred by guilt. After our speed-dating debacle, Brook and I stayed up late drinking wine and drunk-dialing all the old boyfriends we could track down through Facebook. I think we might've broken up at least one bad marriage last night. At least I hope it was already unfixable.

As I roll over to crawl out of bed, I feel fur. It's GG, lying on the bed next to me—on top of Sweater Arms, to be exact. I vaguely remember laying it out on "his" side of the bed before passing out. I read some more of *Feng Shui Love* last night, and it said that you have to clearly announce your intent to the uni verse and make room for it. So instead of sleeping in the middle of the bed, I made room. I chuckle at the thought now as I reach over to pet GG, who darts off the bed and vanishes down the hall. "The Gray Ghost indeed," I moan.

I drag myself out of bed and step over my clothes from last night, strewn across the floor, and wander into the kitchen in search of aspirin and coffee. I find Brook, looking fully awake, pouring over a bunch of papers spread across the kitchen table.

"You're not going to believe this!" she says while making a note on a page. I wince at how loud her voice sounds.

"I can't believe you don't feel like ass," I say with a loud yawn while I rummage through the dishwasher for a coffee mug.

"I'm not as much of a lightweight as you," she says. "Remember, I've been single and boozy for the last decade." She raises her mug in a mock toast. "Besides, I'm too excited. I got an email this morning from *Urge* magazine to do a freelance job. They want me to interview Bon Jovi!"

After pouring some coffee, I locate the aspirin bottle in the nearest cabinet and count out four into my hand, dumping the rest back in for later. "Wow, that's great. Huge. How'd you land that?"

"I don't know. I thought Mitch Ellis had me blackballed by everyone in town. But this will certainly get me back on the road to credibility."

"Maybe Mom's little feng shui rearranging worked after all," I say, popping the aspirin and chasing them with black coffee.

"Well, tell her to get over here pronto and move something else!"

I'm surprised at the exuberance in her voice. "That's awesome news, Brook. Really. And I'd be so much more excited for you if I didn't feel like I have malaria." I rummage through the pantry for saltine crackers.

"Sorry about all the wine, Lil. It's just been so long since I had a partner in crime." She takes a bite out of a cream cheese Danish. My stomach turns a slow somersault when I get a whiff of it.

"You know, as much as I resisted the whole dating thing, I have to admit that I actually had fun last night," I say, finally spying the cracker box.

"Good, then you can go with me to the singles mixer this weekend at the Glave art gallery. I've heard it's pretty good."

"You also heard that speed-dating was pretty good." I take a bite of saltine.

"What? Neal the snorter not quite what you had in mind?"

"I still can't believe he scratched me off his list," I say incredulously.

"I can't believe the little guy didn't kick you in the shins," she says, and we both burst out laughing. Well, Brook laughs; my laughter is somewhere between a chuckle and a moan.

For the next half hour we again go over our scorecards from

last night, regaling each other with our favorite lines from each of the less-than-desirable candidates. We were supposed to turn the card in at the end of the night to Chirpy Woman, so in the event you listed someone who had mutually listed you, she would arrange the date. Seeing how Brook and I had absolutely no one listed, we decided it would be more entertaining to keep the cards for a rainy day or in the event of a funeral when laughter would be sorely needed afterward.

Now that I'm feeling like I might actually live and eat again, I decide to get dressed and order lunch and a newspaper from the corner deli. June is just a few days away so I really need to start looking for a job. Brook really likes the idea of me singing again, although I think mostly it's because she knows how much it would bug Richard. She says she has the perfect place. She knows the owner of a seedy little bar down in the village. "I might even give him a call later," she says on her way out the door.

Hopefully, she's just joking.

As I wait for my delivery, I sort through the thick pile of mail Brook left on the coffee table. I pick up a letter forwarded to me from Dad. Apparently Mr. Janice has fast-tracked proceedings and frozen all of Richard's accounts pending the equitable distri-bution settlement. I'm glad my dad is taking care of this for me. I don't have the stomach for any of this. There's also a note with a smiley face saying that he's swamped, but is still going to try to get back to New York to see his baby girl in a week or so. I know it's corny, but I love that he still calls me his baby girl.

I peruse the rest of the stack, mostly junk mail. Apparently, once you've signed up for speed-dating or online dating or any-thing that remotely screams *single*, your mailbox becomes crammed with invites to every swinging singles event within a hundred miles. It's like the Internet, when you accidentally stum-ble upon something risqué, and then you're inundated with porn sites begging for your business. Brook and I have apparently been added to the pathetic loser list, as evidenced by the pack of match-makers now circling us. Who knew this was such big business?

I'm about to throw them all into the trash when a brochure advertising an adult singles camp catches my eye. I never thought I'd say this, but it actually sounds fun. Camp Wiki Wonder offers a four-day weekend in upstate New York, consisting of three-legged races, chicken fights, volleyball, and canoeing: basically all the things you did at summer camp, only now as single adults. Hey, it might be fun to reconnect with my inner child, I think. Although I'm not sure that's what I'm really looking for in a man. I mean, don't we have a hard enough time getting them to grow up?

It would be a liberating way to celebrate Fourth of July, instead of watching the usual fireworks over the Pentagon with Richard. When Brook comes home that afternoon, it takes exactly three minutes to convince her to go, and she isn't even listening to me for two and a half of those minutes. Believe me, Brook will do just about anything these days if it involves my moving on and wanting to date. In fact, she says it would actually work out perfectly, because she has to interview The Go-Go's the day before in the nearby Catskills.

❂　　❂　　❂

It takes most of June to find the perfect camping outfits, so when we pack up the rental car—a sporty little convertible—and drive up the open road to adult dating camp; we're practically dragging asphalt with all our gear.

Halfway there, I start to hyperventilate. Sometimes I have these mini panic attacks when I realize I really am divorcing Richard, and that I'm going to have to have sex with someone else soon. When I express my fear aloud to Brook, she says I should be jumping for joy at the thought of having hot monkey love again. I tell her that things were hot again with Richard in Barbados...until his cell phone rang.

Brook lays on the horn, blowing at no one.

"What are you doing?" I ask with a startled jerk.

"Snapping you back to reality. Dick is done, remember?" She turns up the radio. "Now hand me the potato chips."

The rest of the way she keeps me firmly planted in reality while we motor along, singing old songs and eating potato chips right out of the bag. With the wind whipping through our hair, I let all memories of Barbados trail out of the car behind us. By the time we make it to the Catskills for the Go-Go's show, we're in full party mode and feeling every bit of our carefree eighties days. We dance to every song, under the moonlight of the out-door amphitheatre. What a blast! Brook was in such great spirits, she actually enjoys interviewing this eighties band. Plus it helps that the women are still cool. We finally pack it in around 2:00 a.m. and head for the nearby Holiday Inn.

Buoyed by the energy from the night before, we wake up early and hit the road for Camp Wiki Wonder. Sadly it's starting to drizzle by the time we turn at the dirt road indicated by the map. We pull over and put the top up, but we don't let it dampen our excitement and hope for our own personal fireworks display this Fourth of July. There's a meet-and-greet campfire scheduled for tonight and rain was not part of the plan. I had pictured us sitting around cross-legged all bohemian-like, singing songs with cool guys strumming acoustic guitars. And my hair was definitely not wet and matted when I crawled into the lap of one of the guitar guys for a passionate kiss. *Who am I kidding? I probably wouldn't do that with perfectly blow-dried hair either.*

When we pull in at the end of the road, we don't see any of the cute little log cabins from the brochure, only dilapidated shacks left over from the fifties, I'm certain. And outhouses! Out-houses for Christ sakes! Seriously, how can one relax and meet their soul mate when taking a poo in what is essentially a cardboard box just a few feet away? For the prices we paid to come here, you'd think they could at least afford indoor plumbing.

"Brook, this can't be right. Do you think we took a wrong turn?"

She squints at the sign, and then checks it with our reservation papers. "Nope, we're here, unfortunately. Guess we could still make a run for it and head for the nearest Hilton."

I am seriously considering this when I'm startled by a rapping sound on the passenger side window. A large wooly man motions for us to roll it down. Tentatively, Brook pushes the button.

"Welcome to Camp Wiki Wonder," he says with a grin. Either he's been chewing black gum, I notice, or he's missing a tooth. "You two must be Brook and Lily, the city girls."

"How did you know?" I venture.

"Well you're the only two on the list who haven't signed in yet. Just park over there, and we'll get you checked in." He motions for us to drive toward a shack with a split door, where the top is open and the bottom has a drive-in tray stuck on it as a makeshift countertop. We consider just gunning it and racing out of there in a cloud of dust, forever being the two mysterious cool chicks from the city. But before we can manage anything so *Thelma and Louise*, Mrs. Wooly Man, I presume, greets us. Greta, as she introduces herself while snatching our bags out of the back (yes, snatching) which I assume is because most people won't drive away without their luggage.

She manages to hustle us into the shack where we're issued our tent and flea collars. "Actually, they're flea bracelets and anklets," we're told, although they did come out of a box with a picture of a dog on the front. "For mosquitoes and ticks and whatnot," Greta informs us. I shudder at the thought of what "whatnot" could possibly be.

When we ask why it wasn't explained in the brochure that we would stay in tents and wear dog collars, Mrs. Wooly answers,

"You're paying to meet quality singles in a fun-filled atmosphere, not for quality accommodations." Apparently some people are so desperate they don't mind sleeping on the ground and relieving themselves in the woods just for a date. No way is Brook doing that. I look to her, waiting for her snappy excuse as to why we'll need a refund, so we can be on our way.

"Oh we might as well stay, just think of the re-tell value." She's actually smiling as she says this and signs our weekend away on the registration form.

What? I think. Then remember she'll suffer through almost anything if she thinks there's a good story in it. She is *so* wasting her talents at *80's Today*. She should be sitting on a couch next to Matt Lauer badgering efficiency experts and politicians.

"If we're staying, you're putting up the tent by yourself," I say as we exit the check-in shack and traipse off into the woods toward the spot indicated on our diagram.

❂   ❂   ❂

The next morning we wake to the sound of what I'm guessing is a bugle. Seriously, what did we sign up for? Oh, did I mention that it rained last night? All night. And what do you think two city girls look like after they've slept in the rain?

Oh right, you're thinking, *what happened to your tent?* Well, apparently, if you don't set it up right from the get-go, it doesn't withstand a little wind and rain very well. So why didn't we just pack it in and head for the highway? We were going to when we lost the car keys somewhere in the dark woods.

So as we crawl out from under our droopy tent, we make a pact to not be defeated by Camp Wiki Wonder! We agree to look at the positive side, and see it as a sign from the universe that we should stay. Surely our soul mates must be here for us to have endured all that we have, and we're only about nine hours into this thing so far.

Needless to say, the campfire was cancelled last night, so they're shooting for tonight instead. Hopefully we won't be too tired after all of the activities that Mr. and Mrs. Wooly have scheduled for us, starting with wheelbarrow races in an hour. I just hope I'm the barrow and not the wheel.

After a much needed shower and breakfast, we head to the top of the hill and anxiously await our pre-assigned race part-ners. It's a gorgeous summer day as the sun glistens on the shoul-ders of a gaggle of guys approaching. Maybe this won't be so bad after all. Nice builds. Cute. Word is they're lacrosse players. Brook and I try to look attractive while doing calf stretches.

The guys are almost to us and they are looking hot. Several are shirtless and I can definitely spot gym bodies when I see them. This is more like it. Wonder if they are planning on joining our little campout? Wouldn't mind making some S'mores with these fellas! Things might start getting interesting around here. As we continue our cute poses, I can hear them chanting. It's al-most like those cadences used in the military. Maybe we have some Marines in our midst! But as they get closer, I realize it's not a cadence at all. I know that song. It's from *Les Miz*! A couple of the guys wave excitedly as they pass by us. "Beep-beep, ladies," one exclaims as he veers around us. I take a closer look. Chiseled bodies, great hair, skin to die for—why, it's a gaggle of gays! For a split second, I consider joining their jog and singing "Master of the House" with them as loud as I can.

"They seem fun, but stay focused on our mission." Brook says, reading my mind.

As we turn our attention back to our group, my breath catches in my throat. The most gorgeous man I've ever seen is tying his shoe a couple of yards away. He looks up from his lac-ing and smiles. Please, oh please let this be my pre-assigned race partner and not a stray from the jogging gays.

"You wouldn't happen to be Brook, would you?" he says as he glances at a small slip of paper. Brook, who has just appeared at my side, smiling satisfaction, starts to speak, but I shove her to the side and thrust my hand forward to shake his.

"It just so happens that I would be Brook," I say with a hearty handshake.

"You would?" Brook says with a look. I ignore her as I feel his manly grasp.

"Mark Walker," he says with a smile.

"Brook, uh Bellevue, and this is my friend Lily, Lily Chamber-layne." Brook rolls her eyes and goes with it. Another reason why I love her. Mark stands to his full height before us, which is well over six feet. With his dark hair and olive skin, he could be a Greek god. Jackpot!

"So, what position is your strongest?" he asks. I don't need to tell you what's going through my mind while I gaze into his dark eyes and slip off into my own daydream, which apparently lasted awhile since Mark followed up with, "For the race?"

"Right, the race. Well, you look like you have good upper body strength, so I'd say you drive and I'll steer," Brook, who's been watching this pathetic scene unfold, lets out a cough-disguised laugh.

"Brook, dear," she says with a deliberate tone that you only hear in bad movies, "can I see you for a minute over here?"

"Of course." I give Mark a light touch on the arm. "I'll be right back."

"I'll be here," he says with a sexy grin. *Camping is awesome!* I practically skip over to Brook, who's sitting cross-legged on the ground now.

"So why'd you steal my Adonis?" Brook asks after I plop down beside her.

"I'm sorry. I don't know what came over me. I guess it's that old broken heart of mine trying to mend." I give her my best puppy-dog face.

"And that trumps my decade of losers?" she asks.

"I'm pretty sure, but I'd have to check the handbook to be absolutely certain." Brook grins and relents. She's just telling me to be sure to tell him my real name as soon as I get back, when a cute guy with longish blond hair interrupts.

"Either one of you Lily?" he asks with a slight British accent. He's wearing cutoff jean shorts and a muscle tee, and there's something about him that screams rebel. He oozes confidence and coolness. Very Richard Branson-ish.

"Lily? That would be me." Brook jumps to her feet brushing the grass from her shorts, and thrusts out a hand, winning by a photo-finish.

"Brad Green. What do you say we kick some wheelbarrow butt," he says while offering her his elbow. Brook links her arm through his and turns toward the starting line. "My thoughts exactly," she says, and smirks at me as the two bound away.

Things are on an upswing from there. Mark, as it turns out, is a doctor, and Brad is, among many things, an aerobatic pilot. Perfect for us. Mine the safe, reliable choice, and the nonconforming seat-of-his-pants one for Brook. Even the two guys hit it off like old school chums. I can't remember the last time I laughed like this. We actually fall over laughing mid-wheelbarrow when I drive Mark into a cooler of live bait. We lose the race, but fortunately not our senses of humor, which is refreshing considering Richard would've lectured me ad nauseam on the finer points of steering. Mark seems to get that it's all about the journey. In hindsight, I've realized how many things about Richard were so mismatched for me. Why did it take so long for me to notice this? Is it just that I chose not to, or did I just have nothing to compare them to?

Well, one thing is apparent: Mark sure seems a better fit for my sweater than Richard ever was. I can't help but notice this fact while I wheel Mark along by his firm thighs, watching his muscular arms knot up and release with every step he takes. In fact, I can already see him wearing the sweater as we gather at my parents' house for Thanksgiving, sitting in front of the fireplace, his arms wrapped around me while he recounts to my father the extraordinary job he did on the triple artery bypass that afternoon. *Mom, Dad, isn't Mark the greatest?*

By the time we sit around the campfire that night, Brook and I have all but forgotten about the name change; we just naturally answer to the other's name by now. When Brad says, "So, Brook, Lily tells me you're quite the singer. Do you know this one?" and starts strumming a familiar song on his guitar, I immediately jump up and proceed with a searing rendition of Pat Benatar's "Heartbreaker." Further prompting from the other campers has me running through a twelve song set list before they finally let the fire go out, and people start dispersing to their tents. So much for my romantic campfire vision, but dang that was fun! After a quick kiss goodnight from the guys, Brook and I wander back to our own tent wondering when we should straighten out the little name mix-up.

"I guess we should've done it right away," I say while practically skipping. I'm so energized from singing.

"Oh they'll probably be flattered and laugh about it. We'll tell them in the morning," Brook says while swatting mosquitoes from her face.

○　○　○

So why isn't there any laughter when we break it to them at breakfast? Why, instead, are their faces crinkling up like we'd just admitted to a serial killing spree and told them where we buried the bodies? This isn't how Brook and I rehearsed it while getting dressed in our little tent this morning. We had planned to just sort of confess the next time either of them said one of our names out loud. So when Brad asked Lily to pass the jam, I jumped in and said, "Sure." To which he replied with a confused look, "Thanks, Brook."

When I told him, "No, you had it the first time, I'm actually Lily," both men looked genuinely confused.

So Brook broke in with a giggle and started to explain how the whole mix-up started and then I jumped in to finish the story. All the while, Brook and I laughed and buttered toast and thought we were being endearing, but Mark and Brad's looks toured through confusion then annoyance before finally arriving at just plain mad.

Brook and I look at each other. We then reiterate how they should be flattered that we found them both so attractive we'd resort to such a girlish prank. But for some reason they're kind of stuck on the whole deception thing, saying that yes, it would have been flattering and funny then, but now it's just plain dishonest. "I can't believe you two think this is funny. I could never date someone so deceiving. If you'd lie about your name, I can only imagine what else you'd lie about."

"But it was just a little case of snowball-rolling, it was completely harmless," I defend. "And as time went on, we just got farther and farther away from the hill." I giggle.

"It just slipped our minds." Brook nods in agreement.

"My God, you are all just like Brenda, my lying, cheating ex-wife," Mark continues to rant. "Lies are not harmless. They hurt people."

Brad chimes in, "Like it might slip your mind to tell about your affair? Or the ten thousand dollars you spent at a cute little boutique in Milan while vacationing with your girlfriends? Something like that?"

Oops. Apparently these two have some issues to work out from their last relationships. This has somehow gone horribly off track. "You could hardly compare the two," I say, and shift nervously in my seat. "One is just a harmless little prank, and what you're implying is quite a leap from there."

The two men pick up their coffee cups and stand. "I think we're done here," Mark says solemnly.

Brad adds, "What a shame, I really thought this was the beginning of something special." And with that, they walk off together. Brook jumps to her feet.

"Oh, but it is special. At least you've found each other. Maybe you two could join the little group on the other side of the campsite!"

Chapter 11

I t rains all the way back to New York. The day, not to mention the weekend, is a total washout. *The Cars Greatest Hits* bounces from the CD player while we ride in silence. When I confess to Brook that I can't help but feel a little disappointed by our dating escapades, she growls, "Get used to it, kid. I had to."

It's a reference that never fails to make us howl with laughter. It's from my seventh birthday party when the clown my mother hired got completely sloshed on a bottle of Boone's Farm. His donkey got diarrhea and candy-coated the yard, so my mother refused to pay him for ruining my day and disappointing me. As he was leaving, he spat over his shoulder, "Disappointment—ha! Get used to it, kid. I had to."

Brook and I belt out the lyrics to "Shake it Up" along with the CD. We start head bopping and finger snapping, and before I know it, Camp Wiki Wonder is a distant memory. And potential Sweater Arms Mark is old news. In fact, we can't stop laughing about it now while we rehash the weekend. "Chuck 'em if they can't take a joke," we say in unison, a phrase we used in junior high. When we get back to the apartment, Brook has my spirits buoyed again. I'm even open to allowing her calling her friend who owns the club in the village. It was so much fun singing at the campfire, I figure why not sing a couple of nights a month. Brook calls and sets it up. When she hangs up the phone, she announces that I'll be singing in two weeks at *Freddy T's.*

I feel renewed and alive and full of possibilities when I bounce into my room. GG is sitting on top of a book on my dresser. I stop bouncing, hoping I won't startle her. I want to try to pick her up. I love cats, and it bugs me that I can't win her over. As I slowly approach, she darts over the side and under the bed. She really needs to ditch that whole hard-to-get thing. It doesn't work.

"*The Rules* went out a long time ago, GG," I brush her fur off the dresser and notice the book she was sitting on, *Feng Shui Love*. I have got to finish reading this. If I'm going to make a go of singlehood, I can't let my little dating disasters deter me. I plop down on my bed, drape ole Sweater Arms around my neck and start flipping through the pages. The big red sticky note is still on the chapter titled "The Love Corner." I re-read the first line: *The single most important area of the home is the love corner. The fate of every relationship can be traced back to the state of this area, which is the far right corner from your entry door.* Here my mother took the liberty of noting in the margin that this was a dark musty closet in my marital home with Richard.

It goes on to say, *The corners must be completely clear of clutter to let the energy flow through easily, and a symbol of love should be placed there as well to invite love into your life. Shades of love, such as reds and pinks, should be present in the area. If you or your partner are not partial to these colors, you can place a piece of fabric or paper under a piece of furniture.*

Mom noted in the margin that I could hang a pair of fiery red panties behind a picture frame to invite great passion into my relationship. I shudder at the thought of Mom's sexy lingerie hanging behind our family photo in her den. I force my eyes back to the page. The book says that, if a relationship is smooth sailing then suddenly runs aground, you should check your love corner. *There could be leaks, or an infestation of insects in the wall.*

Hey, you know, that was probably it. I should call Richard and tell him that all is forgiven. I see now that it wasn't his fault; we just probably have termites! At this point I must call my mother and share my thoughts. When she hears my Richard/termite theory, she points out in all seriousness that if I just take a look at our history, I will see a pattern. When we started out, though I didn't call it anything then, our love corner was in our bedroom, which had two red walls. And we did have great passion. In our next house it was in our bathroom, the one with the toilet that only stopped running if you jiggled the handle. She says she doesn't need to point out the obvious on that one as to where our passion went.

Then we settled into our lovely brownstone, where the love corner was located in a stale, musty closet. When I mention that we did have quite a bit of heat on our Barbados trip, she says that was probably due to the layout of our hotel room. As I recall, the far right corner was where the big white fluffy bed was. And there were red roses on the nightstand beside it. Could she be on to something with this? Could I possibly go back and remodel and everything would be hunky-dory?

Of course Mom says yes, but I'm pretty sure new paint and plaster isn't going to patch up the betrayal and the baby mama. She admits this is a tricky one, but she's sure that a consult with her feng shui expert Justin will help. *No thanks, Mom, that ship has definitely sailed.*

Then I get to thinking. It couldn't hurt to start taking care of my love corner from here on out. A little love insurance, so to speak. The next day, after reading the book cover to cover, I get to work on the far right corner of the apartment, which is in the living room. Now that I look at it with my newly honed feng shui eye, I do see what Mom was talking about that day. All the clutter and pictures in the bookcase must be sending mixed messages to the universe, and I'm guessing the last time Brook dusted the shelves was sometime in the Clinton era.

I take everything down, do a thorough cleaning and place things back strategically this time, using only things that could represent love. I find a rose quartz crystal heart in the hall bathroom and move it to a pedestal in the corner bookshelf. Just so happens that Brook's scrapbook of Italy is bound in a big red leather album, which is perfect for a love corner. We'll keep that one right where it is. I also find a small pink plaque in the back of my closet that says *Let Love In*, and I place it on another shelf.

I accent with as much red and pink as I know Brook will stand, and even find a red footstool in Brook's closet that I move in front of the corner chair. By the time Brook comes home from work, I've totally remodeled the living room. She takes one eye-rolling look and wanders into the kitchen.

"Well?" I venture, following behind.

"If you're referring to the goofy love shit in the corner, I saw it," she says, opening a box of cookies.

"And don't you want to know why it's there?"

"My guess? It has something to do with either your mother or your sweater." She grabs the milk from the fridge.

"I guess you could say it's a little of both. It actually has to do with feng shui." I hand her the book. "Remember? Your job promotion after Mom rearranged the furniture?"

"Oh, yeah," she says while quickly perusing the back cover. She drops it on the table adding, "but didn't you tell me once, that when your mother starts making sense to you is when I should order you two matching straightjackets?"

"I know, I know, but you have to admit, it did seem to work," I say with an eyebrow raised.

"Which means all that pink and red in there might actually help you find the Cinderfella who fits your sweater?" She dunks a cookie in her glass of milk.

"My thoughts exactly," I say as I lean back in my chair.

"Well, Lil, I'm all for anything that will keep you focused on moving on from that lousy union with Dick that you called a marriage."

"Then you'll help me do the rest of the apartment?"

"What do I have to do, clean?" she asks through a mouthful of cookie.

"They call it clearing, and all we have to do is make our intentions known to the universe in all the sectors of the bagua." I hand her the laminated card Mom left for me.

"The bag-what?" she asks.

"It's all there on the card, explaining what colors and symbols to use in each area of your home."

"As interesting as this all sounds, I'm going to pass." She hands the card back to me. "I've got to do some research for an upcoming segment on the show."

"Really? You don't want to help?" I steal a cookie from her and dunk it in her milk. She shakes her head no as she stands and gathers up her stuff.

"Why don't you ask your mother?" I think about this as I polish off the rest of the cookies. What the hell. . .

Mom is so thrilled when I ask that she makes plans to come up for the weekend. She even offers up Justin's services as well. I decide not to tell her about my singing gig just yet, as we're having a nice run of getting along lately.

❂   ❂   ❂

Saturday morning Mom arrives promptly with Justin in tow. After getting acquainted over coffee and bagels, Mom is anxious to get started, so the three of us get to work cleaning and clearing and rearranging, until we've covered every inch of the place. Seeming pleased with the results, Justin says we should see vast improvements.

"Honey," he exclaims with a toss of his ponytail, "your health is going to be solid, your wealth is going to increase, your career will flourish, and your family relationships will strengthen." He puts an arm around both my mother and me and gives a little squeeze. "But most importantly," he says releasing us, "you will find love." He finishes with an open-arm gesture.

After writing out a detailed list of items to pick up, Justin sends us out shopping while he puts on the finishing touches. So off we go to Nordstrom to look at bed linens. Mom and I are eyeing a set of magenta sheets through the window when Dad calls my cell.

"If you're looking for Mom, she's right here," I tell him. Laughing, I add, "And don't worry, she's not spending any of your money. We're spending Richard's!"

He has an odd sound to his voice when he says, "Oh, your mother's there?" like he didn't know this.

"Didn't she tell you?" I watch Mom light up a cigarette. I try to take it from her, but she waves me away. When I ask him, Dad says he's out of town on business. "Again? What'd they do, transfer you to another city?" I ask playfully.

He tells me he's sorry he keeps missing me, and if I need anything to please let him know, but Mr. Janice will make sure that his baby girl's taken care of so don't worry. After adding his empathy for how hard this whole breakup is for me, he asks to speak to Mom.

"Hello, James," she says when I hand it over. "How are things going with the big case?" She exhales smoke into the air. I can't believe my father isn't nagging her to death about her smoking. He strictly forbade my brother and me to ever smoke.

"Yes, dear, I will, dear," she says. A moment later, "For the love of my ass, James, I said I would." She gives me a strained smile, then continues, "Darling, relax, there's no need to rush on this. We've already discussed it and as I recall, you agreed that we should definitely wait on replacing the countertops. Okay, sweetie, got to run. I'll bring you a big bear hug from Lily." She flips my phone shut and hands it back.

"Mom, is Dad all right? He sounded funny."

"Oh, he's just tired of traveling, honey. Look, there's a beautiful comforter in the window ahead." She points.

"I thought you already replaced the countertops."

"We did. He was talking about the ones in the guest bathroom. I was thinking a nice cool lime green would look fabulous in your new bathroom, what do you think?"

We enter the store. "I think Richard would've hated lime green. Perfect," I say with a grin. I'm so thankful that my mother seems to have finally given up on pushing me back to Richard. I'm sure she secretly thinks I'll grow tired of New York soon, and then Richard will show up on his white horse and whisk me back to DC. But that isn't going to happen. For one thing, Richard has stopped calling. Not that I care, but I guess Lee Ann put a stop to that. Anyway, I've got bigger things to focus on, like replacing Richard with Sweater Arms.

When we return home with my new bedding, Brook and Will are sitting on the couch listening to Justin explain the finer points of smudging to clear out bad energy. I notice Justin could pass as a double for Jude Law, if Jude had a long ponytail. Seeing Mom, Will immediately breaks into a big smile.

"Mrs. Stevens, you haven't changed a bit." He stands to take her hand.

"Thank you, darling," She looks like she's searching for his name, so Brook jumps in.

"Lauraine, you remember Will Forrester, don't you?"

Mom looks genuinely stunned. "Weenie Will? For the love of my ass, look at you now. Not so weenie anymore!" She pulls him into a hug.

"Yeah, he lost the weenie a long time ago," Brook says, chuckling. Justin practically chokes on his seltzer water.

"Ha ha." Will playfully punches her in the arm.

As Mom catches up on Will and his family, I can't help but notice how cute he and Brook are together. They have such great banter between them. Richard and I never had that. When Will says he has to leave, Justin decides to go too, so he can share a cab with him. *Real subtle, Justin,* I think. *Too bad you're barking up the wrong tree.*

Mom tells us we have one last thing to do before she leaves. We have to send up balloons. Having read the book, I know why. The book says that once your love corner is clear, you must make your intent known to the universe by writing down all of the qualities you want in a soul mate and attaching the note to a balloon. Mom leaves us to write our requests while she runs out to the party store on the corner for red balloons.

"What are you going to write on yours, Brook?" I ask while she flips through a magazine.

"I'm done. I'm exhausted from Justin's lecture. My feng is definitely shui'd."

"No way," I tell her. "Did I refuse when you dragged me to speed-dating?"

She lets out a long sigh.

"This is it, I swear. Come on, it'll be fun." I sit on the floor at the coffee table and start writing down my wish list of what I want in a man: intelligent, funny, able to banter, successful, financially stable, *definitely* not a lawyer—maybe something in the medical profession this time—sincere, not afraid to show his emotions, a good father. . .

"Let's see, what else?" I mutter. I notice Brook's still reading her magazine. "You're not writing anything."

"I'm reading an article about our old friend Duff and his humanitarian missions to Ethiopia. My God, he's as big as Bono now. I can't believe I had a summer fling with him when we were kids."

"That's great for him, now stop reading and start writing."

I hear a tearing noise, then Brook hands me a picture of the

Duff. "Here, put this on my balloon. I want someone like this: sexy, an artist and humanitarian. This is the whole package for me."

"The book didn't say anything about pictures," I tell her. "That might be against the rules! Besides, how is the universe going to know what your picture means? I think you have to be specific."

"I'll take my chances. At the very least, I'll have a hot Italian guy on order." She gets up and goes into the kitchen. "I'm starved, you want a sandwich?"

"No, we ate while we were out shopping."

"Kitchen's bare. I'm going to run down to the deli." She grabs her purse and heads for the door. "Tell Lauraine bye for me if I'm not back before she leaves."

"What about the balloon launch?" I say

"Just tape the picture on mine and let it loose. See you later," she yells over her shoulder as she makes her escape.

"Okay, but hurry back," I call after her. "I'm creating my online dating profile later and we can do one for you too."

By the time Mom returns with three red balloons, I have practically written a book of what I want in a man. "I hope it's not going to weigh my balloon down." I say as I attach my pages to the balloon string.

"Well at least your odds are going to be better than Brook's." She chuckles as she ties the magazine picture to a balloon for Brook. We open the window by the love corner and I lean way out holding our balloons out by the strings.

"Should I say something?" I ask over my shoulder.

"You already did." She leans out the window beside me and points to the big note dangling from my balloon.

"Good enough then." I release the strings and we watch our balloons float slowly upward. As they near the top floor of our building, I notice something attached to the string of the third one as well, *Mom's balloon*. I turn to her and ask, "Mom, why are you sending one up?"

"It's like renewing your wedding vows, dear." She watches, her face wistful, until the balloons skirt over the roof of the adjacent building and float out of sight.

Chapter 12

If friends had told me a year ago that I'd one day be embracing the Web for love, I'd have told them they were completely mad. However, with a new zest for this whole dating thing after our feng shui weekend, I decide to give online dating a try. I pull ole Sweater Arms around my shoulders and start perusing my search results. Sure, I know I might not find the actual man whose sweater this once was, but I can certainly look for what it always represented to me, the fairy tale.

After a few minutes, I start to wonder if this is a good idea after all, with websites like MealTicketMatches and Golddiggers. Are they serious? Who would post on something like that? And look at this one: DarwinDates, for beautiful people only. You actually have to submit a photo and be voted in before you can use their website. Solemates for people with a foot fetish? *Dear God, what next?* I think, *AnimalAntics?*

I was only kidding. Don't ask what comes up when you type that one in. There's got to be something suitable for regular folks. Oh, here's one. ProfessionalMatchmate. That sounds more my speed. I click on it to view a sample of the men and women listed. I start with the competition to see what I'm up against. And after perusing several profiles of scantily clad women draped spread-eagle over everything from the hood of a Mercedes to a leopard-print couch, and one even lapping water doggie-style from the kitchen sink—I'm not making that up—I have to wonder what sort of profession these women are in. I exit that site and scroll some more.

HeavenlyMatch. Sounds like a safe bet. They promise to find your perfect match by supplying only the men who prove to be compatible based on a personality profile you fill out. Sounds good to me, so I click on it and find that the people are more to my liking. I quickly accept the terms of the site, which I do not read—is that a dangerous move?—and begin the lengthy process of creating a profile.

Urrrrrgh. . .I end up spending two hours just filling out the application. Dear God, I spent less time on my calculus final exam in college. Finally, I hit the finish button and patiently wait while the little hourglass twirls around with the message, *Finding your perfect match.* How exciting! Potential-Sweater Arms guy is just a few seconds away from appearing on my computer screen. A message pops up:

> *We're sorry, but we are unable to provide you with a perfect match at this time. You indicated that you are separated and Heavenly Match requires a faxed copy of a final divorce decree. Thank you, and we hope you will consider us when you are eligible to date.*

My face burns with shame as I read this. Oh my God, why don't they just say, *Hey loser, we know you're out cheating on your spouse and we couldn't possibly risk exposing our heavenly matches to the likes of you!*

I log off and try to compose myself. Wait a minute—why am *I* feeling ashamed? Richard was the one out dating while we were together. Heck, he probably belonged to half a dozen websites. In fact, I should've looked for him on that last one, the one with the drinking-out-of-the-sink lady. He might have been a charter member. I'm sure *they* don't have any paper requirements. In fact, they probably have a box you can check for *married but flirting.* Surely I won't toil in purgatory for having a date or two before I have final divorce papers! I mean really, who knows how long Richard might try to drag this out with financial settlements and whatnot? And why should I have to be alone when he's out stroller shopping with his pregnant girlfriend?

Defiantly, I click back on and continue to scroll dating sites looking for something that sounds a little less restrictive. Not that I don't see their logic; I'm sure they're just safeguarding their clients from people like Richard. Okay, here's one that sounds appropriate. Singleonceagain, for those who never thought they'd have to be out on the dating scene again. Their tagline is, *When life throws you a curveball.* Pretty much sums up my situation. Surely they wouldn't add salt to the wound by making you wait for a final divorce decree. I click on, and start reading. Just pay the $19.95, upload a picture, create a profile and I'm in. No two-hour questionnaire to fill out, no restrictive paperwork required. I'll be up and running in a matter of minutes. Sounds good to me!

I pull up my picture file on my computer and start looking for a good one. Richard and me last Thanksgiving. Richard and me in Las Vegas. Richard and me at my mother's surprise birthday party. Just Richard holding a fish. Richard skiing in Tahoe. Richard petting a dolphin in Maui. Why don't I have any of just me? I think a good therapist might say something about losing my own identity. Our life really was all about Richard, with me being the good wife. I don't think I really thought about it before, but it was. He never really cared about what I wanted. Look at how long he put off starting a family.

My heart skips when I find pictures of us on our second honeymoon in Barbados. Oh my God, this one of Richard and me on the moped was taken the morning of the meltdown. Just a few short hours after this, I found out what a lying rat bastard he is. This one seems appropriate then. I edit Richard out of the picture and am left with a lovely one of just me sitting on the back of a moped in the glorious tropical sun. I upload it onto the site and create my tagline: *Suddenly single and new to the area. Looking for someone to show me around the Big Apple. Must be financially and emotionally stable. Lawyers need not respond.*

It won't win any awards, but it's simple and to the point. I click *Submit* and it's done. I've just stepped into my first cyber singles bar. Now what? Do I wait by my computer, check my watch, and act like I'm meeting a girlfriend?

I start browsing through the profiles of available men. This is kind of fun, like catalog shopping. Worknman54 is a regular everyday type you might see in Sears, while rugged Gowiththaflow44, sitting on a mountaintop with a backpack slung over his shoulder, is definitely more L.L.Bean. And then there's the metrosexual Beenthere305 with his fitted button-down shirt and bright blue tie loosened around his neck, just dying to crawl back into the Neiman Marcus Spring Edition he fell out of—

Ding. Oh, someone just sent me a wink. It's someone named StillGotIt. Okay, Mr. StillGotIt, let's see what you've still got. It says he's 48—not *tooo* big an age difference—has a 25-year-old daughter, is retired, has his own plane. He also goes on to say:

> *I'm looking for the complete package. Someone who's beautiful, sexy, fun, loves to laugh. Likes to dress up for special occasions, but doesn't mind showing some skin when I want her to. She must be very open-minded in all areas, especially the bedroom. I like a girl with a little nymphomania, and if she's bad, doesn't mind a good spanking. She must also have a beautiful best friend whom she would love for me to meet. Okay, maybe I'm asking for too much with that last one.*

Dear God, the audacity of this man! My first wink and it's from some asinine pig twit. Does he think anyone would actually respond to this demeaning piece of drivel? I'm furious. I have to respond.

> *Dear Mr. StillGotIt, I see in your profile that you have a 25-year-old daughter. What would she think of your terribly offensive request? I think I will email it to her. Would you want some slimy jerk sending her a wink like this? And do you really think you will meet decent, respectable women with something like that? Or maybe that's not your goal. Maybe you don't have any respect for women, and are just looking for someone to degrade. Well, I suggest you try another site; in fact, I just saw one with a woman drinking water out of her kitchen sink wearing nothing but high heels and lingerie. Or better yet, take your $19.95 and go buy a lap dance. I only hope your daughter has an honorable stepfather.*

I click Send. There. Maybe he'll learn some manners—
Ding. It's him again. What now?

> *Dear Ms. Suddenlysingle, or should I call you Positivelyprude? I have no idea what you find so offensive. I believe in being open and honest from the start. That was what was wrong with my last marriage, she was too uptight in the bedroom. And as for my daughter, you leave her out of this. I think I'm seeing why you're "single once again." Good luck to you. By the way, what was the name of the site with the woman in her lingerie with the sink?*

Okay, that's it; I'm blocking this animal from contacting me again. I can't believe the nerve of some people. I can't lose focus; I'm here to find Sweater Arms. After scrutinizing several more profiles, I run across this:

Lookn4Love, are you a confident, smart and challenging woman? If so, please read on. I'm looking for someone who stays in shape (but not vain) and is fun (but not shallow). Paraphrasing the singer, Al Green, when things are good or bad, happy or sad, you are one of the ones that commits to working it out, you should be comfortable handling the world on your own, but wise enough to know when the search is over and it's time to move into a steady relationship (with me of course) for stability, comfort, and strength. Does this sound like you? Isn't giving up on the search for true love one of the worst things we can do? Both partners in a committed relationship should absolutely be the other's first choice. I won't settle and neither should you.

"I won't, I won't," I say out loud. This guy sounds like he could be my guy! And looking at his picture, he's cute too. I wonder what size sweater he wears. His profile says he's 6'2", taller than Richard. Good. Richard is always intimidated by anyone taller than him. At 6'1" he was usually the tallest guy in a room of all of our acquaintances.

As I read all the way to the bottom of Lookn4Love's profile, I notice that he has a three-year-old daughter and his wife of ten years passed away in a car accident a year ago. Wow, that's some curveball. My heart turns to mush as visions of my picture-perfect family flood my head: me in a cute yet elegant little red dress standing by the Christmas tree, a tall handsome ex-widower and his little girl snuggled into my side. And in my arms I'm cradling our tiny Santa-suited baby boy. I'm noticing a holiday theme with all my perfect family visions.

Without hesitation I type,

Dear Lookn4love, you sound wonderful.

Chapter 13

After several weeks of emailing back and forth with Herbie—yes, that's his name—we decide to meet for coffee. It seems innocent enough, but I still figure I better do a little research beforehand anyway. You never know, he might have a police record a mile long. As I settle in at the kitchen table with my laptop I feel fur beneath my feet. I instinctively pull my legs up thinking I've stepped on poor GG, but instead I find a purple feather boa lying in a heap on the floor. "Oh God," I groan as I reach down to pick it up. It's from my singing debut last night at *Freddy T's*.

What a flop that turned out to be. Fifteen people turned out, and that was including the wait staff, Brook and Will, who Brook dragged along as filler. Most were more interested in the Yankees game on TV than my renditions of old Bonnie Raitt songs. Except for Marla, a mid-fifties hair piled high former beauty queen turned actress. She joined me on stage when I started to sing "Have a Heart" and turned it into a duet. Marla was really into it, shimmying around with her wild purple boa. She ended up staying for two more songs that she enthusiastically begged me to sing with her, Stevie Nicks' "Stop Draggin My Heart Around" and Tom Petty's "Breakdown." I'd say Marla's had some relationship issues throughout the years. Thankfully Brook was finally able to coax her down from the stage by siccing her on poor Will as a distraction. He was a good sport though, buying her wine spritzers and even accompanying her for a spin or two around the dance floor.

"It wasn't a total bust last night, as least you've got two new groupies." Brook nods at the boa in my hands as she breezes into the kitchen.

"Will doesn't count." I fling the boa around my neck.

"I was talking about the older guy at the bar who couldn't take his eyes off you!" She says grabbing a mug from the cupboard.

"I didn't notice him. Would he fit the sweater?" I ask hopefully.

"Nah," she says while filling her cup with coffee, "He wasn't really your type. Kind of old rocker meets organic farmer."

"I have no idea what that means." I flip open my laptop and turn it on.

"That's why he's not your type." She grabs a banana from the fruit bowl and peels it. "Hey Freddy T told me he wants to book you again, but on a weekend next time."

"Oh, I don't know. After last night I'm thinking it was silly to even consider resurrecting some girlish dream from my youth. Besides, I'm too busy with my quest for Sweater Arms." I type Herbie's name into the Google search engine. Brook rolls her eyes and takes a bite of her banana.

"I'll tell him you'll check your calendar and get back to him. What are you doing anyway?" She peers over my shoulder with a chuckle.

"Googling Herbie before I meet him. Did I mention he's a dentist?"

"You did." She tosses what's left of her banana in the trash and plucks her purse from the chair. "I've got to get to work, email me his vital info in case you go missing. See ya." She grabs her coffee mug and hurries off. I tell her I will and get back to my research. Google is definitely a single girl's best friend. With just a little digging, I learn that Herbie is Herbert Alexander Johnson III. What a great name for a dentist. Richard was afraid of the dentist. Anyway, Herbie was born and raised in Buffalo, New York. He attended Princeton undergrad and went to the University of Virginia for dental school. Herbie also published tons of articles addressing such "interesting topics" as periodontal disease and infected gingival sockets, among other things. I suddenly have an urge to go floss. Thankfully he isn't only interested in all things oral, no pun intended. He's also active in a variety of philanthropic activities. What a guy.

With a few more mouse clicks, I find out Herbie is currently in practice for himself in an office in mid-town Manhattan. I also find Carla's obituary. God rest her soul. Her picture's still on his company website. She was a makeup girl if I ever saw one, big black hair and rouge that screamed out for a good blending sponge. I know that's not nice. I'm just a little surprised I guess. One other thing screams out from the picture, she had an enormous nose. I know she couldn't help it, but I'm just saying that she obviously had the financial means to have it downsized a little, and didn't. I wonder why. *Maybe because she wasn't shallow and insecure like Lily Chamberlayne!*

I do feel a twinge of guilt. Not enough to stop researching Carla though. I also happen upon an article about her tragic death in a car accident. There's a picture of Herbie and their baby daughter, Olivia Grace. Okay, enough about Carla-God-rest-her-soul, it's making me want to cry. I promise, Carla, I'll be good to them—

My vow is interrupted by the door buzzer; must be my cab. I shut down my computer and head downstairs to meet Mr. Lookn4Love. So far he seems to be everything I had put on my balloon. The taxi whisks me away to Le Artisans at the Four Seasons, where we agreed to meet for tea. I recognize Herbie from his photo, waiting outside the restaurant. He seems even taller, darker, and more handsome in person than his picture implied. Eat your heart out Richard "Dick" Chamberlayne!

After we get through the introductions, Herbie takes my hand and leads the way. We talk about my marriage a little, and his practice. We talk about our favorite movies, music and meals, and it turns out Herbie and I have quite a bit in common. We're getting along so well, in fact, that we decide to turn our meet-for-tea into a full-fledged lunch date. We enjoy lobster salads and white wine and more conversation. Things can't be going any better. So why do I bring up his deceased wife?

He starts telling me all about Carla, how they met, how happy they were. He describes Carla as a classy woman, beautiful inside and out. I want to ask about the photo on his website, but think better of it. He goes on and on about how wonderful his Carla Marie Amagucchi was, about what a great mother she was, the best wife, the best cook, his best friend, his soul mate. He recounts their first kiss, their honeymoon to Barbados—does he have to mention Barbados? He even shows me his wallet full of Carla-with-the-big-nose pictures. I start to wonder how I would ever fit into this life. Just as I'm thinking about me, I notice tears running down poor Herbie's cheeks.

Obviously this is a painful conversation, and I'm glad he's not afraid to show his sensitive side, but it's definitely time to change the subject. I venture into territory no man can resist: sports. When I bring up the Yankees, Herbie descends into sobs again and mutters something about Carla and the Yankees and an engagement ring. People begin looking at me as if I'm the cause of all of this poor man's anguish. Check, please. I finally manage to get him together enough to wave down a taxi and send him on his way. He says he'll call me, but I tell him I think he should take some time to heal before venturing any further into the dating world. Poor Herbie, he was so good on paper.

I decide to walk for a while before heading back to the apartment. It's such a beautiful day, and I want to enjoy what's left of my wine buzz. While I stroll along checking out the summer window displays, I start thinking about what I wrote on my balloon. He certainly was everything I'd asked for. Maybe that was the point. The book said to remember that the universe takes you literally, so be careful what you wish for. I did write *sensitive* and *not afraid to show his feelings*. Oh my God, I have to do a balloon revision right away. I've got to find a red balloon ASAP!

Just then, I hear someone calling my name. I turn to see Will approaching. He's dressed in a suit, briefcase tucked under his arm and eating ice cream out of a cup.

"Hey Lily, I thought that was you." He scoops a spoonful into his mouth.

"Wow, you look nice. Where you headed?" I ask.

"Home, but I just came from a meeting. I was trying to wrestle money out of some Wall Street fat cats for research funding for the hospital. You look pretty snazzy yourself. Where are you off to?"

"I'm actually looking for a place where I can buy a red balloon. I just had a date with a crier, and I need to send a new message up right away."

He looks at me for a minute as he continues to spoon ice cream out of his cup, and then breaks into a grin. "This has something to do with that feng shui stuff, doesn't it?"

"Yes, it does. Now, do you know where I can find a red balloon?"

"I think the card shop about four blocks up has balloons." Before he can finish, I've got him by the arm, dragging him along with me. I don't have time to get directions. I have to let the universe know right away that I don't need any more crying dates.

When we get to the card shop, Will asks the clerk to inflate two red helium balloons. "So what is it again that we're doing with these?" he asks while we wait for them to be blown up.

"You're going to do it too?"

"Hey, I don't need any crying dates either." He says while taking the balloons as the clerk hands them over.

We're headed for the register when I remember, "Oh, we need something to write with and on."

"Got you covered." Will taps the briefcase still tucked under his arm. When we reach the register, the clerk tells Will that'll be three dollars. I reach for my purse, saying, "You don't have to pay for my stuff."

"I've got it." He hands the guy the money before I can protest. "So what now?" he asks as we exit the store.

"Now we need to write down the traits we want in a mate and send them up. Only be specific. Apparently the universe doesn't have interpretive skills. I put *sensitive* and *not afraid to show emotion* on my last one, and boy, did I ever get what I asked for."

"So you think this stuff really works?" He raises one eyebrow and hands me the balloons.

"I don't know, but I'd rather be safe than sorry."

"I agree. So what do you say we head to the park and set these babies free?"

What a sport. I really do wish he were more Brook's type; he'd be perfect for her. Maybe I can sway her vote a bit. I'll start talking him up more at home, about how cool he is and so forth.

When we get to the park, we both sit in the grass and Will offers up a yellow legal pad from his briefcase. As I guide Will through the process of placing his order to the universe, he seems genuinely interested, and even asks if he can borrow the book sometime, although I'm sure he's just being nice. As I list my requirements down the side of the page, I notice that Will has used the back of a business card.

"That's a pretty small order." I comment.

"But very specific." He says with a nod of satisfaction. When I finally finish, we tie them to the balloon strings. He looks over at mine and frowns.

"No wonder you got a crying date, who could read your handwriting?"

"My handwriting's fine; let me see yours." He moves it behind his back and reaches for mine.

"Give me that balloon! I think it needs some editing. What you really meant to say is that you're looking for a crier *and* a pants-wetter."

He comes after my balloon with his pen. When I try to pull away, he holds my arm and pretends to write on it. I let go of my balloon and it floats away before he can grab it.

"Oh no," he says, "Aren't you supposed to say some magic words or something?"

"Nope, I already wrote what I wanted to say."

"Well then, here's to finding love." He lets his go, and we watch them float away. "So where'd you meet the crying guy anyway?" he asks as we look skyward.

"I met him online," I say as we stand to leave.

"Online? Isn't that where they catch all the predators?" He brushes grass from his pants as we step onto the sidewalk.

"Stop it. I'm not sixteen, and there are nice guys on there. You just have to find the right match site."

"And which one would that be exactly?"

"I met Herbie on Singleonceagain."

"His name's Herbie? No wonder he was crying." Will takes my arm as we cross the busy street.

"What about you, Willard?" I raise my voice above the street noise.

"Well, that's why I go by Will, Lillian," he shoots back.

I slow my stride. I've never used my real name, ever. "What? Who told you that?" I stop short of the sidewalk, but Will gently nudges me along as the traffic light changes.

"I saw it on your eighth-grade report card. I was a geek, remember? Used to work in the administrative office after school." I break into a wide grin at the memory.

Will offers to walk me home, but I insist it isn't necessary, so we part ways on the corner at the next block. All I keep thinking the rest of the way home is how to get Brook to see him in a new light.

Chapter 14

The next morning I'm feeling optimistic about my emergency balloon launch in the park. The apartment seems to have a new energy to it. I think there is definitely something to this feng shui stuff. All our corners are clear, the love corner is set, and my revised balloon has been sent out to the universe. Life in general seems good. Dating, however, has proved highly exhaustive. No wonder people stay in bad marriages forever. If only they could just turn it over to the universe, like me. This is much better. I'm even feeling highly creative again, like all that clearing brought down all kinds of walls in me. Since my little singing gig was a bust, I really need to find something to do soon, but what? Will said I could help out with fundraising. Maybe I will.

I notice the magazine that Brook left on the coffee table for me. It's *Urge*, that new "in" magazine on the local arts scene. Brook has started writing a monthly column for them, and this is her first issue. I flip to the page she marked and get halfway through when I think I hear a faint knock at the door, I stroll over and look through the peephole. There's a man with flowers in hand, nervously shifting his weight from side to side. My first thought is that this feng shui thing sure works quickly, but no way can this be Sweater Arms. For one thing, he's too old, even though he does have that sexy Kurt Russell thing going on.

I see him reach out and knock again on the door. Should I open it? How did he get through the front door anyway? I start thinking, what if he's an ax murderer? Nah, he doesn't seem the type. I bet somebody buzzed him in and he's just got the wrong door. Maybe he's looking for the nice lady down the hall, Ms. Patterson. I bet that's it. I fling the door open just as he's starting to walk away. The flowers in his hand catch my eye.

"Lilies! How beautiful," I say with a warm smile. "She's going to love them."

The man blinks a few times, starts to speak, then stops himself and stares at me with a look of, well. . .I don't quite know really, maybe surprise. So I venture, "You're looking for Ms. Patterson right? You've got the wrong door. She's down the hall three doors to the left." I point from the doorway.

He still says nothing. What's with the staring anyway? Maybe I shouldn't steer him to Ms. Patterson's after all. Maybe he *is* an ax murderer.

"Actually, I'm wrong, it's the next floor up," I stutter, and start to shut the door.

"Lily, is it really you?"

How does he know me? Something about him does seem a little familiar. "Have we met?" I ask. He starts to tear up. Oh no, not another crier.

"A long time ago," he says, wiping a stray tear. "I'm Walter Rickman. . .Your father."

Either this guy is some kind of con man or a ghost. I grasp the door with both hands, ready to slam it shut. "Well sir, that's not possible, because my father died in Vietnam."

"Vietnam, huh?" He chuckles. "So that's what she told you? Guess I can't blame her. That one sure ties it up nice and neat."

What is this man talking about? I know I should probably be afraid of him being a strange whack job and all, but I'm not. I'm actually thinking he might just have the wrong girl. Yes, my real father's name was Walter Rickman, but I'm sure there's more than one man with that name.

"Mr. Rickman, that was my father's name, but you've obviously got the wrong girl."

"Because *your* father died in Vietnam?" He seems amused.

"Yes, that's right."

"But your name is Lily Travis, born March 9th, and your mother is Lauraine Travis?"

"Yes, but—"

"You have Lauraine's blonde hair and beautiful eyes, but I think your smile's your old man's." He flashes a prideful grin. "Yep, when you opened the door and smiled at me, I knew right away you were my daughter. Smile looks just like me and my sister's. Mary Anne's. Yep, we both got that smile from our momma. Must run in the family."

Okay, what is this guy up to? Travis *was* my mother's maiden name. "What do you want, mister?" I ask, with suspicion. Although I still don't feel any fear, I keep both hands planted firmly on the door in case I need to slam it shut quickly. He keeps talking.

"Sorry, didn't mean to just drop in on you like this, but I didn't think you'd see me if I just called after all this time. Didn't know your mother told you I died. This must be quite a shock for you."

He's still holding the flowers at his chest. His eyes remain on me.

"Mr. Rickman, if that *is* your real name, why should I believe you, a total stranger, telling me that my mother, a woman I've known all my life, would lie to me about something as big as this?"

Now he looks at his feet.

"Oh I'm sure she didn't think of it as a lie, she was probably just trying to protect you. I've been a no-good son of a bitch most of my life. She probably thought I'd just break your heart too. Which I'm sure I would've." He looks up. "But what could I possibly gain by telling you I'm your father if I weren't?"

"Hmm. I don't really know. I guess most cons are going

for money."

"Yeah, I guess they are." He chuckles. "But this is no con. I don't want anything from you, Lily. I just wanted to finally meet you. Guess the guilt of leaving you and your mother has finally chewed a hole in my heart."

I take one breath. Then another. "So you're telling me that you left me when I was a baby and my mother lied to me about it?"

"Seems that way. Hey, if you don't believe me, I still have this." He pulls a photo out of his back pocket and hands it to me. It's a picture of a couple in a hospital bed holding a newborn baby. Definitely my mother. And it does look like a younger version of the man standing before me. Could the baby be me? Could my mother really have lied to me about this? I guess it's not entirely implausible that Mom, who lives her life like she's starring in her own soap opera, could do that. Hell, that might even be where she got the storyline. So if it's possible that this man is my real father, whom I'm having a sinking feeling he just might be, and he did just up and leave when I was a baby, why is he standing here now?

Staring at the photo, I say in a daze, "Wow. Maybe I should've read my horoscope this morning. I'm sure it would have said something about digging up the past."

"Your horoscope, huh? Raine used to read those." He leans on the doorframe.

Raine. Oh my God, only Mom's closest friends call her that. I am in complete and utter shock at this moment, which is the only explanation I can offer for why I breezily invite him in for coffee like he's my old school friend who just stopped by with crullers.

I can tell he doesn't know what to make of this move on my part either. He cautiously enters, but keeps eyeing the place like he's waiting for someone to jump out at him with the fireplace poker, perhaps my mother or my stepfather or even me. Like we've had this grand plan all along; we knew this day would eventually come, and after much meticulous planning, finally our prey has sprung the trap.

"Do you take cream and sugar, Mr. Rickman?" I call out from the kitchen. "Or should I call you Walter or just Walt or maybe Pops?"

Okay, there we go. Sarcasm. That's a good sign. Passive aggression is good here. I was beginning to think I was losing a grip on my sanity, to be so cavalier about old Walt here after almost forty years of parental absenteeism. The expression on old Walt's face when I return to the living room says he was beginning to think the same thing, until now. Now his look says, *Okay, here it comes, this is the part I rehearsed, the part where she cries and asks why I left her, why I didn't love her.*

Well, sorry to disappoint, but I don't need to ask why. If there's one thing I've learned in life, it's that people just feel what they feel and that's that. You can't change it, and they can't change it. It is what it is, whether it's love or hate or envy or lust or just plain indifference. I take a seat on the couch and nonchalantly stir hazelnut creamer into my coffee. "So, Walt, what's going on that you would look me up now?"

"Oh, this isn't the first time. It's just the first time I've actually tried to talk to you. I've looked you up many times."

I'm thinking that whole fireplace-poker scenario I was running earlier isn't a bad idea after all. "Oh please," I say. "Is this the part where you tell me that you were there, lurking in the shadows, for all the milestones of my youth? That you hid in the bushes and watched me learn to ride a two-wheeler, or quietly slipped into the back of the room at my kindergarten graduation? Or maybe you crouched in the lily pads with an inner tube at Miller's Lake the year I learned to swim at summer camp?"

"No, nothing like that," he responds ever so calmly. "I never even made it into the same state. I just meant I looked you up in the sense that I knew where you lived. Never really got much further than that."

He's still holding the lilies. Why does that annoy me so? Maybe it's not the lilies so much as *what he just said*. Is he kidding me? Now I'm starting to get mad. Did he really just tell me that the sum total of his interest in me was looking up an address?

"Really? That was about as far as you got, huh?" So much for my theory on not trying to make people feel something they don't. I grab the damn lilies out of his hands and whack him over the head with them. *See, I made you feel that!*

He looks surprised, but only for a second. Then he actually smiles at me.

"What the hell do you want?" I demand, and throw the remaining stems at his chest, hard. "Answer me! Why'd you finally make it past a street name this time?"

He fiddles with his empty mug, reminding me that I never filled it up in the first place. Good. He doesn't deserve coffee. "Well, I saw you sing the other night at Freddy T's, and I wasn't certain, but I just had a feeling that you were my kid."

"You saw me sing?" I manage to ask, then "Oh my God!" I remember Brook's description of the man she said was watching me from the bar, "old rocker meets farmer" or something. Yep, that's definitely him.

"I was blown away, kiddo. You got some pipes on you. I used to do a little singing myself, but then I had a falling out with the lead singer in my band, so then I—"

I let out a loud "Shhhhh" to quiet him. "Let me get this straight. You saw me sing, had a feeling I was your daughter, and just showed up here? Now?"

"Well, I had to do some research first. Got your name from Freddy, who said you were staying with his friend Brook, so I looked her up on the internet. Got the address and decided, yeah, it was time to stop by." He leans back smugly, clearly impressed with his investigative skills. Damn that Google!

"So you decided it was time to stop by did you? Well, why do *you* get to pick the time?" I say, standing to face him. "What if it's not time for me? What if I want to hang on to this bitterness for another twenty years or so?"

Where is all of this emotion coming from? I had no idea I could feel anything at all for this man. Where is Dr. Phil when you need him? I'd relish sitting on one of his comfy stools right now, with old Walt by my side, hearing Dr. Phil give him one of his famous *how's-that-working-for-you* lectures. And Dr. Phil's wife, Robin, would give me sympathetic looks from the front row. We'd probably have coffee together after the show and laugh about how delusional old Walt is about all of this. Like he can just spring back into my life after I'm a grown woman and expect me to just come to terms with the fact that he didn't want me as a baby. I mean, the baby stage is the cute stage, when you do want them around. I could understand if he packed up and left during the surly back-talking teenage stage.

So what does that say about how unlovable I must have been, for him to not even want me when I was a cute gurgling little ham hock? I know this isn't about me; this is about him. So why can't I stop feeling this incredible wave of rejection and abandonment? And I haven't even begun to explore the betrayal I feel from my mother. Dr Phil would have to book an entirely different show for that one.

"Lily, I really don't know what to say." I was so wrapped up inside my own head I almost forgot he was still here. "I know I have no right to expect anything from you, but I do want you to know that sitting here in front of you, looking at you, I feel an enormous sense of loss and love for you. I've been a fool most of my life, but by far the most foolish thing I ever did was walk away from you."

He starts to say something else, but stops, like he wants to see how I'm digesting this first to make sure I'm going to keep it down before he proceeds to feed me more. I turn my head to look at him. I want to stay quiet, match his stare, and make him incredibly uncomfortable. The thing is, I don't think old Walt is uncomfortable at all. He seems to have his own agenda, apparently just as he's had his whole life. And it's all I can do not to throw my coffee on him. Oh, I'm seriously contemplating it, except I don't want to ruin Brook's lovely moss-green chenille couch. Maybe I could lure him into the kitchen by the sink. Sensing his imminent soaking I'm sure, Walt stands.

"Lily, I'm sorry. I shouldn't have just showed up like this. I don't want to upset you." He pulls a slip of blue paper out of his shirt pocket and sets it on the coffee table. "Here's my address and phone number. Why don't you call me after you've had some time with this?"

Why don't you call me? He said it not as a question, but a simple statement of fact, as though an hour or two after he leaves, I'm expected to pick up the phone.

"Wow, I hope you're in good health, Walt," I say. "Because if I take as much time as you did, you'll be in your nineties."

I intended to sting him. He only nods in agreement and actually pats my head as he passes on his way to the door. After he leaves, I take a deep breath and look around the room, my gaze stopping on the recently freed-up family sector of our apartment where a picture of me as a little girl is prominently displayed on the mantle. My arm hair stands up when I realize the shirt I'm wearing in the photo boldly states across the front, *Daddy's Girl.*

Wow. This feng shui is powerful stuff.

Chapter 15

W hen Brook comes home I surprise her with the guess-who-came-for-coffee story. She's full of questions about my father fiasco. Once she finally gets past the whole I-thought-your-real-father-was-dead scenario *and* that he was the guy at Freddy T's, I'm bombarded with a whole new batch of questions. I think she missed her calling as a prosecutor.

"Where did he come from? How did he know you were here? Why do you believe him? Does your stepfather know?" I shrug and shake my head through her cross-examination, all the while wondering the same things myself.

"Gosh, guess he didn't have time to fill out the questionnaire you left," I say while I watch her pacing the floor.

"You thought the man was dead, Lil, just thought you might be more curious about him," she says when she finally plops down on the other end of the couch.

"I *am* curious. But I didn't want to give him the satisfaction of thinking he mattered at all to me. Tit for tat, I say." I reach for the phone to call my parents. I do wonder if Dad knows, or if Mom told him the same lie.

While I dial, I say, "I know it might seem like a stretch for me to just take this man's word for it, but one, you know my mother, and two, there is kind of a resemblance."

The answering machine picks up right away, which usually means they're screening their calls. After the beep, I say, "Hi

Mom, *Dad.*" I emphasize "Dad" a little too much, but I'm feeling the need to hang on to my reality a little tighter right now. Still no one picks up. I say, "I guess you're out to dinner or something. Anyway, give me a call when you get back. Oh, Mom, I met an old acquaintance of yours today, Walter something, and he was just *dying* to know what you've been up to lately." I hang up feeling a slight vindication, knowing she'll be wondering if I know what she thinks I know.

"You know that will drive your mother absolutely insane. You want a glass of wine?" Brook asks on her way to the wine cabinet, which is precisely in the middle of our newly cleared health area. I hope that isn't bad feng shui. If she and I suddenly become alcoholics, at least we'll know why.

"Why do you think I left that message? And yes, I'd love a glass. . .a big glass."

"So you want to go out tonight? Some rum maker is sponsoring a big singles thing over at this nightclub called Rain." She hands me the wine.

"I don't know. A nightclub? Won't that be loud and young?"

"Not tonight. There's supposed to be a jazz pianist playing, not really what the kids are into."

"You know, I could use a distraction. All this daddy stuff is giving me a headache. Besides, if this feng shui stuff can bring a father I didn't know I had out of the woodwork, imagine how it might fill out a sweater."

"Good. Then go get dressed, something sexy yet casual. Oh yeah, Will's going to meet us there."

"Will? Why's he coming? Could there be a little spark starting?" I ask with a girlish giggle.

"No, he's coming because he's single and he needs to get out more. Besides, it'll be nice to have a man along so he can pretend to be our date if the situation arises. Kind of like having a big brother around."

"I would never bring my brother on a date," I say, heading to my room to change.

"That's because your brother has a giant stick up his butt," Brook shouts after me.

"You know," I call out from my room, "I think Will might have a crush on you."

"No way. Will and I are definitely just buddies. Besides, you're the one he was madly in love with in ninth grade." I hear her chuckling, as she appears in my doorway. "Remember the time he went out and collected seventeen varieties of leaves for you so you'd get an A on your biology scavenger hunt?"

"And I felt sorry for him, so I agreed to go to that pep rally with him? But he came down with the worst case of poison oak ever known to man, so I went with Ronnie Richmond instead, and he gave me a hickey under the bleachers." I hold up a tan skirt for Brook's approval. She shakes her head and makes a beeline for my closet.

"And poor Will was so depressed; he neglected his own biology assignment and got an F. The only time I think he ever failed anything in school," Brook says, one hand holding a black v-neck dress for inspection, a pink ruffled shirt in the other.

"I know, I did feel kind of bad about that, but Ronnie Richmond was the star running back. Who could pass up a make-out session under the bleachers with that?" I crinkle my nose as Brook turns back to sort through my options.

We emerge forty minutes later, me wearing a sleeveless fuchsia jersey dress and Brook in a simple black mini and heels. I think we look hip and young until we arrive to a line a mile long outside the trendy nightclub, mostly consisting of pretty twenty-somethings.

"I thought you said it wouldn't be young," I say as we approach the line.

"It's not supposed to be," Brook says. "Maybe the older people are inside." We join the cattle call. My look to her says *they'd better be after I got all dressed up in hair and makeup.* "Hey if not, we can always try out the whole cougar thing," she ribs. This velvet rope scenario is a little more than unsettling. I mean really, we're supposed to think we'll be picked to enter over these nubile twenty-year-olds?

After waiting in line and fidgeting with our makeup for ten minutes, Brook gets impatient and steps out of line, grabs my wrist and pulls me with her as she strides toward the front of the line.

"Where are we going?" I ask.

"To hurdle the velvet rope," she says with a sly smile.

She'd better be joking.

Just as we reach the front, a large group of exceedingly attractive young men approach from the other side. They're all laughing and drinking from big plastic cups. The lead guy heads straight for the bouncer, who scrolls his guest list, then waves them in. Brook pulls us into their mix and starts chatting them up. One young redheaded guy with a nice build immediately takes a shine to us.

"Hey, where'd you two come from?" he asks with a grin. His red hair and freckles remind me of Opie Taylor from the old sitcom. "Trying to ride in on our coattails?" He puts an arm around us both.

"Is that wrong?" Brook gives him a coy smile.

"Only if you don't let me buy you two a drink," he says while sizing us both up. Brook returns his size-up with one of her own, adding, "Grey Goose martini," and saunters ahead into a mix of colored strobe lights and very loud music. Opie has me clutched tightly under his wing as we make our way to the bar. Once there, he high-fives all of his buds and orders us drinks. I shout over the music to Brook, "This is not the sophisticated singles mixer I was hoping for! Where is the pianist anyway?" Young Opie appears with martinis.

"Did you just say what I think you said? Man, you older babes are fast." He starts moving to the music while he chugs his beer. Dear God, we've fallen down the rabbit hole and landed in the middle of an MTV dance party with twenty-year-olds bumping and grinding each other like gazelles in mating season.

"So what are two lovely, sophisticated ladies like you doing in a place like this?" Opie yells while he continues to slither and gyrate. Brook pretends she can't hear him, which leaves me to respond.

"What are you trying to say, we're too old for this place?" I yell back. And here's the annoying part: he doesn't even say *since when is twenty-nine too old* or anything remotely similar. He just grins and leans into my breast and shouts, "Older women are so hot."

I don't know how to take this; I mean on the one hand, he did say we were hot, but on the other hand, he did call us old. "I think you've been watching too many re-runs of *Sex and the City*," is all I can think to say.

"Well, it does give a boy an education," he says with a wink while he checks out Brook's rear. She rolls her eyes and turns to me.

"We need to go to the ladies' room. Excuse us for a minute, Junior." Just as we head off, Opie appears right in our faces.

"I'll walk you over," he says with a grin, "just in case you have any ideas of ditching me at the restroom."

"Well, it doesn't speak much for your prowess to know that women ditch you at the restroom on a regular basis, now does it, Opie?" Brook says, and pats his chin.

"Who's Opie?" he asks with a genuinely puzzled look. And

why wouldn't he, since he was probably born the year we graduated high school.

"Opie Taylor? Mayberry? Any of this ringing a bell?" I try to explain. He shakes his red head no. "He was a character on a sitcom," I venture. "Red hair, freckles. . ."

"Sorry, I don't get it," he shrugs.

"What's not to get, I just explained it—"

Opie's attention span has apparently expired. He grabs my hand and rushes me to the dance floor.

"I love this song!" he yells over the music.

Okay, it's finally happened, I've turned into my mother, because there's no way anyone could call this music. As for dancing, I'm not sure Opie isn't having some sort of seizure. He's jumping straight up and down, flailing his arms around. I step back to get out of harm's way and scan the room for Brook. I spot her beside a big potted palm chatting up a tall, handsome fellow who looks to be more our age. I try to make my way over but am wedged on the dance floor among a sea of flailing fledglings. I wave my arms to get her attention, but it only encourages Opie to make an advance.

"Look at my old lady groove," he yells while he straddles my legs with his and continues to seize. I know it's loud in here, so I'm going to assume I heard him wrong on the old-lady bit. I'm able to wiggle away and start in Brook's direction when suddenly Opie grabs me by the waist and jumps me up and down to the music with him until he has some sort of spasmodic crescendo, whipping me around with him. When I finally break free, I run toward Brook and the tall guy. As I get closer, I slip on the beer-soaked floor and end up sliding up to them instead, reminiscent of Kramer in *Seinfeld*. I skate right into the tall guy—who turns out to be Will.

Does he look hipper than usual? How is that possible in the midst of all these trendy kids? I feel like a frumpy schoolteacher next to all these half-clothed, half-my-age girls.

"Funny how our worlds keep colliding," he says after he stands me back up.

"Thanks for leaving me with the frat pack, Brook." I punch her arm playfully.

"You were hardly Jodi Foster in *The Accused*. And besides, I thought you might be enjoying the attention." She sips her drink.

"Think again," I say, grabbing her drink and downing the rest of it.

"Well this seems like a bust," Will says. "What happened to the sophisticated singles mixer with the jazz piano player?"

"Apparently it was cancelled, but I never got the email," Brook says. "Sorry guys. Let's go grab a drink somewhere else."

We decide to walk because Will knows of a quaint little place nearby. Right after we sit down and order drinks, Brook's cell rings with a crisis from work and she has to go rewrite some copy that's to air at midnight on her satellite show. With all the excitement from the unknown-dad debacle, I realize I haven't eaten all day and the liquor's starting to gnaw a hole in my stomach. Will offers to take me to dinner somewhere, but I don't feel like uprooting again, so he orders up one of everything on the bar menu. While we make our way through a pile of potato skins and loaded nachos, we catch up on each other's lives. I tell him about the resurrection of old Walt.

"Wow," he says, "to have a brand-new relative appear in your life out of nowhere. I would love that!" He shakes a couple of drops of hot sauce onto his nachos.

"But wouldn't you be just a little bit angry that he rejected you as a baby and deprived you of all those lost years?" I ask, taking a bite of potato.

"Nah, you can't hang on to that. Like he said, you were probably better off." Will takes a sip of his beer. "People change. Why don't you just get to know him as the person he is now, and then decide if you like him or not?" He pops a stuffed jalapeno into his mouth and smiles. I stare at him for a minute, trying to figure out if he's really that highly evolved or just a doormat. When I tell him that, he explains that he and his sister Wendy were estranged for many years because of some silly family disagreement. Then she got sick. He said he'd give anything to have a do-over now. Then he fills me in on the specifics of his sister's brain tumor, and how he came to dedicate his life now to working with non pharmaceutical-funded researchers and doctors to find a cause and cure for such abnormalities.

"Many doctors have speculated that artificial sweeteners were the culprit of the tumor that led to her demise," he says. "She lived off of diet soda, even drank it for breakfast."

Dear God, I think, and when I tell him that I do the same he suggests I come by the lab in his wing and talk to some of the doctors there about the research they're doing on the potential effects of many artificial products.

By the time we polish off all our junk food and have several more drinks, I feel woozy. Will insists on seeing me home, even though I tell him I'm perfectly capable of taking a cab by myself. As we walk along looking for a taxi, Will spots a little dive bar with karaoke. "Come on, Lily, let's go sing," he says, with a gentle tug on my arm.

"What? No. . ." I say, pulling the other way.

"Come on, I know all the words to anything by Elton John." He takes my hand and leads me back the other way.

"Elton John? Really?" I ask, stopping to face him. "Because I've had just enough alcohol to get my rock star juices flowing and if you're going to tempt me with Elton John. . ." I give a little eyebrow raise. He gives a nod *yes*. "And you're going to sing with me?" Another affirmative head nod. "Then what are we waiting for?" I grab him by the arm and pull *him* along now.

To my surprise, Will is actually pretty good. Since they don't have any Elton John to load into the karaoke machine, Will and I tell them we'll wing it, and just grab the mics and do our thing, which turns out to be our own boozy renditions of "Bennie and the Jets," "Rocket Man," and "Crocodile Rock." Will turns out to be quite the crowd pleaser, encouraging people to stand on the tables and sing along. We close out the night with "Don't Go Breaking My Heart," in which Will even plays imaginary piano on the wall of the DJ booth. I had no idea Will could be so much fun. By the time we finally get back to the apartment, we are high on booze and stage adrenaline.

"Wow!" Will exclaims with a little jump as we exit the cab. "Who knew it was such a rush to sing?" He pays the fare, and then turns to me. I point around him as the taxi speeds away.

"You just let your cab go," I say as he turns to watch it round the corner.

"That's okay; I'll call another one after I walk you up. I've got to use the bathroom."

Flimsy excuse, I think as I let him walk me upstairs. He tries to keep the conversation innocuous enough, but I know what he's up to, so when he tries to kiss me in the living room, I'm not surprised. I give him a head push as he's coming in for the lip lock.

"Oh my God," he moans, "I finally work up my courage after two decades, and you give me a head push? Way to permanently scar a guy, Lil." We both chuckle.

"It's nothing personal, I'm just. . ." I hear a hissing at my feet. The Gray Ghost herself has made an appearance. And I'd say she doesn't look happy, judging by the ears pinned back on her head.

"Hey baby. At least somebody likes a kiss from old Will." He picks her up and kisses her head. She immediately snuggles into his shoulder.

"Wow, she really does like you."

"Really, I'm not that bad," he says with a sneeze. After he puts the cat down on the floor, she weaves in and out of his legs.

"No, you're not bad at all. In fact, I was just trying to think of a way to get you and Brook together."

"Brook and me?" He laughs. "But we're just friends."

"But couldn't it be more?"

"That's precisely the question I was going to ask you." He takes both my hands in his.

He's so sweet. Why don't I feel anything for him? I look him in the eyes and wait for something to bubble up. I sigh.

"I'm sorry Will, I just don't feel that way about you."

"Okay then, fair enough. Just promise me you won't humiliate me further by laughing about this later with Brook."

"I promise." Still holding both my hands, he leans down and kisses me on the forehead, then turns to leave. After a few steps he stops at the front door.

"Good night, Lil. And think about getting to know old Walt. You might be pleasantly surprised by what you find underneath."

He closes the door behind him, and I feel like the popular cheerleader all over again, crushing the hopes of the sweet geeky guy who just collected seventeen varieties of leaves.

Chapter 16

What a time to run out of hazelnut creamer, just when I need my coffee the most. After Will left last night, I got to thinking about Walt and had another glass of wine to calm my nerves. I ended up watching the room spin afterward. I've really got to curb my alcohol consumption. I'm not twenty-two anymore.

"Well, I'm off." Brook comes into the kitchen looking like she's ready to run a marathon.

"Where are you going?" I ask while I stare into the refrigerator, trying to manifest my creamer.

"Cincinnati, remember? My big Bon Jovi interview?" She types a last minute email then snaps her computer shut.

"Oh God, take me with you!" I say, not so much for Bon Jovi, but I'd love to check out of reality for another day or two before dealing with my mother.

"I wish I could," she says, "but I'm going with some producer. Ian Milesky. And we're flying on a company jet. I'll be back late tonight, I think."

"Wow, a company jet? Sounds exciting." I drop into a chair at the kitchen table and watch her gather up her things.

"Well I've got to run, wish me luck." She swings her computer bag over her shoulder and heads out before I can even tell her about karaoke with Will. Remembering all the alcohol involved reminds me that I need caffeine! Might as well get dressed and run down to the corner Starbucks. As an incentive, I imagine

Sweater Arms having a double espresso in the corner booth at this very moment.

As I pass through the living room on my way to get dressed, I notice the pink heart that was in the love corner, now sticking out from under the couch. *How did that get there?* I wonder as I reach down to retrieve it. A sudden swoosh of gray darts past me, startling me to jump back.

"GG, you little brat," I call after her as she perches herself on the far arm of the couch. If I didn't know better, I'd think she's trying to sabotage my love life after I rejected Will. I swear she just rolled her eyes at me when I placed it back on the shelf.

❀   ❀   ❀

When I walk through the doors of Starbucks, the smell of assorted coffee drinks puts a smile on my face immediately. Thankfully there's no line, since all the nine-to-fivers are neatly tucked into their cubicles by now. So with lightning speed I am delivered a hazelnut cappuccino and blueberry scone. With steaming mug in hand, I plop down in a corner booth—regretfully, no sign of Sweater Arms—and unfold the daily news. Before I can even take my first sip, guess who plops down across from me? Poppa Walt.

"What are you doing?" I demand, nearly spilling my coffee.

"I saw you through the window, thought I'd say hi," he says with a boyish grin.

I casually take a sip. "There are stalking laws here, you know."

"I don't think this qualifies." He turns to prop one leg up on his seat.

"Well, I don't recall extending you an invitation, or even showing the most remote interest in talking to you." I spread the paper out in front of me without looking up.

"I'm not stalking, I'm just persisting."

"Tomato, tom-ah-to," I say while I keep my eyes on the paper, trying not to let him unnerve me. He takes the lid off his coffee and blows on it. I hope he's not planning to drink that here.

"So who's the guy you took up to your apartment last night?"

I look up with a jolt. "What? Oh my God, you are stalking me."

"I'm not," he says, raising both hands in surrender. "I just stopped by to make sure you were all right after the bomb I dropped on you. And I saw you stumbling in with some schmuck."

"First of all, he's not a schmuck. I knew him when we were kids, which you might've known if you'd stuck around. And second, I don't think you have any right to judge who I go out with. If I want a character analysis on my dates, I'll ask my dad, the attorney, not you, the. . . I'm sorry, what is it that you do?"

"I'm a drummer." He takes a sip of coffee before continuing. "Well, used to be. Now I'm just a bartender in the Village, little place called Rosco's. Have a room on the second floor—"

"Charming." I flick my paper wide open in front of my face.

He chuckles, adding, "You do remind me of Raine."

"Stop it, just stop it." I slam the paper on the table and stand, collecting my purse and coffee to go.

"Okay, don't get yourself all in knots," he says, shifting to the end of the booth. "It was just an observation."

"Well, stop *observing* me, okay? You don't know me, or my mother. You made your choice, so live with it." He motions for me to sit back down, but I don't budge.

"I hear what you're saying, kiddo," he says looking up at me. "Ever since I saw you singing that night, it just reminded me. . ." He sighs and lets the thought roll by as he puts the lid back on his coffee and stands to leave. We face each other, a mere foot apart. Seconds pass before I break his gaze and quickly sit back down, turning my attention back to my paper. He shuffles a few steps away.

"Guess I was hoping you were the kind who believes in second chances. Maybe. Someday."

When I'm sure he's walked away, I look up and watch him retreat to the door, feeling the good mood I had going slip right through my skin. Just as he puts a hand on the door to push, he turns and raises his coffee to me in a mock toast. He gives a wink as he pushes the rest of the way with his back, then disappears outside down the sidewalk. I feel a lump in my throat start to rise. No, I am not going to let him get to me. Logically, I know he shouldn't matter to me, and what he thinks shouldn't matter to me. But logic seems to have taken a holiday, because I can't stop feeling this nagging little tug at my heart. Now I see where I got my one dimple from. He has the same one, on the same side. Not that it matters—just an *observation*.

My phone rings just in time to save me from myself. I check the caller ID. Not available. I don't usually answer those, but since I still haven't been able to confront Mom about her big lie, I click it on. "Hello."

"Hey, Lil, it's me." The familiar voice sends my stomach into a back flip.

"Richard, what do you want? Need me to help you pick out baby names?" I pull a blueberry off my untouched scone.

"Ouch. I told you that baby isn't mine, and I'm going to prove it as soon as it's born. The DNA test will show you."

I roll my eyes and scroll through the index to the newspaper, looking for my horoscope. It has got to say something about old wounds bleeding like hell.

"I shall anxiously wait to exhale then," I say, flipping to page thirty-two and setting my sights on Pisces.

If you can, just stay in bed today, preferably with the covers pulled tightly over your head! Communications could prove to be stressful. Take a deep breath, be patient, and all will smooth out by the end of the week.

I knew it. I take a deep breath and realize I haven't heard a word Richard just said. "I was reading my horoscope. Did you say anything worth repeating?"

"Yes, Lily, I did. I said that the divorce property settlement papers came today, and that I really can't bring myself to sign them. Lily, you know I love you, and I can't bear to lose you."

"Richard, please don't be a dick about this. Just sign the damn papers." I take another breath and stare at the ceiling.

"No. I have to see you first. I can't give up without a fight. If I'm nothing else, I'm persistent."

There's that word again. Maybe they should start a club or something. Those *persistent* people could do great things if they got enough members.

"Good," I say. "Then you'll understand my *persistence* in requesting that you sign the damn papers!" I shout this, not meaning to, and the cute coffee guy looks up with alarm. I mouth sorry to him and smile sheepishly.

Richard continues for the next ten minutes about why I shouldn't give up on us, about how we had such a good thing, blah, blah, blah. I bet he's really good in the courtroom, badgering the hell out of the witness until he gets a full confession, because I find myself, against all logic, agreeing to meet him in New York one last time before signing the final papers.

"Whatever. It's not going to change anything," I say before hanging up. And I mean it. I've completely moved on from my old life with him. I just wish I had a boyfriend to dangle in his face. *Sweater Arms, where are you when I need you most?* Maybe I'll just make one up. Maybe I'll tell him I'm dating a brain surgeon or something. Just the thought of seeing his face when I wish him the best with Lee Ann, seriously, and tell him how I hope he wants the best for me too with—oh, I don't know, with Doctor Scott. My cell phone chirps. Caller ID says it's Brook.

"Hey there, you clear for takeoff yet?" I say.

"The flight got pushed back to noon, so I came back home. I need to leave soon, but your mother's here." I notice that she's using her fake smiling voice.

"My mother?" I ask, as if the concept is foreign to me.

"Yeah," Brook responds. "You know, the woman who got varicose veins carrying you and has never let you forget her sacrifice. She's sitting in our kitchen drinking sherry."

I check my watch. "At 10:30 in the morning?"

"Apparently, she's got a lot on her mind. I've got to get out of here, so could you come home please, now?" Brook says with just a little desperation.

I begrudgingly pack up my things, and leave my lovely daydream behind. I take my time walking home, collecting my thoughts and ammunition. I can't let Mom turn this thing around and deflect blame. It's so like her to say that whatever outrageous thing she's done was somehow for my own good. Like the time she cut my hair in a pageboy style when I was eleven so it wouldn't get caught in the roller coaster at the state fair, for my own good.

When I finally reach the apartment, I hesitate outside the door. After several deep breaths I reach for the doorknob, only to have Brook fling the door open. Her ESP forever intact, I see.

"Good luck, got a plane to catch," she whispers as she buzzes past me. Before I'm even fully in, Mom comes out of nowhere and embraces me like I've just come back from Iraq.

"Oh honey, just let me hold you. I know this must've come as a terrible shock to you darling, but I was only trying to protect you." She squeezes me tighter. I decide to toy with her a bit before going for the kill.

"Mom," I say, the word muffled through her arm, "What are you talking about?"

She releases me and looks me in the eye, searching for any hint of recognition. "The message you left on the machine." She proceeds cautiously.

I give a little headshake that says, huh? She presses on tentatively. "The one referring to someone named Walter dying to know what I've been up to. . ."

I purse my lips and give a look of pondering. "Oh, you must mean *Wally*, the little boy who lived in our neighborhood when we lived on Skipwith Road. Remember? He's all grown up now. I saw him at a bookstore, he asked about you." I'm a little impressed with myself at how easily I just made that up off the cuff.

Mom looks surprised, then relieved realizing how much time she's wasted fretting and perfecting her defense when it wasn't what she'd thought it was after all. I say, "Why, what did you think I was talking about, Mom?"

"Oh nothing dear, let me make you a cup of tea." She breezes into the kitchen. I breeze in behind her, wondering when I should pounce and tell her about the real Walt. Oh what the hell, now's good.

"No tea for me, Mom. I just had a latte with Dad at the corner cafe."

Crash. There go the teacups.

"Oh right, I didn't have a chance to tell you about the miraculous resurrection of Walt, did I?" I wait while she bends down to pick up the pieces. I notice a slight jitter in her hands. I stay silent, hoping to unnerve her further. After a few moments of silence on her part, she starts to tremble, then heaves herself over on the floor in a fetal position and starts to cry aloud.

"All these years of being married to a defense attorney, and that's the best you've got?" I say while stepping over her to retrieve an apple from the fruit basket. "What response, exactly, are you trying to elicit from the jury? Sympathy?" I take a bite of the apple as she continues to sob, only now it's the jerky, silent kind. I pick up the latest issue of *People* from the counter and step back over her to leave the room.

I have no idea how long she wallows on the floor in there before she notices I'm gone. I become engrossed in an article about a one-handed woman softball player in Oklahoma. She's the pitcher. Apparently she holds the glove with her arm against the left side of her body while she throws it with her right hand. She then immediately slides her hand in the glove and is ready to catch by the time the ball is hit. Her team won division champions four years running. Amazing.

Mom finally wanders in and takes a seat on the other end of the couch, all red-eyed. I peer over my magazine at her while I deposit my apple core on the coffee table beside me.

"Darling, let me start off by saying how very sorry I am for having lied to you. It was certainly never my intent to hurt you." She takes several deep breaths. "I was only trying to protect you."

We say the *only trying to protect you* part in unison, to which she gives an eye roll and says with a dramatic head toss, "I'm not even going to bother if you're just going to be flip."

"Hold on a minute," I say leaning forward. I slap the magazine down on the couch for effect. "You're not the one who gets to be mad here. *I* am. And I *am* mad. So you can climb on down from center stage, Miss Drama Mama, and explain how it was better for me to think my real dad died in Vietnam. I even went to that damn wall and looked for his name on two separate occasions!"

I'm fired up now. I jump up and grab my purse and rummage for the picture I've carried around all my life. "And who is this anyway?" I shove the picture of a handsome soldier sitting on top of a military tank in her face. She squints at it for a few seconds before recognition.

"Oh, that's William Holden, dear, from a scene in *The Bridge on the River Kwai.*"

"What? Are you kidding me?" I ask incredulously.

"No, that's Bill Holden," she says, gazing at the picture. "I always loved that movie. Did you ever see it?"

"Well, apparently not, or I would've recognized dear old Dad, now wouldn't I?" I grab the picture back from her and start to tear it up, then think, *what the hell; I don't have anything against William Holden.* I put it back in my purse, and start pacing. "Does that not even bother you? Did you think that was some kind of joke, letting me mourn for a man who in reality didn't want me?"

"Well that's precisely why I didn't tell you that the son of a bitch was still alive!" She jumps to her feet now. "For the love of my ass, how is a child supposed to reason with that?" She does her head-toss thing again for punctuation.

I continue to pace. "I'm not saying you had to tell me when I was four, but what about when I was older?"

"What age would you suggest is appropriate to tell your child that her no-good biological father doesn't give a rat's ass about her?" She's doing her own pacing opposite of me. "When she's ten? Twenty? Thirty? When?" She throws both arms up in the air. "What about now? Is it any easier to hear now? Hmm?" she asks while grabbing me by my shoulders and forcing me to face her. She has a point, I guess. It certainly isn't easy to hear at any age.

"Darling, I didn't want you to ever find out that your father would rather roam around the country chasing some silly dream of being a musician than raise his baby girl. What good could've possibly come from it?" She wipes a tear from my cheek that I didn't even realize had leaked out. I quickly retreat, wiping my eyes as Mom lowers herself back to the sofa with a look of concern.

"You might have turned out completely different had you known," she says as I go back to my pacing. "You could've been one of those promiscuous girls with a daddy complex. You know, always dating older men—usually married—trying to recreate something you had absolutely no control over." I feel sick to my stomach as I flash back to Adam, wondering if people just inherently know things without having to be told. "This way," she continues. "You were raised in a loving home with two parents who desperately loved and wanted you."

"Did Dad know?" I stop pacing and look at her.

"Of course not. He would have tracked that bastard down and broken his legs for you." She's right, he would've. And I realize she really *was* only trying to protect me. My bottom lip starts to quiver. She stands and motions for me to come to her. Without hesitation I lunge for her and let her hug me madly. She might be a stark-raving loon, but at least she's my stark-raving loon.

"I'm mad as a hornet that he came sniffing around upsetting you. What does he want anyway?" she says into my hair.

"He said he just wanted to see me." She gently releases me and cups her hand to my cheek.

"Well, he's seen you, so why is he still hanging around?" She looks genuinely concerned with this.

"He lives in the Village, bartends at some dive and lives over top of it."

She shakes her head in disgust. "Oh darling, see why I didn't want you to know him?" *Yes and no.* On the one hand, he's a loser rat bastard. On the other, he has a certain charm about him that I can't quite pinpoint. Maybe it's just my romanticizing of the situation, I don't know. I mean, I did think he was a fallen war hero my whole life.

"How do you think he found you?"

"He said he just knew I was his when he saw me singing, so he asked the owner—"

"What? Where on earth would he see you sing?" Guess I never told her about that.

"In the Village. Some friend of Brook's has a bar there. Apparently Daddy Dearest wandered in." It dawns on me as I watch her start to pace now, that *that's* why she never wanted me to sing. . .because of Walt! Then a thought occurs to me. "Mom, you didn't happen to do a little singing yourself back in the Walt days, did you?"

"Did he tell you that?" She stops dead in her tracks.

"You did! Didn't you?" I ask as I make my way around the couch toward her. She heads for the kitchen, trying to avoid eye contact. I leap across the chair and cut her off at the doorway. "You were the singer in his band!" When she heads in the other direction, I jump up and down yelling, "You were! You were!"

"I did not sing in his band!" She proclaims indignantly, finally turning to face me from her spot by the mantle. "It was his friend's band, and I played tambourine." I break into a fit of giggles as I stumble toward the couch and perch myself on the arm.

"You played tambourine?" I double over, suddenly finding this hilarious. She starts to chuckle herself as she comes over and plops down on the couch beside me.

"Wore go-go boots and everything." She breaks into a full-blown laugh as I fall backwards into her lap. We are both yukking it up pretty good about her band days, when my guffaws turn to something else.

"Darling, what is it?" She asks through furrowed brow. I grab her tight and cry into her shoulder. Then I tell her the thing that I've never told anyone else, except Brook. I tell her about Adam, and all that followed. Although she is shocked, she understands. Probably better than anyone she tells me. As I sit, snuggled in her arms, I flash back to the day Justin feng shui'd the place, specifically the family sector, and how he said family relations would be strengthened.

"Mom, I think I've had enough of this whole dead-dad business for now." I stand then offer her my hand. "Can we just go and have a nice lunch somewhere?"

"Of course, darling." She stands and loops my arm through hers, walking me toward her purse. "And afterward we'll go shopping and buy something insanely expensive on Richard's credit card. Then you can come stay with me at the Plaza tonight. We'll order room service and watch old movies, and tomorrow we can spend the day at the spa."

"Sounds perfect," I say leaning into her. "Maybe we could even rent *The Bridge over the River Kwai.*" We both laugh as I jump away, avoiding her playful swat.

Chapter 17

Surprisingly, the weekend at the Plaza with my mother turned out to be quite energizing. The whole dead-dad scenario seemed to invoke some long overdue mother-daughter bonding, which I think Mom needed most; the idea that my brother's baby will be calling her "Grandma" soon seems to have her a little frazzled. So when she insisted on dropping a thousand dollars to cleanse and revive our bodies with acupuncture and Ayurvedic treatments, I didn't refuse. I opted for the Diva Sapah Luna: the Divinity Moon treatment. I think it was the description in the brochure that reeled me in.

A gentle stream of oil infused with flower petals flows over the third eye, also called the moon eye (center of forehead). When the moon eye is awakened it brings forth greater intuitive awareness. This treatment is followed by a relaxing massage to the scalp, hands, and feet, encouraging a sense of well-being.

Wow, they weren't kidding. I feel fabulous and my third eye is definitely open. I enter the streets of New York a peaceful Cyclops. I'm thankful to the universe. I'm thankful that my mother and I were able to get past the whole daddy thing. But mostly I'm thankful she's on her way back to Philly. Not that we didn't have fun, but for the love of my mother's ass, she can be a handful.

Uh-oh, I feel my inner peace start to slip when I step out to hail a taxi and Manhattan madness hits me in the face. Horns blowing, people hurrying by, and the stench of the trash truck all work simultaneously to put a damper on my Zen buzz. My third eye is starting to squint while I try hard to stay centered and in my "happy place." In the window display across the street, I catch a glimpse of the *Bewitched* movie playing on several big-screen TVs. That was my favorite show as a child. I so envied Samantha, and would often fantasize about how much easier life would be as a witch. Just snap my fingers and create a twin that I'd send off to school while I spent my days at FAO Schwarz or Disneyland. Most days, I think I still carry that fantasy. If only I could twitch my nose and go back to life before Lee Ann.

Or would I? Now that I think about it, if I could have my perfect life, I don't think Richard would be a part of it. Looking back, I never really had that "peaceful easy feeling," to quote the Eagles song, the feeling that was so prominent in the Sweater Arms dream.

I guess if I'm really honest, I felt like I had to always please Richard, even if that meant giving up my own identity. Samantha and I probably have more in common than I realized. I mean, look at Darrin; he was a nice enough fellow, attractive (well, at least the second actor was), had a good job, and was a good provider. But he would never let Samantha use her witchcraft. Talk about a control freak. What red-blooded American male wouldn't have taken advantage of a hot blonde who could do magic and make his life easier? An egotistical oppressive bastard, that's who. He and that astronaut who found Jeannie should've been dropped into an alligator pit in the final episode, with Samantha and Jeannie giving each other a high-five.

Wow, where is this all coming from anyway? Something must have jiggled loose while opening that third eye. I never realized that I resented giving up so much for Richard.

Unable to flag down a taxi, I decide to walk a few blocks until I find a Starbucks to indulge in a skim mocha latte. That's the closest I've got to a happy place these days. I enter to the smell of espresso, which always reminds me of Italy. Maybe Brook and I should plan a girls' trip back there sometime soon. Who knows, maybe this time I'd find the actual man in the airplane seat and not just his sweater. After flirting with the cute coffee guy for several minutes, I finally settle in to a cozy booth with my latte and the paper. I breathe in the sweet aroma while I flip to my horoscope. Yes, I'm definitely feeling my Zen buzz return. I take a sip of my latte and realize it is all wrong. I slide begrudgingly back out of my booth.

"Excuse me. You've forgotten the whip on my skim mocha," I point out to Cute Coffee Guy as I hold my cup across the counter for him to take back. He looks genuinely confused.

"Sorry, ma'am, most people who want skim skip the whip. I mean, it makes perfect sense if you're going for the low-fat drink."

He didn't just call me "ma'am," did he? His cuteness factor just plummeted a few hundred points. "The way I see it," I say smugly, still holding my cup out, "if you sacrifice the whole milk you can indulge in the whip."

He gives me a scrutinizing once over as he reluctantly takes my cup back. "You sure? I mean the calories in the whipped cream are like triple what you'd get in the whole milk."

"That's why I get the skim!" I say. "So the calories average out." Am I the only one who sees this logic? His young coffee-girl coworker snickers something in his ear while he adds a dollop of whip cream to my brew. I'm not going to let them bother me. Having just had my third eye opened, I'm going to choose instead to send them loving light. Speaking of which, when I return to my booth and newspaper, an article about the starving people in Africa catches my eye. *I* should try to do more when it comes to the plights of the world. Look at Will, trying to make a difference with all of his research funding. Really quite admirable.

As I take a sip of my *whip* skim mocha, I realize it is criminal the amount of money we'll pay for a cup of coffee. My God, it could probably feed a whole village for a month in some of those struggling countries, but it is good coffee. You have to admire Bono and Oprah for all the hard work they do giving back and trying to make positive changes in the world. Now I feel bad that I bitched about getting whip on my latte.

Oh look, Nordstrom is having their half-yearly sale. Kate Spade New York is giving twenty percent of every purchase to the Feed the Children fund. Maybe I *can* do my part after all! I mean, the likelihood of me partnering up with Bono or Oprah is pretty slim, but I do have plenty of "Richard cash" to buy shoes for a good cause.

❂   ❂   ❂

As I enter Nordstrom, I pause to take it all in: the live piano music, the fragrant perfume displays, and Kate in all her glory, ready to save starving children. Then it smacks me in my third eye—summer is over. It's been almost six months since I left Richard. I think my third eye is struggling to hold back a tear as I approach the shoe display and force myself to start looking over the fall arrivals. I wish Brook were here to laugh at me.

As I peruse the selection of suede stacked heels, I notice an Italian hottie looking my way. Dark eyes, dark hair, and olive skin wearing a fitted white t-shirt displaying his great pecs and biceps. His look is a combination of John Stamos and Goran Visnjic. Or maybe I'm just giving way to my TV doctor crush. Best of all, he isn't wearing a wedding band!

He casually makes his way around a women's shoe display, picking up a green suede flat and inspecting the heel. He must have a girlfriend. I catch him glancing my way before he nervously turns and picks up a black stiletto heel. I pick out several pairs of shoes, lining them up like contestants in a beauty pageant. I ask the salesgirl to please bring me the matching purses as well. Italian Guy hovers closer. Wow, he is cute. All that's missing is the sweater. Maybe it's him! After all, I did just revise my balloon request, and my love corner has been clear for days.

Or maybe he's some serial killer with a foot fetish, and he scouts for victims in the shoe department. I retreat back a few feet, remembering a case one of Richard's friends had involving a serial killer who had a fetish for women with milky-white feet. He'd kill them and cut off their feet to display in a trophy case in his basement.

"The two-tone chocolate ones are very attractive," Italian Guy says, startling me from behind. I breathe in sharply as he quickly recovers, "I'm so sorry, I didn't mean to frighten you. I was just admiring your taste."

"Oh right, thanks." I try to size him up. He's too handsome to be a serial killer. I know, I know, whose mother hasn't warned them about Ted Bundy?

"So, shopping for your girlfriend?" I ask still holding the brown shoe.

"No, actually my son." He fidgets with a purple mule.

"Your son likes stilettos?" I ask, pointing to the shoe.

He lets out a nervous laugh. "Oh no, he's only eight. But if he did grow up and discover a fondness for stiletto mules, I'd love him just the same." He gives me an amazing grin, more like John Stamos' Dr. Luke than Goran Visnjic's Dr. Luka.

"Well, how very liberal of you." I smile back and am holding his gaze when the salesgirl reappears with my shoes.

"I'll let you get back to your shopping," he says. "I just saw you from across the room and had to say hello."

I can't help but grin like a schoolgirl while he asks the salesgirl where the kids' shoes are. She directs him to the third floor while I slip on the two-tone brown ones Dr. Luke is so fond of.

After plunking down a week's worth of Richard's billable hours on several pairs of shoes and matching purses, I feel good. I haven't frivolously spent this much money on myself in a long time, if ever, come to think of it. Starting to feel quite liberated, or maybe it was the little crush I was feeling for Dr. Luke, I take a stroll up to the third floor and see if I can run into him again. I hope that doesn't seem desperate.

I scour the store top to bottom, all four floors, twice. No sign of the good doctor. I'm exhausted and in need of an iced tea, so I head for the in-store coffee bar on the first floor when I recognize the tune being played on the baby grand by the escalators: "Dream a Little Dream of Me." Could it be a sign about the guy in my dream? If the universe wants me to find Dr. Luke, I decide, he will appear.

I nearly fall out of my seat when, two minutes later, who should walk in just as I'm squeezing lemon into my iced tea? He smiles in my direction and gives me a wave with his shopping bag. I wave back and he heads toward me.

"Would it be terribly forward if I asked to join you?"

That sexy smile again. Please don't be a Ted Bundy. Although I doubt the universe would be so cruel. "Only if you swear that you do not collect women's feet for some trophy case in your basement."

"I swear I don't have a basement." My third eye confirms that he's definitely not a killer. We both smile, and I move my shopping bags to make room for him at the table. The chemistry's so thick you could study it in a petri dish. His name is Robert Crescioli, and he confesses to scouring the store for the last half hour himself. He's definitely Italian, he's from Pittsburgh, and he's a neurosurgeon. Oh my God, he really *is* a doctor! I think I even put that on my first balloon: that I wanted someone in the medical profession.

He has one son, but desperately wants to have more. He's been separated for two years and his divorce is finally coming down to the wire. When I asked what had caused the demise of his marriage, he explained that his wife was clinically depressed and spent most of her time on the couch. After six years, he just had enough. Since the son is the same age as the marriage, I have to wonder if it was a shotgun wedding. To my surprise, I actually ask this out loud. He tells me no, he was just anxious to have children. He goes on to tell me that they met at the hospital, of course, and as the cliché rolls on, she was a nurse.

After we get through the brief history of my marriage, we move on to lighter topics and spend the next hour laughing and regaling each other with silly stories spanning from kindergarten until now. Robert doesn't even flinch when I tell him about my newfound feng shui and the balloon request to the universe. In fact, he wants to know what I asked for. I tell him, "I don't think I should say just yet, since I think it's similar to making a wish before you blow out the candles, and it might not come true if I tell." He then asks if he can take me to dinner. As tempting as it is, I decide to make him wait. I don't want to seem too eager.

We exchange email addresses and phone numbers instead, and he offers to get me a cab. As we stand to leave, I brush up against his arm and wait to feel some electricity or something, some sign this might actually be Sweater Arms. I don't feel anything, but I chalk it up to him not wearing a sweater. I toy with the idea of just asking him to come with me to the men's department and try on a sweater. He could stand behind me and wrap his arms around my waist like in the dream. If it isn't him, I can save us both the trouble of proceeding further. I decide against it, realizing it sounds like something my mother would do. Besides, I figure I can maneuver it in on our first date instead.

Once outside, he puts me into a cab and prepays the fare. He says he'll definitely call me soon, and could I please wear the brown two-tone shoes to dinner? I ask him how he knows I bought those, and he says he didn't, but he's been picturing me wearing them on our date ever since he sat down with me for tea.

When I get home, I check my email. I didn't think he really would have written already, but. . .bingo, one message waiting from NeuronDoc. How cute.

> *Dearest Lily,*
>
> *I can't believe my luck running into you today. Or was it fate? I can't stop smiling. Please don't make me wait too long to have dinner with you. Your laughter is truly addictive and I'm already feeling withdrawals. You name the time and date, and I've got the perfect place.*
>
> *- Rob*

Wow, thanks universe. He's just what I ordered.

Chapter 18

Dating Dr. Rob has proven to be everything I'd hoped for. Although I haven't been intimate with the good doctor yet, it's now the end of October, so I've managed to get his sweatered arms around me many times. And I have to say, it could be him. As for Brook, she's been on fire lately. She got a new job as a DJ on a satellite rock-radio show that records live from New York, and has been dating Ian, the music producer she flew with to Cincinnati a while back. She's also become a big believer in feng shui. She even painted the far left corner of the apartment purple because that's the color the book said would ensure the flow of money into your life.

With Brook's new job and Richard sending me a big chunk of money recently for no apparent reason, I'd say the feng shui is working. We still haven't settled up on our divorce because Richard still insists on seeing me first, but I just haven't had time with dating Rob and taking on a volunteer position with Will's research department soliciting donations. I never knew that life could be so fulfilling. I'm having a blast, I'm doing work that matters, and I think I'm falling in love. I've even booked a new singing gig. It's only ad jingles for Brook's station, but at least it pays well. Hey, I know I'll never be Bonnie Raitt at this point in my life, so I figure I'll just have fun with it.

As I turn down our block on my way home from the hospital, I see Will coming out of our building. I know there's nothing going on between him and Brook, but I can't help rushing up behind him.

"Did I catch you on your walk of shame?" Startled, he turns and gives me a grin.

"Hardly. I just dropped by with some pictures Brook needed for a meeting today. I'd borrowed them for a proposal I was pitching for a fundraiser."

"I don't know. Your hair looks kind of slept in," I tease.

He gives me a mock frown. "That was the look I was going for, thought it was stylish."

"Yeah, *was* being the operative word." I reach up and muss his hair. He rolls his eyes, putting his hands in his pockets.

"I guess I never was much of a fashion bug." I give him the once-over and decide he definitely looks better than he did in chemistry class.

"I'm just kidding you. You look fine." His face flushes slightly and he changes the subject.

"So what are you doing home? Shouldn't you be slaving over the phones back at the office?"

"I'm a volunteer, remember? I don't have a set schedule." A cold breeze kicks up and blows my hair into my mouth. I brush it aside. "Besides, I have a date tonight that I need to get ready for." I struggle to find the invisible strand that's stuck to my lip gloss. Will reaches out and pulls it away, tucking it behind my ear.

"Well then, I won't keep you," he says. "Have a good time." He takes a few steps backward with his hands in his pockets before turning to head up the sidewalk. "And be careful," he shoots over his shoulder.

"Thanks, I will," I say, bouncing up the front steps. What did he mean by "be careful?" I'm not going out into the streets alone. He really needs someone of his own to worry about. Since the universe obviously answered my request, maybe I should send up a balloon for Will. Wait, he did already, that day in the park.

Maybe he didn't know what to ask for, or wasn't specific enough. I'll have to remember to ask him what he wrote.

When I enter the apartment, Brook is gathering her stuff to leave. "Hey there," I say while tossing my keys into the big red heart-shaped glass bowl I acquired for our new feng shui décor. Brook picks hers up from the same bowl.

"Hey, you're home early," she says. "Sorry I've got to run, but do you want to hang out with Will and me tonight?" She props the door open with her foot. "Ian's out of town, so Will's bringing over *Halloween*, and a bunch of sequels. We'll probably get a pizza and hand out candy to the kids, it'll be fun—"

"Can't, got a date with Dr. Rob." I plop down on the couch and kick off my shoes.

"Ooh, is *tonight the night*," she sings, doing her best Rod Stewart impersonation.

"Stop. You know I plan to take things slowly when it comes to that."

"Yeah, but there's slow, and then there's just plain torturing the guy. What are you waiting for? Don't answer that, I've really got to run. We'll delve further into this tomorrow." She points a finger at me while closing the door behind her.

"Okay, Dr. Ruth, I look forward to it," I call out as I slump back on the couch and stroke my chin in contemplation of whether tonight *could* be the night.

Dear God, what is that huge monstrosity on my chin? I jump up and run to the hall mirror to find myself looking at the biggest pimple known to mankind on the side of my chin. Where the heck did that come from? And why didn't Brook tell me I had a goiter growing on my face? It's so unfair that women seem to have a reintroduction to pimples when they're already fully enlisted in the war against wrinkles. It's cruel indeed that all of a sudden we are forced to dab drying agents on our faces when we are so desperately trying to keep from drying out.

I examine the goiter on my chin. I swear it's the size of a penny. Oh well, at least the doctor's not squeamish, I presume. I spend the rest of the day experimenting with different camouflage techniques. In the end, I find that there are only so many layers of concealer you can put on before it starts looking like a dab of Silly Putty stuck to your chin. I consider wearing a mask; after all it's Halloween. Damn, there's the door buzzer. At least my dress should direct his attention elsewhere: an original BCBG Max Azria turtleneck mini sweater dress, quite sexy with my new leather knee-high boots and chain belt. I figure even nice girls can look a little naughty on Halloween.

When I let Rob in, he devours me in a passionate kiss while slamming the door behind him. Wow, he is *definitely* hot. (I could never really say that about Richard.) When we finally break apart, he hands me the bouquet he's been holding. Flowers. When was the last time I got flowers? Excluding the dozens of roses that Richard sent while he was trying to suck up—these are different. Not to mention, they're my favorite, Star Gazer Lilies, and they're for no reason at all. Brook would probably call them his hopeful panty peelers. When I told her last week that I thought he and I were both enjoying the return to just making out—when kissing seems magical, mysterious, and like you both just might explode—Brook said that's all fine, "As long as Dr. Rob doesn't explode on my chenille couch."

God knows *he's* been a good sport about it. I'm the type who could never have meaningless sex very easily. Not that I didn't when I was young, there was that whole Adam incident of course, but even back then it made me feel a little queasy, like I'd just stolen a pack of gum from a convenience store. So here I am, a decade-and-a-half older and still not comfortable with stealing gum. Although the more I'm crushing on this man and feeling things that resemble the L-word, I think the time is definitely near. If it weren't for the spackled growth on my chin, I might just lead him back to my bedroom right now.

After putting the flowers in water and making out for a few more minutes, we're off into the city. Rob picked the quaintest French restaurant, La Champlain, which has outside garden seating. Outdoor gas heaters take the autumn chill from the air, and it's easy to forget we're in the middle of a bustling city here, with crushed-gravel floors under our feet and a vine-draped trellis overhead. The tables are dressed in floor-length linen topped with white floating candles. And you know how good candlelight makes a girl look. I had to wonder if Dr. Rob picked this place after noticing my enormous pimple. Maybe he thought he could stomach me better with a hazy glow. After two hours of conversation consisting mainly of Rob bragging on his son Ryan, we decide to call it a night. I don't really mind all the talk about his son. I'm impressed that he's such a doting father, as long as there's room in his life for me.

As we approach the door to the apartment, we hear laughter inside. I'd hoped no one would be home so we could have another little make-out session before the night is over, but from the sound of it, Will and Brook are still watching movies. He has really become a permanent fixture around here, which is good in some ways—heavy lifting and such—but terribly awkward too, seeing how Brook said he still has a crush on me. Rob doesn't seem to notice, although he has pointed out on several occasions that a man wouldn't be hanging around so much unless he had designs on one of us, to which I offered up Brook of course.

We enter to find Brook and Will lying on opposite couches watching my all-time favorite movie, *When Harry Met Sally.*

"What happened to Halloween Scary Movie Night?" I ask.

Brook laughs. "We couldn't take Jamie Lee Curtis making

such foolish decisions, so we switched to chick flicks."

"Cuz no foolish decisions there," Will exclaims with an eye roll.

I've never known a man comfortable enough to watch chick flicks unless he was trying to score major points. Maybe Will does have a thing for Brook after all, and she just doesn't notice. He certainly isn't awkward or gawky around her though. There's a nice, easy feel to their presence. They talk and hang out like girlfriends, which makes me wonder for the first time about Will. He hasn't had any girlfriends since I've been in New York, and he does make a mean soufflé. Maybe he's gay. I never thought about it before, but now, watching him laugh at Meg Ryan. . . I don't know.

After Rob has as much as he can take of Harry and Sally, he politely makes his exit, citing early rounds at the hospital. We kiss in the hallway like two hormonal teenagers until Mrs. Barnhart from down the hall passes by with her snarling poodle. Nothing kills a mood faster for a man than a little frou-frou dog.

He nuzzles into my neck—Rob, not the poodle—and kisses me below my chin. I so *do not* want to let him go. I think about suggesting we go to his place, but since he's never asked me before, that might be a bit forward. Oh, I'd been to his place of course, a penthouse on the Upper West Side, but he never tried to keep me overnight. I think we're both becoming afraid of my virtue. Mom would be so proud.

"I had a great time, the restaurant was amazing," I pull him closer, taking in his hint of cologne. I'm gaining the courage to invite myself over to his place when the door flings open to reveal Will munching potato chips right from the bag.

"Your brother's on the phone," he says between handfuls. It feels more like my brother is standing in the doorway.

"Tell Todd I'll call him back," I say while I try to hypnotize Rob with my eyes.

"I think they had their baby," he says between crunches.

"It's okay," Rob says. "I've really got to go. Take the call." He gives me a peck on the cheek before he leaves. I turn to follow Will's trail of crumbs.

"Don't worry, I'll get those up with the dust buster before I go," he says, plopping back down on the couch. Brook's engaged in phone conversation with my brother, so I sit down by her feet to wait.

"So, how was the date?" Will asks, offering me the bag.

I nod it away. "It was great, perfect. He's perfect."

"Just be careful, Lil. It's been my experience that when someone seems perfect, they're actually the ones with the biggest secrets." I reach over and take a handful of chips.

"Oh I don't have to worry about Rob, we don't have any secrets." No sooner do I say it than the phrase *famous last words* flashes in my head. I hate to challenge the universe like that. I'm thinking of some clever way to rephrase it when Brook hands me the phone. I almost don't want to take it now, with that last statement hanging in the air like a baited hook waiting to be swallowed whole by a passing fish

"Hey, Todd, great news," I say through my fake smile.

Chapter 19

It's been two weeks since my brother had his baby boy, and I still haven't made it down to visit. Mom keeps begging me to come to Philly for Thanksgiving to see the new baby. I'm just not up for that yet. Will and I have been swamped, trying to tie up loose ends for a big fundraiser ball we have coming up in December. Kelly Ripa's emceeing it, and Brook used her clout with her new job to get Bon Jovi to play. It feels good to have a purpose again, although it has been limiting my Dr. Rob time tremendously. I think Will secretly likes this. He's been flirting with me a lot lately, which is fun; it makes the time pass quickly. But I'm desperately missing the arms of the good doctor.

"You okay?" Will says from his mound of paperwork. He has a small office in the hospital oncology wing, and now we share it.

"Sure, why do you ask?" I continue to sort through files of prospective donors.

"I don't know, you were looking at me funny."

"Funny? What do you mean?" I lay a stack of files on his desk.

"Moony, starry-eyed, something like that." He turns to tack a business card onto the bulletin board behind him.

"Oh, you wish," I say.

He raises an eyebrow. "I wasn't implying it was over me. I was going to rib you about Dr. Rob. But now that you've given yourself away. . ." He lets it hang in the air with a smile.

I almost don't have the heart to tell Will that Rob invited me to go with him to Bermuda next week for a medical conference he has to attend. I think I'll send up another balloon for Will. I think the last one got hung on the roof of the building next to ours, because I keep seeing something red flapping in the breeze. No wonder true love hasn't swept in for him yet. He does deserve someone special. I can't believe how selfless and giving he is. And how consistent. That's an important thing with women that I don't think men understand—consistency.

Suddenly, I realize how that might've sounded if I'd said it aloud. Look at how I'm going on about him; you'd think I was the one with the crush. I almost wish I did like him like that, because I know how good he'd be to me. But I don't. It's just lack of chemistry, I guess. And besides, I have a dreamy neurosurgeon to spend my time fantasizing about. Not to diminish what Will does, with all his efforts to bring attention to his sister's research fund. I think it's quite noble.

"You know, actually I was thinking of you a minute ago," I say crossing to where he's sitting and taking his head in my hands. He looks at me, surprised.

"I was thinking you'd look really good with your hair cut short and kind of flipped up here." I pull my hands through his hair and muss the top up a bit. I step back and try to visualize the cut. "Yeah definitely, it would look hot." Will flattens his hair back down self-consciously.

"You think so?"

"I do," I say while I return to my spot by the window. "I'll go with you sometime to have it cut if you want." I imagine how handsome he'll look for the girl who'll come along after my next balloon launch for him. We can double date even. I'm sure she and I will become great friends and have coffee together on Saturday afternoons when our men have to work.

"Well sure," he says. "It's been a while since I've changed it up, I guess." He looks up from his papers, "Maybe we could go today after lunch?"

We had started a sort of ritual lately: Mortie's deli for soup and a sandwich, and Starbucks for a latte on the way back. It's a nice break in the day. I only worry that he might be getting too attached to me. It sure would be nice if he were gay; I've always wanted a gay best friend. Not that I'd trade Brook—I mean in addition to, a Will to my Grace. I always envied Grace on that show. In Will she had her own personal stylist, makeup artist and fellow chick flick fan. Not to mention the snappy repartee and shoulder to cry on when yet another man broke her heart. Although I guess I've been lucky there, since it's only been Richard so far. So then I'd be *his* shoulder to cry on when yet another man broke his heart. If only Will knew what I was day-dreaming about right now. I chuckle at the thought.

"What?" he asks from his desk.

"Nothing, I was just thinking about *Will and Grace*," I answer while I try to look busy. His look says he has no clue what I mean. "You know, the TV show?"

"Ah yes, funny stuff that show was," He spins around to file something.

I spend the rest of the time before lunch envisioning our sit-com life, both searching for love in the big city, both usually ending up eating ice cream and barbecue potato chips on the couch watching *Letterman* together. In the sitcom version there isn't a Dr. Rob because everyone knows once the lead character snags a love interest, the ratings plummet and cancellation is usually not far behind. Why is that?

By the time we head out for lunch, I have managed to make a few phone calls and mail a couple of media kits we made up earlier in the week. Will and I go through our usual lunch routine, but make a pit stop in Barney's before hitting the barber shop on our way back. Will needs to pick up a few new shirts for some client meetings he has scheduled this weekend.

"Something hip and casual to match my clients, and I'd love your opinion," he says.

I end up steering him toward a trendy brown button-up number with a subtle tan swirly design extending down from each pocket. When he tries it on, he says he's a little self-conscious with the way it's tightly fitted. I tell him he shouldn't be, that he looks fine. And he does. I think he's been working out lately. I grab another, similar shirt in midnight blue, and a sexy gray pinstripe shirt to show him before proceeding to checkout. According to Will if I like them, it's good enough for him.

After Barney's, we head to the barbershop where I explain the cut to the barber. Once he's underway, and everything looks to be going as planned, I run out to get our daily lattes. When I return, I nearly walk right past Will paying at the register. I do a double take. How could one little haircut make such a difference? Will looks great. The butterfly has been released from his cocoon.

He nervously runs his hands through his cut when he sees me.

"So, what do you think?" He takes the latte from me; I break out in an approving smile.

"I. . .love it." And I do.

We leave the shop and head back toward work, sipping our lattes. Just as we're about to turn the corner back to the hospital, he says, "Let's play hooky."

"What?" I ask with my cup poised to drink.

"Come on, we don't have to answer to anyone. It's a beautiful day, we should be outside. Don't get many days like this in November."

He does have a point. "What would we do?" I ask.

"We can do anything we want. How about stroll through the park and feed the ducks, then wander over to the petting zoo?"

"Petting zoo?" I ask, then down the rest of my latte.

"What? You got something against petting little lambs?"

"No, lambs are fine," I say, hesitant.

"It's the ducks then. You have some strange phobia about their rounded little bills. Oh, the horror!" He puts his hands up in front of his face to ward off the imaginary creatures. I slap him on the shoulder playfully.

"It's not the ducks, I like ducks, it's just that—" I fumble for the right phrase, something that won't hurt his feelings, but he reads my mind.

"What? Dr. Rob has a duck allergy?"

"I just don't want to feel like I'm doing anything unfaithful, and feeding ducks feels sort of, you know, intimate." He breaks out in a chuckle.

"It's ducks, Lil, not an afternoon in a hotel. But it does make one wonder what sort of *fowl* things you've been doing with your boyfriend."

I throw my empty cup at him. He deflects it with his arm.

"Look," he says while he bends down for my cup, "I already know you're gaga over Dr. Rob, and that we're just friends. I got it the day I went in for the kiss." He playfully rubs his forehead. "So let's just enjoy the nice weather before it's gone."

I think about this for a second.

"Okay, good. Now that's out of the way, lead on to the duck pond."

"Jeez, the ego on you. Do you think every man who sees you is in love with you?" He points to a suited businessman crossing our path. "Oh, don't look him straight in the eye; we might never ditch him once he falls under your spell."

I jab him in the ribs as he takes off in front of me, calling out, "Oh, what about that homeless guy that's lying next to the wall? Don't get too close, Lil, he might end up sleeping on your doorstep."

He leaps out of the way of my lunge and takes off again with me in pursuit. When I finally catch him at the next block, he throws me over his shoulder and carries me across the street to the park where we enjoy the glorious weather feeding ducks, and yes, even going to the petting zoo. There's definitely something to that petting therapy they use in nursing homes and hospitals for kids. No matter what's gone wrong in the world, it's hard to stay mad or sad when a cute little animal nudges you with its wet nose, begging to be petted some more.

Will is struggling to stay kneeling while a rambunctious little goat keeps knocking him over. "This is it. I'm going to start a petting program at the hospital in the oncology wing," he says. "Can't you just imagine how much the kids would love it?"

"I don't think they're going to let you bring smelly goats into the hospital," I point out.

"Ha ha. But they *will* let me bring a smelly dog."

"Oh yes, smelly dogs are always welcome at hospitals. In fact, Dr. Rob was just telling me the other day how he found surgery much more enjoyable with a smelly dog at his feet—" Without warning, Will tackles me and rolls me over, holding my face in front of the goat.

"Give her kiss," he coos. I squirm wildly when the yucky goat tongue licks my face.

"Let me go, Will Forrester!" I yell between licks.

"But he loves you, Lily. I guess he can't help himself. He must be under your spell too," he says, holding me still for more goat licking.

"You are so dead when you let me go!" I yell through goat slobber.

He finally releases me and runs like a wildcat out of the animal pen. I'm up on my feet and chasing him in a matter of seconds. He darts behind the public restrooms with me not far behind. I'm constantly scanning the ground for something disgusting to wipe on him. I come around the corner of the restrooms, and scan the bushes. No sign of him. Just as I'm turning toward the ladies' room, he jumps down from a tree and grabs me from behind with a growl.

"Ouch! You shocked me," I squeal as he twirls me around.

"How could I shock you?" he asks as he gently sets me down.

"It must have been static from your sweater. I am *so* getting you back when you least expect it."

"I'll be ready," he says with a mischievous grin.

"Just for that, you're buying lunch for the rest of the week."

"Okay," he says, chuckling.

"*And* the lattes," I say, and wipe my face on his sleeve. I notice the time on his watch. "Well, as fun as this little goat-love afternoon has been, I've got to get home. I'm meeting my soon-to-be ex for the signing of the papers."

"That shouldn't take long, seeing how you're covered in goat spit. I'd imagine he'll wonder why he didn't sign them sooner."

"It's a wonder you're still single, Will Forrester."

"Hard to believe, I know," he says as he loops my arm through his. "I'll walk you home. As it happens, Brook and I are doing the new Chinese place around the corner from you tonight. I'd ask you to join us, but I'm not sure I could eat with the goat stench." I slug him once more in the side.

Chapter 20

We return to the apartment to find Brook and a friend in the living room having wine. Her friend's about our age, tall and leggy with long wavy auburn hair and beautiful hazel eyes that sparkle when she smiles. I could swear I'd seen her before on some hair color commercial. And I can also smell the setup for Will as soon as Brook leaps from the sofa to introduce them.

"Hey guys, this is Maddie Walsh, the one I was telling you about, Will."

So this is Maddie. Brook's mentioned her a few times before, mostly about how she was the only other sane person working at *80's Today*, but not once did she mention how beautiful she is. Will practically hurdles across the coffee table to take her hand.

"Nice to meet you finally," he gushes. She eyes him appreciatively and says something about the pleasure being hers. I step forward and extend my hand, saying, "Hi, I'm Lily."

She gives me a winning smile and takes my hand into both of hers, then pulls me into a hug. "Oh Lily, I have heard *so* much about you. I feel like we're old friends already!" She releases me and gives my arm a squeeze. "Brook has told me all about your awful Dick. That must've been terribly painful for you." Before I can even answer, she adds, "But I understand you've found Prince Charming in a certain sexy neurosurgeon. Yay for you!"

She flips her fabulous hair over her shoulder and sits back

down on the couch. Will takes a seat beside her. "Have some wine, I brought it back from Napa," she says while crossing her leg so that it's grazing Will's. "And you are joining us for dinner, aren't you?"

"I wish I could, but it just so happens that I have to meet my awful Dick to finalize divorce papers tonight." I take my wine and perch on the arm of the chair across from them, suddenly feeling self conscious with goat spit in my hair.

"I didn't realize that was tonight," Brook chimes in while pouring Will a glass. "Well, don't give him any wiggle room. He's a rat bastard and should compensate you accordingly."

Will seems absolutely mesmerized by Maddie. I have a sudden urge to snap my fingers in front of his face. "I know I'll get what's fair," I say, distracted by Maddie's spell on Will. "He might be a lot of things, but cheap has never been one of them."

"Yes, but cunning and manipulative are his strong suits, so I'm just saying. . ." Brook leans back and sips her wine. Maddie and Will clink theirs in a silent toast.

Suddenly I feel defensive of my awful Dick. I think it has something to do with not wanting Maddie to think I'm an absolute dolt for having spent almost a decade and a half with such a cad.

"I trust Richard won't try to hurt me any more than he already has," I say. "I mean, we did have many wonderful years together before we drifted apart."

Brook gives me a look like I've been smoking crack. I must admit, even I take a quick glance around for the pipe when Maddie says, "Of course you did. No one would even suggest otherwise."

Brook starts to object when Will gives her shin an inconspicuous kick beneath the coffee table. Maddie refills her own glass of wine as she continues.

"My first husband became so controlling and jealous toward

the end that I was embarrassed to take him around anyone I knew for fear of what they would think of me. Isn't that crazy? He's the ass, and I end up having to feel like one myself for being with him." She looks at me and lifts her glass. "So don't you worry, Lily, no one will think less of you for someone else's behavior. Believe me. I know they all can pass themselves off as princes in the beginning."

Brook raises her glass to clink Maddie's and gives me an apologetic look. I know Brook loves me and that she wasn't trying to put me down, especially in front of company. And she's the first to admit to having been involved with the jerkiest of all jerks. I give her a reassuring smile when Will says, "Gosh, I'm starting to feel a bit uncomfortable sitting here in my man skin." Maddie gasps.

"Oh Will, I'm sorry, I didn't mean to sound bitter, because really I'm not, ask Brook." Brook nods in agreement as Maddie continues, placing a hand on his arm. "I just know how Lily feels and don't want her to be defensive on my behalf." She smiles in my direction as Brook turns to Will and asks, "Man skin?"

Half an hour passes before Brook announces she's starving and really must have some food if she's going to drink any more wine. They all get up to leave, much to my relief. Maddie gives me a warm hug and tells me how happy she is to have finally met me, and looks forward to our new friendship. Brook clinks my wineglass with hers as she passes by, and Will dashes around the other side of the couch to help Maddie with her jacket before giving me a quick "See ya" without even looking back. He didn't even notice that his biggest fan, GG, had slithered out to say hi. After the door closes behind them, GG sits down and gives me a dirty cat-look.

"Hey, don't blame me," I say, "It was Sally Sunshine who was sucking up his atmosphere." I felt a little slighted too. God knows why. This is what I wanted for him.

Oh well. I've got to get ready to see Richard. I really wanted a little phone time with Dr. Rob before heading off to my meeting, but now it's too late. I'm starting to feel a bit nervous about seeing him. I don't know why, but I'm even a bit melancholy. I guess that's only natural because really, I meant it when I said that we had many wonderful years together. We did. I just didn't know then what I know now; which is what it's like to be treated like a princess. I'll just give Rob a quick two-minute call to tell him I miss him.

I dial on my cell while I pick out an outfit for my paper-signing dinner. What exactly does one wear to finalize their divorce these days? I decide to wear one of the few dresses I still have that Richard gave me, a black, fitted number that will also show him how svelte I am in comparison to what Lee Ann must look like now. Although, truth be told, I wish it were me all blown up and ready to give birth. It should've been me. But then how weird would that have been to have us both pregnant at the same time? At least I found out before *that* bad soap opera played out.

"Hi handsome," I say into Rob's voicemail, "I was hoping to catch you before I headed out for my meeting with my ex. You're probably busy saving a life, so I'll try not to be too disappointed that I missed you. Call me later; I'll be a free woman." I hang up feeling slightly buoyed just by the few seconds of the sound of his voice. I really am lucky, I think as I head for the shower.

❂   ❂   ❂

Thirty minutes later, I bounce down the front steps and grab a cab at the corner. I speed off to Koi, a hip uptown eatery, to meet my ex. My *ex.* Wow, it's really happening. I'm having a good hair day, my dress fits like the proverbial glove, and Richard is going to rue the day he ever cheated on me.

He's waiting for me on the street in front of the restaurant.

Damn. I wanted to make an entrance. You know, have him see me from across the room, then sort of glide toward him with all eyes in the room on me, wondering if I were some celebrity. Then I'd slide in next to him and flash a seductive grin and say something about, is he feeling all right, he looks a little pale. But no—here he is standing outside my cab, peeling off bills to pay the driver after he opens my door. I guess it's just as well; nobody ever thinks I'm a celebrity, and now my ride's free.

Richard takes my hand in his as I exit the car. I give him a quick hug then start to pull away, but he holds on tighter. When he finally releases me, I notice his eyes are watery. I will myself to feel nothing. This is the man who betrayed me, who broke our vows, and who I've happily moved on from. But he's also the man I loved dearly for many years.

"My God, Lily, you look fabulous," he says while he gives me an approving look. "I've missed you some kind of bad," he adds.

"You look pale, Richard." I turn and head to the front door adding, "Let's eat, I'm starved." I feel a bit of excitement watching his look of enthusiasm fade like a sinking sun.

"Okay, I get it, the look-at-what-you-lost attitude," he calls after me. "Believe me, Lily, I know what I've lost." He catches up and stops me at the door, trying to meet my eyes. "And I will do anything to get you back."

I give him a snippet of eye contact, and then look past him into the restaurant. "Is that Uma Thurman?" I say as I breeze by him.

He chuckles, then follows me in. "Okay, I'll play along. I'll admit I deserve the attitude."

Once we're seated, drinks ordered and breadsticks delivered, he leans forward.

"So. . .most expensive thing on the menu?"

"What?" I'm not sure if he's trying to make some sexual innuendo about me, or if he's asking me to guess the priciest item

Feng Shui Love ♥

they have here.

"That's how this is going to go, right?" He leans back in his chair. "Most expensive wine, most expensive meal. It's part of the punishment." Before I can answer he takes his wallet out and lays it on the table. "You can have every last penny I have if you'll forgive me and come back." I roll my eyes.

"Richard, don't you get it? I do forgive you, but it doesn't matter anymore. I realize now that I was only settling with you. I have—" I almost say *I have Rob*, but catch myself. Instead I say, "I have something real now. A job. Independence. A freedom I didn't realize I was missing. And I really do wish you and Lee Ann the best." I give him a sympathetic smile and pick up my menu. "I think I'll have the sesame-crusted salmon, what about you?"

Richard takes a sip of wine and studies my face. "So you felt like you were settling with me?"

"Well, not at the time, no. But now I realize what I need in a relationship, and you could never give it to me."

"And what exactly is it that I can't give you?"

"Red velvet cake." I snap my menu shut and lay it on the table.

"That's what you're having for dinner?"

"No, that's what you can't give me."

He replies with a confused headshake.

"You know how people say that passion in a marriage is like your favorite dessert, and no matter how much you might adore, let's say, red velvet cake, you're going to get tired of it if you eat it every single day. And sooner or later you're going to see key lime pie on the menu and wonder, hmmm. . .maybe I'd like that better." I fiddle with my napkin, waiting.

"I get that Lee Ann is the key lime pie in that scenario, but beyond that, I've missed your point."

"The point is, I could eat red velvet cake every day of my life and never wonder about the key lime pie. I'm sure it would taste fabulous if I had some, and I would no doubt want it again, but if

I made a commitment to myself and to my red velvet cake, I would stay faithful. Because no matter how many times I might have it, even when I'm not particularly in the mood for cake. One thing is undeniably true, it *is* good cake, which is why I wanted it in the first place." I give a nod to punctuate.

"And you don't think your new guy would be tempted?" he asks with a boyish grin.

"Maybe, but I think he would take the initiative to experiment with the cake recipe first or serve it with a different topping once in a while before he would ever abandon it for some apple tart. My Dr. Rob is not selfish." There, I said it.

"Ooh, a doctor." He does the scary hand-wave.

"Well, actually no. He's a surgeon, a neurosurgeon," I say proudly. Then I realize I've been dreaming of this moment all week, and frankly the look on Richard's face was worth the wait. My mother's words pop into my mind: *So what if he can't keep his pony in the pasture, at least he's got a good job and takes care of you.* Maybe that's why she hasn't been on my back lately about getting back with Richard; because Rob-the-neurosurgeon trumps Richard-the-attorney any day.

"So you think your neurosurgeon is so golden he'd never be tempted by some voluptuous nurse?"

I shake my head while Richard chortles and leans back in his chair. "Well, tell me this," he says. "I'm guessing your neurosurgeon was married, kids, big fluffy sheepdog, the whole nine yards, right?" He crosses his arms behind his head.

"I don't believe he had a sheepdog," I say, twirling the stem of my wine glass.

"So what do you think busted up that nice neat little picture?"

Before I can answer, he quickly leans forward and says, "I'll tell you what ended his marriage. Key lime pie. And orange sherbet, and tiramisu, and chocolate mousse, and whatever else he happened upon on the dessert trolley."

"No, that is *not* why his marriage failed. His wife was clinically depressed."

"I bet she was, married to a guy with such a voracious sweet tooth." He sits back again and smugly props an arm on the corner of his chair.

Before I can retort, our waiter arrives. Richard orders the salmon for both of us and asks for no salt and extra sesame seeds on mine. He remembered. I guess he brought his A-game for this one, thinking it's his final shot.

"And we'll have the red velvet cake for dessert," he says as he hands the waiter the menus.

I pick up my wine. "Kiss-ass."

He raises his glass to mine and gives me a wink as the waiter leaves.

"So you were saying. . ." He leans forward on the table with a glint in his eye.

"I wasn't saying anything." I take another sip of wine. I was hoping we were done with analyzing Rob's marriage, because honestly, Richard kind of struck a nerve. I don't really know why Rob's wife was so depressed, but now I'm starting to wonder.

"About Dr. Feelgood and his clinically depressed wife," Richard prods.

"Well, that was it. She was depressed, they grew apart, and the marriage ended. Just like us." I take a big sip this time.

"We might have grown apart, Lil, but that wasn't what ended our marriage." He swirls his wine around his glass a few times. "Men don't leave their marriages because they've *grown apart*. Men leave their marriages two ways and two ways only. They either leave for another woman, or they were thrown out on their tails after being caught with another woman."

"That's not true," I protest, but do faintly remember hearing that on *Oprah* once.

"Sorry sweetie, but statistics show that to be true." He finishes off his glass. I'm starting to feel like downing mine, but refrain since I've only had one breadstick and statistics show that intoxication is imminent for me in these conditions.

"It's not a hundred percent," I say defiantly.

"So your Dr. Bob—"

"Rob," I correct.

"Whatever. So he's in what, some ten-percent group?"

"Well, someone has to be."

He gives me a smug grin while he refills our glasses. "I only hope you don't take all my money and run off to Vegas to bet those odds, Lil." He tries to take my hand in his. I pull away.

"Now that you brought it up, where are the papers? Let me sign while my handwriting's still legible," I say, and giggle. Damn, this wine is going straight to my head. Richard smiles and pulls a single piece of paper from his jacket pocket and hands it over.

"That looks awfully thin. Did you just give me everything?" I unfold the paper and lay it in front of me, trying to focus on its content. It's not our divorce papers. It's the paternity results for Lee Ann's baby. Richard was ruled out as a possible match. I look up from the paper to his beaming face.

"I told you she was lying," he says. "In the handful of times we did it, I always wore protection." He apparently never tried that line aloud in the mirror before saying it.

"Is this supposed to make some kind of difference to me?" I toss the paper in his direction.

"Well, it exonerates me." He hands the paper back.

"From paternity, not betrayal." I ball it up this time.

"But we can get past this," he says quickly. "I screwed up. I'm an ass, but I learned a huge lesson. I'll never again take our marriage for granted. If you let me, I'll cherish you and our children for the rest of my life."

He puts two fingers over his chest, Scouts' honor-style, then slides down on his knees, slipping his arms around my waist.

"Red velvet cake forever, Lil, I swear."

I swallow the lump in my throat and realize I've definitely had too much wine. The waiter appears with our fish just in time.

"Richard, get up," I whisper.

"Don't leave me, Lil," he begs, not moving an inch. "Please. You can still be home in time for the holidays."

I smile awkwardly at the waiter while he nervously sets our plates down then stands, poised over my salmon with his pepper grinder.

"Yes, please," I nod as I nudge Richard under the table. "Do you want pepper?"

Chapter 21

W ell, here we are," I say when we sway up the steps to my building's front door.

Richard looks around. "This is it, end of the line?"

I give a little nod in response. I'm certain he expected me to invite him in, which isn't going to happen. Dinner seemed to go on forever, as did the flow of wine. Richard made a good case for himself, but I did a pretty good job myself with his prosecution. Oh, I admit, he had his moments of cuteness, but betrayal is something I just cannot tolerate.

"Well, I can't just leave you off here on the stoop," he says. "What kind of cad would I be if I didn't deliver you to your door safely? There could be muggers waiting in the stairwell." He gives a double brow-raise for emphasis.

"Does that gesture mean to suggest that it might be fun to come across deranged muggers?" I say, pointing to his brow and teetering slightly on my heels. He puts his arms around me, providing stability. I breathe in his cologne, feeling something familiar stir inside of me.

"Okay, good night," I say, pulling away for the door. But Richard, with his A-game firmly intact, grabs my arm and takes my key to unlock the door. Before I can protest, we're inside the building and heading up the stairs. He has his arms around me again, and is kissing my neck as we ascend. *Stop, stop,* I think. Why can't I say it out loud? *Because it feels pretty good,* I think to myself as his lips find their way to mine. I would try to talk myself out of kissing him back, but I was raised not to talk with my mouth full.

After several passionate minutes of groping and mauling each other on the stairwell, *pink light!* pops into my mind. This time the thought makes its way to being out loud. "Pink light, pink light, pink light," I say while I struggle to get myself free of his arms. He gives me a confused look for about the fifteenth time tonight.

"I was just supposed to send you pink light, not give it to you literally," I sputter.

Surprisingly, his confusion doesn't clear.

I try to explain. "The book. *Feng Shui Love* says—" He cuts me off with another lip lock. I eventually pull away and continue, "I've been sending you pink light all week so we can heal our wounds."

He continues to grope me and kiss my neck, whispering, "Whatever. Who knew it would work so well?"

"But you don't underst—"

"Oh, Lil, please explain this one some other time," he says as he pulls me into another kiss.

"Pink light," I say louder, jerking away again. "I can't do this, Richard, I can't do this to Will."

He pulls me close and gently kisses my chin this time. "Can't do what? Kissing your husband is certainly no crime." He kisses me again and says, "And I thought his name was Bob."

"Rob," I say dreamily between kisses.

"Then who's Will?" he says before planting another kiss.

"What?" I say, snapping my head back to meet his eyes.

"You said 'Will' before."

"No, I didn't, I said Bob, I mean Rob. . .didn't I?"

A wide grin spreads across his face. "You said Will. Who is he?"

"He's just a friend of *Brook's*," I punctuate her name.

"Uh huh, so where were we?" He moves in for another kiss,

which I dodge.

"No, no, we're done here," I say, pulling myself out of my liquid fog. "Our night is officially over."

"Why? We were having such a nice time." He takes my hand in both of his and raises it to kiss the meaty part under my thumb. I don't know why that's always turned me on, but I take my hand back.

"We were feeling the effects of alcohol, which I'm sure was the plan, right?" I say.

His face registers something that looks like genuine hurt. "Come on, Lil, we were about an inch away from reconciliation." He slides an arm around my waist and gives me a hopeful look. I search his face, trying to read him. Is this just some sort of game to him, or is he sincere about loving me? Is he genuinely sorry for his mistakes, or is he just trying to hold on to his nice, neat little life? I can't sort through this right now.

"No, we were about an inch away from divorce, remember?" I pull away from him and head up the stairs. He doesn't try to stop me this time, which stirs a tinge of disappointment, though I'm not sure why. I glance around. He's just sitting there on the steps, looking at his hands intertwined in his lap. I can't tell if he's sad at losing me, or if it's sadness at losing his case. I gulp back the lump in my throat and hurry up the rest of the stairs.

Safely inside the apartment, I head to the kitchen for some water. I need to clear my head and decipher what just happened back there. I honestly think something could have happened between us if he hadn't brought up that Will remark. And why did I say *Will?* I certainly didn't mean Will. He's the last person I'm thinking about right now; Dr. Rob is my focal point. The prominent neurosurgeon with the thriving practice, the penthouse in the sky and the house in the Hamptons—well, his wife has that one now, the lazy ex-wife he'll have to support for the rest of his life.

Where is this negative thinking coming from? And why was

I so close to doing the Turkish tango with Richard? Maybe he put roofies in my drink. I think all the wine tonight has pickled my brain. As I down my second glass of water, I notice a menu lying on the table. It's from the new Chinese place where Brook, Maddie, and Will went. *I wonder if it was any good? I wonder if they use white meat in their chow mien.* As I pick it up, a little slip of paper falls out.

Love is right around the corner.

It's a fortune. I wonder if it was Will's. My head is starting to spin, and I suddenly realize I've got to go to bed.

The next morning, I'm exhausted from a fitful night's sleep. On the plus side, I think I burned three-hundred calories with all the tossing and turning. My head is throbbing as I roll out of bed and head for the kitchen where Brook is reading the paper and munching on a piece of toast.

"Hey there, party animal, wanna go with me to look at paint colors?" she asks, "I'm feng shui-ing Ian's apartment this weekend."

"I'm going to pass," I moan. "I have a date with some strong black coffee and aspirin at the moment."

"Yeah, Richard's quite the headache inducer," she says taking another bite.

"It's more from all the alcohol he plied me with." I steady myself against the countertop and pour my coffee, which amazingly makes it into the cup.

"It's so like him to try to get you drunk for one last roll in the hay."

I lower myself into the chair across from her and visualize the dark brew chasing the alcohol from my veins. "Actually, he brought me DNA papers proving that Lee Ann's baby isn't his." I take a long sip.

"So what does that prove? That he's a lecherous cheating bas-tard, but wore a condom?" She turns the page of her newspaper.

"I know, that's what I said, but he seemed—"

"Sorry?" Brook offers.

"Yeah, I think so," I say feebly. I decide to let the thought stream away, because honestly I don't know what to make of it yet.

Brook decides differently. She folds her newspaper and flings it at me. "He's only sorry he got caught! Please tell me you're not getting sucked in by his crap!"

"I'm not. But I, I did sort of kiss him in the stairwell." I can almost hear her eyes rolling. I wince.

"*Sort of* kissed him?" Her voice goes up a couple of octaves.

"Okay, we made out like two flipping foxes in heat, but I felt something that I can't explain." I force myself up to make cheese toast. I can't have this conversation on an empty stomach.

"Oh, *I* can explain it. It's called abstinence, and it can make you do crazy things. You just need to get laid. And you have a perfectly good doctor just waiting. You don't need Richard."

"Well, gee, Brook, I was thinking maybe it had something to do with feelings, since I was married to this man for a decade and a half. But when you put in scientific terms like that—" I open a cabinet and retrieve the bread.

"*Feelings?* Really, Lil, you don't need to over-think this one. Just scoot on over to Dr. Rob's for a little afternoon play-date, and you'll feel brand-new before the ink dries on your divorce papers. I don't know what you've been waiting for anyway."

The divorce papers! We never got around to that last night. In fact, I don't even know if he had them with him. Guess he thought the paternity test would bowl me over and he wouldn't need them.

"I guess I'm just waiting for the right time to sleep with Rob," I say while I slather my toast in butter and place two slices of cheese on top. "I want him to view me as a viable option for a mate."

"But how can either of you make an accurate assessment if you haven't tried out the merchandise? You've got to take that car for a test drive before you buy it, Lil. What if you find there's too much slack in the clutch cable, or there's an annoying little noise in the tailpipe every time you accelerate?"

"Oh God, stop," I shudder, "I'm already feeling queasy, and that analogy might just send me over the edge." I pop my toast slices into the microwave and set the timer for twenty seconds.

"I'm just saying. . ." She gets up and walks to the sink, carrying her mug.

"And I'm just saying, when the time is right, I'm sure I'll find his clutch cable operating at peak performance. Now could we please move on from this auto metaphor? Because I refuse to address any tailpipe issues while I'm trying to eat."

"All right, all right. Only trying to help. Hey, did I tell you I got an invite to a record release party next week for the Boss himself, Mr. Bruce Springsteen?" Brook says while she washes her mug. "Chalk another one up for feng shui."

"You've really jumped on board the ole feng shui train," I say, returning to the table with my cheese toast. "It wasn't too long ago you thought I was crazy for adhering to the feng shui principle of keeping the drain plugs closed at all times."

"Now we're both crazy. Did you notice the new Jade plants I added to enhance our wealth area?" She places the mug in the drying rack by the sink, and wipes her hands on a nearby dishtowel.

I smile at her. "Yes, I did. Not to mention, you've been keeping the toilet lid practically bolted shut at all times."

"Well, it's so close to the career corner. I can't take a chance of having my professional life go down the drain again."

I nod in agreement as I take a bite of my cheesy concoction

while she gathers her purse and notepad to leave. As she exits the kitchen, she says something about watching Lenny Kravitz shoot a music video after she's done at the paint store with Ian's colors. When I hear her pick up her keys from the heart bowl, I remember and shout after her, "Hey, forgot to ask, how'd your setup with Will and Maddie go?"

"Great," she shouts while opening the door. "She's going with him to the animal shelter today to pick out a dog. So I'd say it's off to a good start. See ya later."

As the door closes, I say to no one, "I thought I was going with him to pick out a dog." Not that he came out and asked me, I just thought it was implied. I push the thought from my mind and finish my toast and coffee. I make a few calls about the big fundraiser, then decide that maybe Brook's right. Maybe I do need to get on with this whole sex thing. Maybe that's why my brain feels so cluttered with Richard and Will and Rob. I need to de-clutter, and Dr. Rob is a good starting point. With renewed spirit I shower, throw on a cute outfit, and head on over to the office of Robert Crescioli, MD.

When I arrive, I'm greeted by an impressive steel building with lots of curves and angles. Nice. I pop through the lobby and take the elevator up to his floor. Then it occurs to me that maybe I should've called first. What if he isn't even here? Maybe he's at the hospital doing neurosurgeony things.

The elevator doors open with a ding. Well, I'm here now. If he's not, I'll just leave him a message. I take a deep breath and make myself keep moving. Down the hall, around the corner, I'm like a beagle on the scent of a pheasant. I've never been here before, but I seem to instinctually know where I'm going. I get to his office reception area, and see him standing behind the counter writing in a chart. As I enter, he and the receptionist both look up. A big smile spreads across his face, and I know immediately that I must have sex today. Yes, this is the man for me, this man who works miracles and saves lives, and looks damn hot in blue scrubs.

"Hi gorgeous, did I forget a lunch date?" he says while his receptionist gives me the once-over.

"Nope, just thought I'd drop in and say hi." I try to look cool as I approach, while butterflies swarm in my stomach.

He comes around to the deserted waiting room and gives me a peck on the lips. "Come on in and see my office." He escorts me down the hall by the hand. Once inside, he closes the door behind us, drops his chart on the floor and devours me with a kiss. As he pins me against the door, I think *Oh yes, this feels right*. Not like the alcohol-induced stairwell incident of last night. I feel a wave of guilt about that when Rob squeezes me tighter, but mostly I feel the doorknob jabbing me in the small of my back.

"Wait, wait," I say as I gently push him away. "What time is your next patient?"

"I'm done seeing patients for the day."

"Oh good, then you won't object if I want to borrow you for the afternoon?" I plant a cool kiss on his neck.

He grins. "Well, I did have Mr. Bryant scheduled for surgery at four, but what the heck, he's paralyzed, it's not like he's going anywhere." He pulls me in for a kiss.

"Rob!" My reflexes push him away.

"Just kidding," he says while he puts my arms back around him. "I guess it's too soon for the neuro humor, huh?"

"I'm sorry, I'm just jumpy today. Can we get out of here?" I pull him toward the door.

"Absolutely," he says into my hair.

∞ Chapter 22 ∞

O h. My. God.
That was as close as I've come to a religious experience. Afternoon delight turned into a full night of
passion. Why have I never had sex like that before? Not that
I haven't had good sex, because believe me, I have. But this
was different, this was urgent, this was excessive, and this was
explosive. I guess a therapist would tell me I had a lot of stuff
bottled up that I needed to let out. I don't know, and I don't
care. I am on a cloud, riding it down the sidewalk as I leave Dr.
Rob's fabulous penthouse apartment. I catch a glimpse of my
reflection in a store window and think, *That Girl Is glowing!
That Girl looks great even on the walk of shame.*

Pink light, pink light. I'm sending everyone I pass pink light.
I want the whole world to let love in. I think I'll make t-shirts with
that slogan and hand them out on street corners.

Okay, I've got to get my head back to earth. I pull out my cell
phone and turn it on to check messages. I'm sure Mrs. Barrett
from the catering service doing the fundraiser is jumping up and
down wondering where I was yesterday. Maybe I should just tell
her the truth. *Yes, Mrs. Barrett, It's Lily. Sorry I didn't make it by
yesterday, but I just had to have sex. Yes, that's right. It's been
months and I just couldn't wait another day. What's that? Try
going a decade? That's very funny Mrs. Barrett— What's that?
Oh, you weren't kidding.*

My cell phone chirps. New messages. I flip it open. Six new

ones. *People, please, get off of my cloud.* First up is Brook, reminding me that our first yoga class is tonight. We decided it would be good feng shui to get clear physically as well.

Next is Mom. She's in town, staying at the Plaza again, wanted to meet me for lunch. Yesterday. Sorry Mom, had to have sex. I wonder what she's doing here.

Will's next, wondering if I could drop off the color samples for the new children's wing. Sorry, Will, I had more important things to do, like SEX. Except that sex is *not* more important than the poor children having to look at those wretched yellow walls. I feel guilty about missing that one. Damn Will. I was nowhere ready to feel guilty about lazing the afternoon and evening away playing doctor. But now, I do.

Ooh, speaking of, next is Rob. When did I miss a call from him? I was with him all night. I check the time of the message. Oh how sweet, he called me when I went to the bathroom to tell me how awesome I am. I'm such a lucky girl.

Next message. I stop smiling. Richard says he'll send me the papers if I really want them. He sounds so sad. But then again, why shouldn't he? He ruined the best thing that ever happened to him, not to mention missing out on the best SEX ever. As I'm about to hit delete, a new call is coming through. It's Will, might as well take it.

"Hi, Will," I say into the phone as I bounce along.

"Lily, did you forget?" He sounds a little perturbed. "You have a meeting in five minutes with Donald Trump to talk about funding the new wing," he says. "Where are you? I wanted to go over some stuff with you first."

"Oh crap, I did forget!" I check my watch to see if I can grab a cab and still make it. Close, but doable. I glance in a store window to see how I look, and there's no way I can have a business meeting looking like this, with my just-slept-in hair and all my makeup rubbed off long ago. Now that I really see myself, I wonder why I was waltzing around in public at all.

"Will, I'm so sorry, I, uh, I had a bit of an emergency to attend to this morn—"

"Are you all right?" he asks, his annoyance now alarm. Damn, I hate to mislead him like that.

"Um, yeah, I'm fine now."

"Oh good. What was wrong?"

"Oh, just uh, female stuff." Not entirely a lie. This female needed to get laid. Urgently.

"Don't worry, I'll take the meeting with him and call you later."

"Will, thank you. I'm so sorry I let you down." And I am.

"I'm just glad you're okay. Hey, there's something I want to talk to you about, but not over the phone. Could you meet me later today, maybe at our Starbucks?"

He sounds kind of serious. What could he want to talk about? And he said *our* Starbucks. Like he wants to talk about *us*. Not that there ever was an *us*. It's just that Brook always used to say he had a crush on me. But it can't be that, because whatever tiny flame he might have had at one time was certainly doused by Maddie. Well, whatever it is, I'll find out soon. I tell him I'll meet him at three.

Okay, back to my best-sex-ever high. I take deep-cleansing breaths while I walk the final block to the apartment. I feel all school-girly again by the time I enter to find GG sitting in the middle of the living room looking like the cat that just swallowed the canary. No, really, there's a tiny yellow feather sticking out the side of her mouth. I approach her slowly, careful not to spook her, all the while looking around for evidence that maybe Brook got a bird while I was gone.

As I step closer I notice another feather, this one light green, sticking out from under the couch. When I reach down to pick it up, GG lets out a loud meow and wanders around to the other side of the chair. Two seconds later I hear a shredding sound, then she darts off like a bullet with her ears pinned back. Looking wired, she leaps onto the side table, and then banks herself off the back of the couch before darting down the hall like she's been smoking kitty crack. When I look behind the chair I find a taupe suede cropped jacket lying on the floor. Shredded. The few decorative feathers left are hanging precariously from the neckline. Brook is going to kill her.

I pick it up to see if it's salvageable, but it doesn't look good. I wonder what provoked her to go all Bruce Lee on Brook's jacket. Maybe we ran out of Fancy Feast. I fold it up and contemplate calling Brook, but decide it can wait. I didn't get much sleep last night, and I'm thinking a nap's in order before I go meet Will for the big talk. I head into my room and plop down on the bed. Maybe he's going to fire me. Can you fire a volunteer? That can't be it. I'm doing a good job around there, other than the little mishap from today.

Oh, I bet I know what it is. He probably just wants to ask advice on something to do with Maddie. Sure, that's it—although I'm not real versed in how to handle drop-dead-gorgeous women. I'm sure she must be more high-maintenance than us mere mortals. I hope Will knows what he's getting himself into. *Again, not my problem,* I think while I feel my eyelids drift closed.

I awake to the sound of purring. GG has perched herself on the pillow next to me. I guess she's sucking up since she knows she'll need an ally when Brook gets home. Actually, she *is* home, I realize, hearing familiar sounds. I stretch and then make my way into the living room.

"Hey there, sleeping beauty. What are you doing napping in the middle of the day?" Brook asks while she looks over some papers.

"Because I was up all night having sex," I confess as I curl up on the opposite end of the couch.

"You did? Good for you. It was with Rob, wasn't it?" She makes a note on a page.

"Of course." I playfully kick her.

"Just checking. After that whole Richard thing in the stairwell—"

"It was ten times better than any Richard-sex ever was."

"I'm surprised Richard could even have sex at all with that stick up his butt."

"Stop. He wasn't that bad."

She gives me a fake smile, and then changes the subject. "So, when's the big Bermuda trip?" She asks while gathering her papers into a neat pile.

I smile. "Next weekend, which will be perfect. I have a great excuse for missing Thanksgiving with my family, and we'll both be tanned for the big gala event."

"Well that *is* the important thing about that night," Brook playfully quips while getting up. She heads for the kitchen. Uh-oh. I left the shredded jacket on the table in there. Better warn her.

"Um, I think GG is mad at you," I say and follow behind her.

"Why do you say that?" She breezes into the kitchen where the jacket is laying out on the countertop.

"Because of that." I point.

"Oh that's Maddie's. She left it here the other night. I guess the feathers were just too enticing for ole G." She gets an iced tea out of the fridge. "Haven't told Maddie yet. I was hoping to find another one like it so I could replace it first."

"Hmm. Maddie's, huh?" I chuckle as I hold it up again.

"Why do you seem pleased by this?" She takes a sip of her tea and leans against the countertop.

"I'm not. It's just kind of funny how GG has such a thing for Will, and then she went after his girlfriend's jacket." I toss it back on the table.

She eyes me, then points a finger at me. "I think you might be the one with the thing for Will."

"Don't be ridiculous. I'm madly in love with Rob." I grab an apple from the fruit basket and take a big bite.

She keeps eyeing me like a prosecutor. "You sure about that? Because I think you're deflecting." She takes a step toward me.

"What?" I ask as I take another big bite.

"That, that right there," she says, moving her pointing finger to my apple. "You can't keep a straight face, so you stuff an apple in it."

"You are insane." I sidestep her and sit down at the table.

Just as I'm about to take another bite, she grabs the apple from me and holds it behind her back. "So tell me again that you don't have a thing for Will."

"You are crazy," I say with a chuckle. She waits with raised eyebrows.

"Okay, okay." I roll my eyes, trying hard not to laugh, then open them wide and say, "I don't have a thing for Will."

"All right then." She hands the apple back with hesitation. I grab it back from her and burst out laughing.

"Lunatic," I say taking another bite. "However, Will does want to talk to me about something important in an hour. He said he couldn't discuss it over the phone."

"What do you think it is?" she asks, wiping her hand on her jeans.

I never did tell her about the attempted kiss that night. I guess I didn't want her razzing him about it. Poor Will took enough torture in high school.

"I don't know what it is. You're the one who said he had a crush on me. Maybe he wants to tell me."

"Nah. He did, but he's so into Maddie now he probably can't remember your last name." *Ouch!*

"Then maybe he wants advice about her?" I suggest.

"I doubt he'd ask you. I'm the one who knows her."

"Well then, no clue. But I'll find out soon enough." I stand and toss my apple core in the trash. "I've got to get a shower before I go."

"Okay then, I'll meet you at yoga later. Don't forget, six o'-clock," she yells after me.

I emerge from the apartment forty-five minutes later, the spring definitely back in my step. The good doctor called before I got into the shower to tell me how much he's missing me already. We talked about getting together again tonight, but he has rounds at the hospital and has to get caught up on charts later. It's just as well. Honestly, I don't think I could take another night like that again so soon.

When I enter Starbucks, Will is reading the paper with our requisite lattes already on the table. I scoot into the booth across from him.

"Hey there, how'd the meeting go?" I say. I can see by his face, not well. "Oh Will, I really am sorry, I should've been there. I've had such a good rapport with Trump's people over the phone—"

Will shakes his head and cuts me off. "No, Lily, the meeting went fine."

He looks so somber. "Well, *what* then?"

He fidgets with the folded newspaper on the table beside him.

"What, did somebody die? What?" I lean forward.

His eyes widen for a second, seeming to confirm what I'm thinking. He exhales deeply while looking me in the eye. "Not yet." He looks down at the table and slumps forward on his elbows. My initial reaction is that it must be him. I grab his hand.

"Oh my God, Will, are you sick?"

"No, no." He takes his hand back, shaking his head. "I'm sorry to drag this out, but I just. . .oh hell, I'll just say it. Lily, I think your father is dying."

It doesn't register what he just said. How would he know about Dad's health? All I can manage is, "What?"

"I've seen your father in the oncology wing twice now. I didn't say anything the first time because I wasn't sure it was him, but it is."

"You don't even know what my father looks like now. He's changed considerably since high school. And Mom would've said something." I reconsider this. "Well, in light of recent developments, maybe not—"

"Lily, I'm talking about Walt. I saw Walt at the hospital."

He takes my hand. It takes a few seconds to register before I pull my hand away.

But the response is easy. "First of all, Walt is not my father. Second, it's really none of my business what his health issues are. Wait a minute, you've never even seen him."

Will's face reddens as he looks down. "Well actually, I have."

He must have heard my gasp; he sits back against the booth and says, "In fact, I saw him right here. It was after you left one day and I was finishing my coffee. He sat down and introduced himself. He asked me to try to get you to see him again."

"What?" I practically scream. "Why didn't you ever tell me this—"

Will shushes me. "Because I thought you might be mad. Apparently I have good instincts." He looks around to make sure I'm no longer drawing attention. "Anyway, I never did try to get you to see him, did I?"

I let out my breath and try to crack my neck. I was feeling so relaxed this morning, despite being twisted into more positions than Gumby last night. But now I'm so knotted up, I can hear my shoulder blades crackle when I roll them backward.

"Lily, it all makes sense now," Will says. "That must be why he came looking for you. He didn't just happen upon you singing. He's dying and wants to make peace."

I can't fathom what to say to this. I shouldn't care about what *he* wants, the man who abandoned me. On the other side of the coin, I do feel a little bit sorry for him. I lean forward on my elbows, my forehead in my hands. I feel Will's hand on my back as he scoots in next to me.

"Lil, I know he's not any kind of father to you, but he's a dying man. Would it be so hard to give him just one lunch date?" Before I can speak, he goes on. "Believe me, the worst feeling you'll ever know is regret after someone is gone for good. There's no way to make it up once you've missed your chance."

I lean over on his shoulder and feel a tear slip down my cheek. He pulls me closer and holds me to his chest.

After a minute, I pull away sniffling. "I'm going to need some time with this one before I can say what I'm really feeling."

"I understand." He says, keeping his hand on my shoulder. "You okay for now?"

"Yeah."

He gives me a closer look. "You sure? Maybe I should go get that goat again."

I give him a little jab in the ribs as a small chuckle escapes me.

"Okay then. You call me if you need me. I've got to run. Maddie's making dinner." He slips his arm from my shoulder and stands to leave.

"Oh, so that's going well, huh?" I ask while I dab my eye with my napkin and look up at him.

"It's going great," he says all moony-eyed.

"I'm glad. You deserve it." I slide out of the booth and stand to face him. I get a whiff of his cologne and it stirs something in me. Maybe Rob was wearing that last night. We walk to the door together while I try to process this latest wrinkle in the almost-dead-dad scenario. Outside, Will gives me a hug before heading off in the opposite direction.

I wander the streets for a while, thinking about when I was a little girl. I'd imagine myself at my father's funeral, saluting the dark car carrying the casket while it slowly drove by. I'm sure I just transposed myself mentally into the Kennedy funeral footage I saw somewhere as a kid. I'm too big to star in that vision now. And besides, since Walt never was in any war, I'm sure his real funeral will be far from the grandiose one I saw as a child, with sad faces lining the streets and waving. Actually, I wonder how many people will even attend Walt's funeral. He seems alone in this world.

Before I know it, I'm digging through my purse looking for the card Walt gave me with his address. A subway ride later, I stand outside the bar where he said he works. It isn't the dive I had envisioned. Once inside, I see it lacks any real décor, but it does have a decent-sized stage and advertises live music on weekends.

I ask for Walt at the bar, and I'm told that he's off today, but I can try upstairs. Apartment number two. Go back outside and into the alley to get to the stairs. Thankfully it isn't dark yet. After scaling the wobbly stairs and venturing into a gloomy hallway that reminds me of something I'd seen on *CSI*, I find myself staring at door number two. Maybe I should opt for what's behind door number three instead, Monty.

Okay, I can do this. I have no idea what I'm going to say, but I've come this far, so I knock. A voice from the other side yells that's he's coming.

Okay, think. . .what am I going to say? What am I going to say?

Before I can come up with anything, the door flings open to reveal Walt; hair disheveled, a robe draped open over his boxers. I look away, and my new line of sight leads directly behind him to the woman in his bed with the covers pulled up around her.

"Mom?!?!" I scream.

Chapter 23

"Hey there, kiddo," Walt says, but he's not able to continue because *my mother* is shrieking like she's just seen a rodent run across the carpet. (And judging from the room, it's not all that unlikely.) Walt steps aside and gestures me inside while Mom and I shout in unison, "Oh my God, oh my God, oh my God!" Walt looks on in amusement as he ties his robe shut.

"What are you doing here?" We shriek simultaneously.

"Mom, I can't believe you're cheating on Dad with. . . *Dad?*" I give Walt a disgusted look as I enter the room. Mom scrambles out of the bed, wrapping herself in the sheet.

"It is not what it looks like, darling." She approaches me looking like she just got back from a toga party at the local frat house.

"Well, it *looks* like you're having sex with ole Walt here." I gesture his way as he lights a cigarette and takes a seat in a nearby chair. Mom grabs the cigarette from his mouth and stubs it out in the ashtray. "I told you, I cannot kiss a smoker," she scolds.

"Well hey, looks like the party's pretty much over to me," he says, running his hands through his messy hair.

"Hello, remember me?" I manage a shaky wave from my place by the dresser.

"Oh baby, I *wanted* to tell you, but didn't want to upset you!" She rushes to my side and tries to embrace me, but I pull away.

"Upset me? What about Dad?" I start to pace beside the bed.

"Hey, I'm cool with it," Walt says while he leans back in his chair and crosses his arms behind his head.

"Not you!" We both say in unison again.

"Darling, please," Mom pleads while she paces beside me, "Just let me explain."

"I can't imagine what explanation you could possibly have for being here. You're the one who said he was a no-good rotten son of a bitch, and that I was better off without him."

"Well, that was true. Then." Mom shoots him a look.

"But now? He's this really swell guy now, is that it? So swell, in fact, that you had to cheat on my father?" I push past her, heading for the door, when I remember why I came. Suddenly I gasp and cover my mouth with my hands.

"You know, don't you?" I say, turning and pointing a finger at her.

Her eyes somehow manage to show innocence. "Know what, darling?"

"And you!" I turn my finger on Walt. "You used that to get her into bed."

Walt looks to my mother and shrugs his shoulders with a confused look on his face.

"That is *despicable*," I say. "And to think I actually came here because I felt sorry for you." I grab Mom and usher her toward the door.

"Darling, please, what are you talking about?"

"I'm getting you out of here." I nudge her once more toward the door.

"But I'm not dressed." She grabs onto the dresser as we pass it and pulls herself free from my grasp.

Walt stands. "Look, I don't know what's going on here, but maybe we should just talk about it—"

"Like you don't know," I spew. "Using your, your *tumor* to woo her into your bed for one last roll in the hay."

"My tumor?" He laughs.

Mom looks genuinely surprised. "Do you have a tumor, Walter?"

"Or whatever it is you're dying of," I say.

"Where'd you get an idea like that?" he says, putting another cigarette between his lips. Mom gives him a stern look. He rolls his eyes and puts it back down, muttering, "Nothing worse than an ex-smoker."

I say, "My friend said he's seen you in the oncology wing a couple of times, so he thinks you are dying."

Walt lets out a hearty laugh. "Hell no, I was just visiting my buddy Chopper. He's got melanoma. I told that bastard to use sunscreen."

"So there's nothing wrong with you?" I ask.

"Well, that's a matter of opinion." He grins as Mom puts her arm around me.

"So that's why you came here, dear?" she asks. "You thought he was dying?"

I nod, and she gives my arm a squeeze and says, "That is so sweet, darling."

"Wait a minute, you." I turn to look her in the eye. "If you didn't think he was dying, why are *you* here?"

"I came to confront him about tracking you down, and insist that he leave you alone."

"So, what? You made a tradeoff? Sex for leaving me alone?"

They both snicker as they exchange looks "No, darling. We started talking, and after a while we realized that we're very different people from who we were back then. One thing led to another, and before we knew it," she gives me a weak smile, "we were waltzing down memory lane."

"I don't think your *husband* is going to appreciate your little nostalgic dance," I point out.

"I thought you said you were separated," Walt says with furrowed brow.

"Mom! You told him that?"

"Darling, we have to talk," she says while adjusting her sheet. "Your father," she glances at Walt, "James left me eight months ago."

I lean my hand on the dresser just in time before I collapse. "What?"

"It's true. At first we didn't want to tell you because of the whole Richard thing, and then I didn't want to tell you because I was hoping that James would come back."

I feel like someone just tossed me a bowling ball, I forgot to hold my hands out, and it connected square in my gut. I'm not sure if I'm even standing upright as I make my way to the door. When I open it, I hear her ask me to wait, that she'll get dressed and come with me. I pick up speed as I leave the door open and take the stairs two at a time on my way down.

I rush out into the street and start running. I have no idea where I'm going; I just need to use up some of this adrenaline pulsing through my veins. What is it about me that makes her think I'm so fragile?

I see a subway sign and dart down into the stairwell. My heart is pounding as I cross the turnstile, more so from my mother than the run. Then I think about my father, not the so-called dead/dying one, but the one who raised me. Why would he leave Mom after all these years? I wonder if she drove him away with more of her *omissions*. It would serve her right. I decide to call him when I get off the subway and tell him how sorry I am.

As I emerge into the street a few blocks from the apartment, I pull out my cell and dial Dad's number. A young woman answers on the third ring. She has to say hello several times before I finally ask for Dad. She very cheerily tells me she'll get him, and then proceeds to call him "Honey."

"Hey, sweetie, everything okay?" he asks a little awkwardly.

"You tell me. Who was that?" I slow my pace and nearly get

trampled by a guy walking a dog.

I hear a rustling sound like he's got his hand over the phone before he finally answers. "That was my friend Carly. So, I take it your mother finally told you."

"Well, sort of. I'd like to hear your side of it." The side I was fully prepared to take until this Carly person answered the phone.

"Now's not really the time, sweetie. Could I call you tomorrow?"

"Dad! I just found out you and Mom split up almost a year ago, but failed to tell me." I start walking again, my building in sight.

"Well that was her idea. She kept insisting that we wait. I wanted this whole thing out in the open. I was honest with your mother right from the start. I knew it would only cause more stress the longer we went on with the charade, not to mention how it was making Carly feel."

Since when does this Carly get a vote, is what I'm wondering. "Dad, what the hell are you talking about? Who is Carly?"

"I thought your mother told you."

"She didn't mention a Carly." I stop walking, having reached my building. I balance on one foot off the edge of the bottom step, waiting for him to explain.

There's a bit of silence before he finally answers. "Carly's my. . .well, girlfriend."

I take a deep breath and sit down while he continues with his side of the story. He's in love with Carly and wasn't about to cheat behind my mother's back. It may not be fair, but that's just the way it is. He can't help what he feels and he hopes that I will understand.

What I wish I could understand is how this day could have started out with my head in the clouds, and is ending with a pile of family crap being dumped in my lap. Thank God Rob and I are heading to paradise soon. I need some distance from reality for a while.

Oh my God. Speaking of reality, Mom must've been devastated when Dad left. I can't believe she didn't tell me. I could've helped her through it. We could have helped each other. Why doesn't she believe that I can handle things?

Then it hits me. She doesn't believe that *she* can handle things. . .so she doesn't!

For the love of her ass, my mother is a big damn scaredy cat!

∽ *Chapter 24* ∽

I'm about to call Mom and apologize when Brook comes bouncing down the steps beside me on her way to meet me at yoga. I fill her in on the day's latest events, and understandably, she's speechless. She sits down beside me, mouth agape, when Mom comes strolling around the corner. I give her a weak smile as she approaches and see it was the last thing she was expecting. As she reaches the steps, I jump up and give her a big hug. She cautiously hugs me back.

"Darling, what happened? You were so mad at me," she says.

I release her and look her in the eye. "I called Dad. Carly answered. He told me why he left. Mom, I'm so sorry."

She gives a dismissive hand wave into the air. "Did he tell you that she's twenty-seven?"

"Dear God," Brook says as she gets up. "Did he get the red sports car too?"

Mom chuckles and shrugs her shoulders. I send Brook off to yoga solo, turning my attention to Mom instead. I knew some mother-daughter time was in order, so we decide to head to the sushi place for some overdue girl talk. As we commiserate over dragon rolls and yellow fin about cheating husbands and past musician flings, Mom confesses that she's never really gotten over Walt. Seems she's wondered about him often throughout the years, and she thought it more than ironic that he showed up right after our big feng shui weekend, when she went home and moved Dad's picture out of her love corner. Finally accepting that he was gone, she thought the picture was blocking real love from finding her. Since it was apparent he wasn't coming back now that he was living with Carly, she sent up her own balloon asking the universe to bring her true love. Then bam, just like that, she gets the call from me that Walt showed up at my door.

"So you didn't go over there to tell him to cease-and-desist his efforts to see me?" I say over a piece of yellow fin poised for a bite.

"No, really I did!" She takes a sip of sake. "That was my story and I was sticking to it, but when I got there he was so happy to see me. He said he couldn't count the number of times he wanted to contact me over the years."

"I see. He wanted to get in touch with you over the years, but not me." I don't know why this is such a sticking point with me.

"Darling, don't take it personally. He didn't know you, and he certainly didn't know how to be a father. He didn't want to have kids back then—hell, we *were* kids. He just wanted to chase his dreams."

"But now he's ready to be a father, is that it?" I stab at my food with a chopstick like a petulant child.

"Oh, heavens no. He knows you have a wonderful father, and you always will. He was just hoping you'd give him a chance to get to know you now." She reaches over and takes my chopsticks. "Aren't you even the least bit curious about him?" Actually I'm a lot curious, but I'm not ready to admit this just yet.

Mom ends up staying in the city the rest of the week, which surprisingly, turns out to be quite fun. By the end of the week, I finally work up the courage to tell her that I am going with Rob to Bermuda for his conference, then staying through the weekend for Thanksgiving. Amazingly, she doesn't put up much of a fight. That's really odd for her, but I'm not going to question it, I'm just relieved. On the final day she's here though, I figure out her angle. She gets me to agree to lunch with her and Walt. It's weird seeing a man who reminds me of myself, but what's really weird is watching the two of them together. They have great chemistry. The way they bounce off one another's thoughts reminds me of Harry and Sally.

At the end of lunch, Walt thanks me for coming, and for a minute he looks like he might cry. I actually feel like I might too, as I imagine us on one of those reality shows where they reunite long-lost relatives who were torn apart by uncontrollable circumstances, never again knowing what happened to the other. Only that's not the case here. So I gulp back the lump in my throat, will my tear ducts to freeze, and offer a handshake instead of going in for a hug. I see the disappointment register on his face, but Mom looks pleased that I'm at least here. I give her the hug instead then head home to pack for my trip. I keep picturing the two of them together while I'm trolling around in my closet and bathroom, collecting my things for Bermuda. I just can't believe how happy Mom seems with Walt, after all that's happened with them. Only it's like it never did!

I shake my head in disbelief, at them *and* the fact that Rob and I leave tomorrow and I hadn't even thought about packing until now! I'm always amazed at how men can pack for an eight-day tour of Europe in a single carryon, while I need three suitcases and a cosmetics bag to make it through a long weekend. It's always been a pain to pack, but now with airline regulations and their 3-1-1 rule. Are they kidding me? Obviously, there are no women in power in the Transportation Safety Administration. Hey, I understand the seriousness of the threat to airline security, but three-ounce containers in a one-quart plastic bag, and *one* per passenger? They're killing me.

I sit on the floor surrounded by miniature bottles, with everything from a facemask to Pepto-Bismol, and I start to think *when did I get so high-maintenance?* Or maybe it's a sign that I'm getting old that I need so many products now. Either way, I don't need the negative energy...*pink light, pink light, I'm surrounding myself in pink light.*

Okay, back to the task. I look at the numerous beauty products I've carefully selected and lined up like soldiers on the floor around me. There's no way all of these are fitting into any little plastic bag, so I'm going to have to take my chances and pack most of it in my checked luggage. I'll just bring makeup items in the plastic bag. That way if our luggage gets lost, at least I'll still be able to put my best face forward even if my hair is a frizzy mess.

Oh, how I long for the days of our youth when Brook and I never wore makeup and tousled long locks were all the rage, like the summer after our first year in college when Brook and I rented an apartment at the beach. We lived off of the samples at the grocery store and Ramen noodles. Remember those? They were like five cents a package. Times were so simple then. Life really is made up of memories, and you're lucky if you can build up a bank of happy ones to dig into when the going gets tough. I smile thinking of all the great memories I plan to create with Rob, starting this weekend.

I climb across the landmine of stuff on my bedroom floor and trip on my MBT shoes lying in front of my closet door. Brook calls them convalescent shoes because they have this huge thick sole that makes you feel like you're walking in sand. They promise to tone your butt and reduce cellulite if you walk in them regularly. I ordered them online, express delivery, the day Rob told me about the trip. Heck, as much as I walk now living in the city, I figured I could have the butt of a 20-year-old in about two weeks.

Granted, they do look like orthopedic shoes, but once you achieve that 20-year-old butt, who's looking at the shoes? I glance at my rear view in the full-length mirror. Admittedly, I'm not good with guessing ages, but I'd have to put it around 28. The shoes are definitely working. Now all I need is a little self-tanner, and I'll be beach-ready for Rob in a couple of hours.

"Uh-oh, something went wrong." I say to my reflection. Why can't I do a simple little thing like apply self-tanner without looking like a poorly striped tiger? Dear God, is that a handprint on my thigh? The chirp of my cell phone sends me running for my robe when I see that it's Rob calling. I feel my face flush when I answer. "Hello?" I have no idea why I'm being so neurotic; I know he can't see me. No response. "Rob, is that you? I can't hear you." He must be in the elevator. I click it off and run the humiliating striped sex scenario through my head. What if the handprint won't come off?

There's my phone again. Again, no response to my hello, but the caller ID says it's the good doctor. "Rob, can you hear me?" I say. No one responds, but I can hear someone talking. I don't recognize the voice so I hang up. A minute later, it rings again.

At least this time he speaks. "Hey baby, it's me," he says when I answer. "I'm running a little late, surgery took longer than I thought, you still want to grab dinner?"

"Don't worry, sweetie, I know saving lives is unpredictable." I open my robe and wince at the sight of my zebra legs. "I've still got tons to do before our trip, so why don't we just skip it?" I mentally count the hours it might take to reverse my tanning debacle.

"Okay, I understand. I'll pick you up in the morning for the airport then. Can't wait." He blows a kiss through the phone.

"Me too. Hey, what's going on with your phone? You kept calling but weren't there."

"I did? Must be this new BlackBerry. I haven't quite mastered it yet." He chuckles. "I'll get my son to give me a lesson when we get back." He concludes the call by telling me he'll be counting the hours 'til we touch down in sunny Bermuda, and we blow kisses back and forth like grade school kids before hanging up. Thank God Brook isn't here to witness our obnoxious behavior.

I head back to the bathroom for some major exfoliation when I hear a tone coming from my cell phone. I flip it open, and the display reads: *1 new text message*. I hate texting. I press okay and the message pops up. It's from Rob. *I can't wait to get my hands on you in Bermuda!*

Well, well, well, isn't he the little eager beaver? I wonder if I could pass the handprint off as his. I'd text him back, but it would take half an hour on this old phone. And I'm still far from being ready for his hands, but isn't that cute? Again I imagine Brook making barfing noises if I showed her.

I spend the rest of the night soaking and scrubbing and re-peating the procedure until my stripes and blotches finally fade away. Of course so did my tan, but hey, I'm happy to wake up pale and handprint-free this morning, ready for the good doctor to examine me later. I wheel my suitcases by the door and take a seat on the couch to finish the last of my coffee while I wait for Rob to pick me up. My cell phone makes that chime again. I open it and read, *Frenchy's at 3?*

What on earth does that mean? We should be at the hotel by then. Maybe it's some kind of sexual innuendo. The knock on the door startles me. I see through the peephole that it's Rob and swing the door open. He grabs me into a big hug.

"How did you get in?" I say when he puts me down.

"I coat-tailed in on one of your neighbors. You ready? We don't want to hit traffic."

He grabs my suitcases and heads into the hall. I snatch my purse from the side table and gleefully follow behind him, for-getting to ask about the frenchy thing. All I can think about is what a lucky girl I am. Who would've thought eight months ago when I was picking up the pieces from Richard, it would really be a blessing in disguise? And not only did I trade up, but I got everything I wrote on my balloon! I don't care if people think feng shui's a bunch of baloney; I'm jetting off to Bermuda with a sexy neurosurgeon because of it. Not bad in exchange for reading a book and moving some furniture, huh?

Chapter 25

Richard wouldn't have been caught dead with anything as girly as my pink luggage, but Rob didn't even flinch when I loaded him up like a pack mule with my brightly colored bags. I know I shouldn't make comparisons, but it's difficult to hide my smile while he zips through the terminal proudly rolling my belongings behind him. When we take our seats on the plane, I snag a magazine from the seat pocket and hesitate. Can you believe it? It's the latest issue of *InStyle*. Do I dare?

I can't help myself; I flip to the contents and find the page. *These days you don't need to read between the lines because it's all being spelled out clearly enough. Be grateful for clear communication; a deeper relationship results.*

That's certainly better than my last departure horoscope. I settle in with my pillow and blanket. After takeoff, Rob pulls out his conference materials and starts to read, so I decide to take a nap. After being up all night packing, I drift off easily and only awaken when the captain dings the seatbelt sign for final approach. Rob's sweatered arm is around me, and I can't help feeling a twinge of nostalgia when I gaze out over the blue water surrounding our destination. The last time I saw the Caribbean, I was excited about starting a family with Richard. I look over at Rob and wonder what our babies might look like. He's made no secret of the fact that he wants more kids, which is another checkmark in his column. I squeeze his hand as we touch down.

While taxiing in, I turn on my phone and immediately get that tone again. I open my new text message: *About to take off now, counting the minutes.* I flip the phone shut and give my hand some man a big hug.

"You are such a sweetie," I coo into his shoulder.

"What's that for?" he asks while he packs up the conference materials he'd been reading.

"All your little text messages. I'd text you back, but it would take me forever." He looks at me blankly for a minute, and then nods his head in agreement.

The Fairmont is everything the brochure promised and more. A balmy breeze flows through the open lobby as we enter to check in. Everything is so magnificent and tropical. A brawny bellman offers me a drink while he takes my coat and hangs it on the cart next to our luggage. Rob hands me a twenty to tip him and suggests I go up and get comfortable while he runs over to the banquet hall to sign in for the conference.

When the bellman shows me in, I decide it's the most beautiful hotel room I've ever seen. The king-sized bed is outfitted in cream-white bed linens draped with a gold satin overlay, piles and piles of satin pillows, and fresh flowers on the bedside table. This is definitely nicer than the suite Richard and I booked in Barbados. I can't explain why, but I start to feel a little nervous. I tell myself nothing can go wrong here, but I'm not taking any chances this time. I whip out a rose quartz heart and place it on the dresser in the love area of our room. After unpacking, I slip into a nice bubble bath with the windows open, overlooking the sea. I can't remember the last time I felt so happy and relaxed. Just as I'm about to drift off, Rob comes in and kisses the top of my head.

"Sorry I took so long, but I'm glad to see that you're enjoying yourself." He sits down on the edge of the tub.

"I'd rather be enjoying you," I say, and take his hand. "Why don't you hop in with me?"

"Oh, I wish I could, but I've got to meet an associate at 3:00. But after that, I'm yours for the rest of the night."

"But I thought we were going to have frenchy's at 3:00," I pout. He gives me a vague look. "Your text message," I say. "Forgive my lack of hip-ness that I don't know what a frenchy is, but I bet I could guess." I release his hand and run a soapy finger up his thigh.

"Did that message get sent to you too?" He jumps up and moves to the sink to wash his face. "I'm sorry," he says through soap and water, "my new BlackBerry really does have a mind of its own. Frenchy's is the name of the café where I'm meeting my colleague."

"Oh." I give a disappointed sigh while he dries his face. But then I smile as he hangs the towel on the rack above my head, "Well, I like my interpretation better."

"Me too." He gives me a quick kiss, "I just have to get some business out of the way first." I watch him brush his teeth and run a comb through his hair. "I shouldn't be more than an hour or two." He blows me another kiss before heading out of the bathroom door. I try to return to my happy place, but I can't shake the feeling of rejection. I know it's silly. I mean, the man did come here for business. I guess it's just hard for me to see how anybody could think about business in such a romantic spot.

After my bath, I call down for a massage on our lovely balcony. By the time Jeremy is done kneading my knotted muscles, Rob is back and eager to take me to dinner. I throw on a slinky sundress and the brown mules he admired on our very first meeting. When I step out of the bathroom, he gasps and tells me how touched he is that I brought them. The rest of the evening is ripped right from a fairy tale: romantic dinner overlooking the sea, a barefoot walk on the beach, followed by a serenade from a Spanish guitar player while we sit around a fire pit beneath a sky full of stars. The evening couldn't be any better. . .unless we had sex. Which we don't. Rob's exhausted by the time we get back to the room and says that last glass of wine did him in.

"No worries," I tell him. "Morning sex has always been my favorite anyway." So we cuddle up together and he's off to dreamland in about forty-five seconds. I listen to him emit soft little baby snores while I stroke his John Stamos hair. Eventually I drift off as well.

When I open my eyes the next morning, I roll over to an empty pillow and a note:

> I'm so sorry I had to run, got a message there was a cancellation and now I have to give a speech first thing this morning. I'll make it up to you double when I get back. xoxo.

Ah, the life of a doctor's girlfriend. Better get used to it, I suppose. Oh well, no use letting all that sunshine outside go to waste. I decide to book a snorkeling expedition for the day. I've always wanted to swim with sea turtles. Richard and I actually booked one in Barbados, but it was scheduled for later in that tragic week. I get dressed and leave my own note for Rob on my way out the door, feeling a little guilty that he'll be cooped up all day while I'm frolicking with sea turtles.

After a light breakfast on the veranda, I head for the boat dock. It seems like a simple enough walk until I wind up at the wrong place three times. By the time I finally arrive at the right dock, I find the boat left without me. I fight the overwhelming urge to be pissed and tell myself instead it's just the universe saving me from some unexpected aquatic disaster. Maybe fate just stepped in and ripped poor, unsuspecting me from the jaws of a hammerhead. I'll just grab a smutty novel and hit the beach instead. I'm sure the plethora of oiled-up cabana boys will be just as scenic as a bunch of old sea turtles.

After two hours on the beach, I'm lonely. I wish Rob could be here. I wonder if he'll drop by for lunch. I whip out my cell and dial, thinking he might be on a break. No answer, so I leave a message telling him how much I miss him. Then I try calling Brook, but again, no answer. Next I try Mom. Voicemail. What a waste to be sitting in paradise and have no one to share it with. Before I put my phone away, I decide to try one more number. A voice answers on the second ring.

"Hi, Will! How's the weather?" I chirp from my chaise lounge.

"Only a really mean person would call me from a sunny island when it's thirty-five degrees and raining here," Will says.

"I'm sorry. I won't rub it in then. What are you up to?"

"Just having my mid-day latte and going through a bunch of old pictures of me and my sis."

"Oh, how sweet. Are there any from back in your Weenie Will days?" I ask as I wipe my sunglasses on a towel.

"There is, as a matter of fact. Here's one of me, Wendy, and her best friend Ellen." He starts to chuckle.

"What's so funny? Your hair?" I ask with my own chuckle.

"Ha ha. No, I was remembering when Wendy and I went to church with Ellen one time when we were probably in junior high. We'd never been to a Catholic church before. Wendy noticed the people before us would all stop in the same spot behind the last row of pews, bow their head and make the sign of the cross. When she approached the same spot, she bowed her head and curtsied."

We both burst out laughing, and Will continues. "Ellen asked her later if she saw the Queen Mother instead of the Holy Mother when she entered." We laugh even harder. People around me are starting to stare as I continue to cackle. Then I realize that Will's laugh has changed to something else, something more guttural.

I recognize the sounds of sobbing.

"Will, what is it?" I ask.

"I just miss her," he says through a sniffle.

"Oh Will, of course you do." My eyes start to tear up.

"I just wish I had spent more time with her," he says, just as I hear a chime through my phone.

"Will, I'm sure Wendy always knew how you felt about her," I say.

"I know. It just hits me hard sometimes, like today. It's the anniversary of her death."

"Oh Will, I'm so sorry. Is there anything I can do for you?"

"You're doing it, by helping me raise money for her research foundation. I really appreciate all you do, Lil," he says with a smile in his voice. I can't help but smile back.

"You know what you need?" I say. "You need to pet a goat."

"Well, it'd have to be a wet goat today. I don't think it would have the same effect, but thanks for thinking of me from your sunny spot on the beach."

"You betcha," I fire back.

"I better let you go before the doc sends out a search party."

"He's at his conference," I respond while flipping over to sun my other side.

"All right then, stay out of trouble and remember to flip over every twenty minutes to cook evenly."

"Just did," I reply.

"You're such a punk," he counters.

I grin into the phone. "You too. See you next week."

We hang up on a high note, thankfully. I guess I forget sometimes that his life's work is based on his sister's death. That's got to be hard for him, I think as I stare at my phone. That's right, I forgot I had a message come through while I was talking to him. I flip it open and read: *Enough of this hide-and-seek, ready or not, here I come, Love D.*

I stare at the message for a few seconds. Who is D?

I scroll back up and see that it was actually a forwarded message. It was sent to Rob, from someone else. Someone who signed the message, *Love D.*

Oh no. It can't be. Not again. I jump up from my chair and throw on my shorts. I head up to the room stomping sand from my feet as I go. I know he's not there, but I need somewhere to pace while I think.

When I reach the room, I put the key in the slot and the door swings open to. . .Rob! Standing in the middle of the room in my lingerie! And his wide feet are stuffed into my two-tone brown mules!

Chapter 26

L ily!" he shouts. "I uh, I. . .I thought you were watching sea turtles." I am trying to blink away the image before me. It isn't working.

"You're stretching out my shoes," is all I can manage when a buff blond man bursts out of the bedroom wearing nothing but his Calvin Klein undies. First, I scream. Then he screams. Then we both shriek, "Who are you?"

"Darien," he says while smoothing his hair.

I look to Rob, who sheepishly steps out of my mules and pushes them in my direction with his foot.

"I don't understand," I say, the understatement of the year. "You're gay?"

"No, this isn't what it looks like," Rob begins, but Darien interrupts with a loud sigh and an eye roll.

"Robbie, please, I am not going through this again," he says, picking up a robe from the bed. "I had to play second fiddle to that wife of yours for the past eight years, and I'm through with this charade. I'm not kidding this time." His look says he means it, as he ties his robe and has a seat on the bed.

Rob starts to say something, but I put a hand up to silence him. The next minute, I'm flinging clothes in my suitcase, throwing each piece more forcefully than the last. I glance around the room to see if I missed anything, and notice the sun glistening off the pink feng shui heart sitting in the love area. I suddenly lunge toward it in a rage, grab it and throw it against the wall as hard as I can. But it doesn't break; it actually sticks in the plaster. "Damn it!" I shout in frustration

"Lily, please," Rob begs, but Darien cuts him off again.

"Let her go with some dignity, at least. She doesn't need to get tangled up with you and all your drama."

"Thank you, Darien," I say, zipping my pretty pink suitcase.

"Don't forget your shoes, sugar, they're fierce," he points toward them.

"That's okay, Darien. Rob's been eyeballing them from the day I met him. He can keep them." I lift my suitcase from the bed and wheel it to the door. "Think of them as a parting gift."

I sling the last sentence in Rob's direction as I slam the door behind me. Thankfully he doesn't come after me as I numbly tromp through the airport for what's become a familiar drill.

⚙   ⚙   ⚙

After my second island vacation obliteration in a year, all I want to do is crawl into my bed. But after struggling upstairs, dragging my pink wheelie bag behind me, I see that the apartment is wide open and men are scurrying in and out with tools and bundles. Inside, I see Brook on the phone in the middle of a mess that used to be our dining room.

"What on earth is going on?" I yell to her over the noise. She snaps her phone shut as she approaches, and gives me a hug.

"I've been trying to reach you, Lil, thank God you're back early." She ushers me past the mess and into the kitchen. "Why *are* you back so early?"

"Island travel is apparently the kiss of death for my relationships. I'll tell you about it later. What's going on here?"

"Oh God, where do I start?" She rubs her temples. "Well, first, while I was out in LA at Springsteen's record release party, our ceiling fell in. Seems the plumbing broke in the apartment above us and it leaked into ours."

I peek out of the kitchen and survey the area, but turn back at her next words.

"And the water damage extends all the way over to the corner. . .our love corner. Oh, and Ian's married."

"What?" I look around. "I've got to sit down."

Brook joins me at the kitchen table. "Yep, his Greek wife came back unexpectedly from her six-month visit home to Santorini. She wanted to surprise Ian by coming back to celebrate the Thanksgiving holidays with him. She stormed the party, creating quite a scene. Oh, and I was fired."

I'm shocked, and this surprises me: After the catastrophe I just came back from, I didn't think I could be.

"Oh, Brook, I am so sorry," I say. "You must've been so humiliated. Did Springsteen notice?"

"I don't know, but I heard his head of security say something to the effect of 'been there, done that' while Ian and I were being ushered out by our elbows." I cringe for her.

"What about Ian's wife?"

"Oh, she'd already made her exit after shot-putting a crystal punchbowl at Ian's head from across the room."

"What did Ian have to say about all of this?"

She shrugged. "There was nothing he could say, and I mean that literally. I whacked him in the jaw with a coffee mug."

I gasp. "You didn't!"

"I did, but he's not going to press charges. Fortunately it was a female cop who showed up, who'd just been dumped herself, *and* wasn't looking kindly on cheating men at the moment."

I giggle at the thought of Brook punching anyone. "Married huh? How did he hide all of his wife's stuff when you'd come over?"

"He didn't. I found out from some PR girl that he and his wife live in LA, and he only rented an apartment in New York after he met me on that trip to Cincinnati."

"Unbelievable." I shake my head in amazement.

"I know. The lengths a man will go to keep a secret," Brook says as a workman sticks his head into the kitchen.

"Hey, lady, you won't believe the size of the dead rat we found in your wall. Come look."

"What?" Brook screams as we both jump up and follow him into the living room. There it is, the size of a dachshund, lying on the crossbeam of our torn-out love corner.

"Did he drown in the plumbing leak?" Brook asks while she watches a guy wearing gloves pull the rat out and stuff it into a garbage bag.

"Nah, he's been there a while from the looks of him," the workman says, shining a flashlight up into the surrounding area.

Brook turns to look at me. "This could explain a lot."

"No kidding. I haven't even told you about that rat Rob and the unfortunate BlackBerry incident yet."

❂   ❂   ❂

Later that evening over room service at the Plaza, I fill Brook in on the debacle with Dr. Denial. Since we had to clear out for a few days, Brook and I decide to lay low through the holidays until our ceiling and more importantly our love corner are put back together. After what we've just been through, it's a treat to be able to unwind and relax. Except for GG, who's still fuming over being smuggled into the room in Brook's duffle bag. At least there's no worry of housekeeping finding her; the chances of any-one cleaning under a bed in a hotel are pretty much nil.

After seven nights of sporadic sleep, I finally give in and take a much needed anti-anxiety pill. Eleven solid hours later, I wake to the smell of coffee. Brook's already ordered room service, and is now sitting cross-legged in the spacious windowsill reading the paper.

"Hey there," I yawn from the giant fluffy bed. I notice GG has stuffed herself behind my pillow; only her tail is sticking out. "Your cat is definitely strange." I roll out of bed and toward the coffee pot sitting on the table.

"I ordered you pancakes. I hope they're still hot," Brook says from her perch.

"Why are you up and dressed already?" I remove the silver cover from the pancakes and take a seat at the table.

"Already? It's almost noon!" she says while she folds up the paper and hops down from the window. "And," she adds cheerfully, "I'm going to go beg for my old job back."

"But you hate that job," I point out while dipping my finger in the syrup for a little taste.

"I have faith it's only temporary. Once they get the ceiling back up in our career sector, I'm sure I'll have a better offer in no time."

"That's the spirit," I cheer her on as I shovel a big bite of pancake into my mouth.

"Not to mention the prospects that will be banging on our door now that the big rat has been removed."

I give her a thumbs-up since my mouth is too full to speak. I'm so glad she's taking all of this so well. I am not so optimistic right now. I just had my dreams for the future dashed again, and I'm not feeling so confident that a little rodent removal and new plaster can turn this thing around for me. It's not that I'm not open, Dear Universe, but I'm just tired of one-way, last-minute air travel.

After she leaves, I decide it's best to distract myself with work and start making calls to finalize arrangements for the big fundraiser. I'm so thankful that I have a million things to keep me busy this time. Not that I would take to my bed for a month of mourning over Dr. Rob. I didn't know him long enough for that.

But a breakup still hurts, no matter how long or how much you knew of each other.

I decide to drop in on Will at the hospital to see if he needs to get me up to speed on anything, but when I get to his office he's not there. So I spend the bulk of the day making final arrangements and returning phone calls, anything to keep my mind off Rob. I wonder where Will is. It's not like him to not come in by now. I decide to give him a call to make sure everything's all right. He answers on the second ring and immediately asks how my trip was.

"Oh, it was fine. I'll fill you in when you get here. Where are you?"

"Oh, we're in Connecticut. Maddie and I came up for the holiday, and then her mom fell and broke her ankle yesterday, so we're still here helping her out."

Wow, he's meeting the family already. "That's nice of you, how long will you be?"

"I'll be back tomorrow, but Maddie's staying through the week." After a few minutes of small talk, I hear Maddie giggling and prompting Will to get of the phone. "Well, tell Maddie I said hello, and I'll see you tomorrow."

I hang up and sit on the edge of his desk, fidgeting with his paper clips. I notice a picture of him and Maddie taped to the side of his lamp. It's really not fair for one woman to get so many stunning features. Will's holding a dog in the arm that's not clutching Maddie's waist. I wonder if that's the dog they got from the shelter. He never mentioned getting one. It seems like things are going awfully fast with those two: getting a dog, meeting her mother. Oh well, it's not my problem. I think I'll go back to the hotel and get a massage. Fortunately, Richard still hasn't cut off my credit cards yet.

After a deep-cleansing mud wrap to detoxify Dr. Rob from my pores, I head back to the hotel room to find Brook packing.

"I got my old job back," she says as I enter.

"Where are you going?" I collapse in a nearby chair. Ridding myself of Dr. Rob is exhausting.

"On assignment. *80's Today* is doing a piece called "Searching for Steve," where I track down Steve Perry in one of those where-are-they-now type shows."

"Steve Perry from Journey?" I ask with the enthusiasm of a fifteen-year-old girl.

"That's the one," she says, giving me a look that says calm down, goober. "Seems he's a bit of an enigma these days. No one's seen him in years. He won't do interviews, and there're all kinds of weird rumors floating around about him."

"Oh, he was so cool back in the day." I jump up and break into song. "*Don't stop believin',*" Brook gives me another look while I head-bob to the silent tempo in my head.

I dance over and shove my imaginary mic in her face. After an eye roll and a head shake she dives right in with me, "*Street light . . . people, living just to find em-o-tioooon!*"

We're both into it now, arms interlinked, dancing in a circle like we're about to swing our partner at a hoe-down.

We finish the chorus by both jumping up on the bed as our stage. As she hits the final note, she raises one arm up high above her head like Steve used to do. We both collapse on the bed, laughing hysterically.

"Dear God, we're insane," she says.

"Yeah, but we do kind of have an excuse, with our post-traumatic stress and all," I say as Brook jumps up and starts rifling through her backpack.

"What are you looking for?" I roll over to face her.

"You'll see. I just downloaded this today." She pulls out her iPod and pops it into her portable speaker. She motions for me to get up, and as soon as the familiar tune starts, we both run to the middle of the room and sing along, "*Shoulda been gone. . .*"

"Remember how *we* used to sing it?" she reminds me, and I

jump in without missing a beat. *"Cinnamon gum, knowing how it made you feel. . . Cinnamon gum, after all the curb appeal."* We fall into each other laughing, and wait for the song to advance to the part we loved the most.

"Oh Barry, now I know, you lying skank," an old reference to Barry, Brook's high school boyfriend who broke her heart in tenth grade. We sing it again for good measure until we're all laughed out, and fall back on the bed catching our breath.

"So what exactly is your assignment?"

"I have to investigate all the weird urban legends about him."

"Like what?" I cross the room and grab two waters from the mini bar.

"Silly stuff. Like, one rumor is that he joined a cult in California, something similar to the Branch Davidians."

"That can't be true." I hand her a bottle of water.

"And another one is that he's a caretaker at some animal rescue place, living in a little shack and going by a different name."

"That one could be true, I guess. Celebrities love animals."

"Oh, and then there's the classic: that he actually killed Sherrie, and keeps her dead body in his basement so he can sing to her forever." We both laugh hysterically.

"And they want you to seriously report on this? Who actually dreams this stuff up? Can't the man just retire to a beach house somewhere and live out his days swinging in a hammock humming old Journey tunes?"

"Apparently not, because they're sending me out on a flight tonight, with a cameraman, to document everything." She swigs the last of her water, and goes back to her packing.

"Tonight? Are you going to be back in time for the fundraiser?" I ask, thinking how I don't want to go to it alone after bragging to everyone about my awesome doctor boyfriend.

"I guess it depends on how fast I can track him down." She zips up the duffle bag and swings it over her shoulder. "You don't happen to have an article of his clothing and a bloodhound I could use, do you?"

"Hey, you're the best bloodhound I know when it comes to sniffing out rock stars. So I'll expect you back by Friday at the latest." I give her an encouraging slap on the back and walk with her to the door.

"Don't forget the Gray Ghost under the bed when you check out." She points with her chin toward the bed.

"After hearing us sing, GG probably clawed her way into the room below us."

I give her a hug as she turns to leave.

"I've got to drop by the apartment to pick up some stuff, then I'm off to the airport. So I'll see you when I get back," she says.

"This weekend!" I yell down the hall after her.

$\mathscr{C}$hapter 27

The next day I get a call at the hotel from Martin, the Sheetrock guy, saying he's been trying to reach me on my cell. He's almost finished with the apartment repairs and I need to bring him a check. I start to pack up everything including GG, when I remember to turn on my phone. There are at least a dozen missed calls, mostly from Rob.

I think until now I was just numb to what happened. I feel failure slap me in the face, hard, like an icy snowball. I'm so disappointed, but I'm also mad, mostly at myself. I didn't feel particularly unique in having a husband who cheated on me. But what did I do to attract a gay man who wants to wear my shoes? Why would the universe play with my heart like that? Maybe it was my red balloon. That second one, when I was in such a hurry. I must've put something weird on it, some inadvertent codeword that the universe saw and said, *You've got to be kidding me*. And then, *Oh well, we don't judge requests around here, we just fill 'em*.

I try to recall the exact words I wrote on that last balloon before I sent it to the universe. I pick up the pink heart Brook left on the bedside table and toss it in the air a few times, trying to remember. Oh who am I kidding? I can't blame anything on balloons or rats in the wall. This feng shui is a load of crap, just like my relationships. I chuck the heart toward the trashcan under the desk but miss. GG runs after it.

"Don't bother, GG, it doesn't work!" I crumple on the bed and

217

start crying, then sobbing. I start pounding the pillow and kicking my feet like a two-year-old who didn't get the shiny toy. GG pounces on the bed next to me, startling me upright. She looks terrified, or maybe pissed. I'm not sure what she's trying to say when she lets out a funny sounding *meeeeeooowwww*.

Then she does something completely out of character. . .she crawls into my lap and gives me a squinty-eyed look. I can't tell if she pities me or just thinks I'm pathetic. Knowing GG, probably the latter, and I don't disagree.

"Oh GG," I say stroking her fur, "I'll be fine. But you must agree that those were two really bad jokes from the universe. First Richard and Lee Ann, and now Rob! It has to be karma." She lets out another meow as she climbs up my chest and head-butts my chin. And I can't help it; I start to lose it again.

Between sobs, I sputter, "It is my karma, isn't it? How do I make it go away? I was so young when that whole Adam thing happened, how was I to know that it might be my only chance to have a child of my own? I didn't mean to blow it, I didn't mean for it to happen in the first place! Shouldn't my karma be clear by now?"

Tears mix with runny nose, so I hobble to the bathroom and grab a roll of toilet paper; it trails behind me while I continue to wail and pace. I'm letting it all out now. It feels good to purge my frustration. "What is it about me that acts as man repellant!?" I shout to no one. GG chases my toilet paper trail. Apparently she's tired of me as well. I roll off another length of toilet paper and blow my nose.

"Okay, snap out of it," I tell myself. I need a distraction. I grab the remote and start scrolling TV channels, when I come across a promo for *It's a Wonderful Life*. That was always my Aunt Pammy's favorite movie. She explained it to me for the first time when I was only three and made me watch it every year until I was an adult. Though I balked at watching it in later years, the message I kept getting was that every decision you make affects other people somehow. Maybe that's why I've always felt so responsible for my actions as an adult.

"Gee thanks, Aunt Pammy." My thoughts are interrupted by my cell phone chirping, probably Martin wondering where I am with his check. I drag myself up, grab the phone and check the ID. It's Rob again. I might as well get this over with. I click my phone open and answer.

"Hello, Rob," I say with a sigh. No response. Here we go again. Just as I'm about to hang up, I hear voices. It's Rob and someone else, maybe Darian. I know I should hang up since it was obviously another pocket-dial, but I press the phone tighter to my ear instead because there's a lot of muffling. I hear Darien's feminine voice shouting, "Rob what are you thinking? You just got out of that miserable marriage, and now you're starting this all over again. You're a liar to the world, Robert Crescioli. But the worst part of all of this is your lie to yourself. Rob, you are a *gay man*! Come out of that closet you're hiding in. Don't you want to live a life that feels right for once?"

I'm starting to feel a little nauseous, but I force myself to listen. I hear Rob's voice say, "You don't have children. I do. And if I come out, my son will be teased and tormented in his prestigious school. This is real life, Darien. How is my kid supposed to deal with a dad who's bisexual and likes to wear women's clothes? I want my son to have normal, happy childhood memories. I sure can't show up at his graduation with my *gay lover* by my side."

Until now Rob's voice has been unshakeable, firm and familiar. Now I hear it wavering as he says, "Look, Darien, I don't expect you to understand any of this. You grew up with ponies at your birthday parties and summers in the Hamptons. You're a trust-fund baby, you don't have to work. I've had to bust my ass for everything I own. My son is more important than anything. I can't let him down again. Children can explain divorced parents, it's perfectly acceptable. But in the real world, children can't explain 'my two dads.' I don't expect you to understand—"

"All I *understand*, Rob, is that you're lying to yourself! And then you bring *yet another* innocent woman into it!"

Rob's voice is shaking harder, and I think he's crying when he says, "I love Lily, and now I've ruined it with her—" There's a rustling sound before the connection goes dead. I look at the phone in my hand. Then I look up at GG, who is still sitting on my bed, tail switching, eyes lasered on me.

"Well, that was. . .interesting," I say to the cat. I really feel kind of bad for Rob. Although I'm mad that he deceived me, I realize it must be torture for him to feel so confused. My phone rings again, and just as I'm thinking I need to block Rob's number to avoid any further humiliation from his inadvertent dials, I see it is Martin. "I'm coming," I say to the chirping phone.

⊛ ⊛ ⊛

When my taxi pulls up in front of my building, I see another taxi waiting. I can see Rob is in the backseat. When he sees me, he leaps from the cab, throwing bills at the driver, who quickly speeds away. I struggle with the duffle bag containing GG, who's now turned into a Tasmanian devil.

"Lily, please can I just talk to you? I tried to call." I continue to struggle with GG, while trying to dig money from my purse. "Let me," he says while peeling off two tens and handing them to the driver. "Keep the change," he adds, then extracts GG's bag from my shoulder and grabs my suitcase from the backseat as well.

"Rob, you don't have to. . .you don't need to. . ." For once, I don't have a clue what to say.

"Can you just give me five minutes, Lil? Please?" He puts the bags down and takes my hand. His eyes on mine nearly derail me. Why is it that weepy men make me so damn weak? I can't think of anything else that ever gets to me like that. I think of how distraught he sounded on his accidental call to me earlier, and I figure I can at least hear what he has to say.

I tell him I need to drop my bag and GG off at the apartment, and then we can go for a walk. He volunteers to do it while I wait outside. I hand him my key and he's back in a flash, before I can even get an emergency call to Brook for advice. I smile awkwardly and shove my phone in my pocket. We walk for a while before coming to rest on a bench in the park nearby. I notice men hanging holiday lights on the trees. Wow, Christmas is almost here. Alone at Christmas. Good thing I'm skipping holidays this year. I take out a tissue and hand it to Rob, who's been doing most of the crying on our walk.

Between sniffles, he manages to squeak, "Lily, you are the perfect woman. I never meant to hurt you. You've been a wonderful friend to me and I know I let you down."

No kidding, I think but don't say out loud. Why belabor the obvious? He stares at the ground, then back to me, then back to the ground. "I've been having this, um, *thing* with Darien since med school."

"You don't need to explain this to me now—" I interject, feeling the need to spare myself the details.

"Please, hear me out." He wipes tears. "I don't want you to have to wonder about this. I want you to know that it has nothing to do with my attraction for you. You're the one I love. More than anything else, I *want* a normal life. With you. We can be so happy together, Lily. Please give me another chance—"

"Stop it!" I put my hand to his mouth. A tear falls down my finger. I have to be strong. "Please don't say anything else. You actually pocket-dialed me earlier, during your conversation with Darien, so I know everything you're going to say, and it doesn't matter."

"It does matter, just listen—"

I keep my eyes on his. "Rob, it's over. You don't really love me, you're. . .confused. I hope you figure it out and have a good life, but I can't be part of it." I take both his hands in mine and hold them to me. I feel a tear escape, but nothing more. The reality of his situation has completely put out the flame for me. I just feel sad for him now.

As he begs me to please give him another chance, I hear the words to the old eighties song "Cruel to be Kind" playing in my head.

I stand up, give him a kiss on the head, and *poof!* My fairy tale romance vanishes, just like that. I ignore his pleas as I walk away, glancing back only once with a look that says *I mean it.*

Chapter 28

Well, it's been a week. The big event is tomorrow night, and guess who's not back? I called Brook first thing this morning hoping to hear that she was making her way through the terminal to catch her flight home. But no. She's been trekking through a California desert for the past two days, looking for some hippie commune that prays to a white wolf or something. So far no sign of Steve Perry, though she said she wouldn't be surprised if she ran into her mother out there. Speaking of, she suggested I ask my own to come with me to the gala to save me from going alone. I suggested she put down the peyote pipe!

I pour another cup of coffee and wander into the living room. My eye is pulled immediately to the new red ceiling and burnt orange walls in the dining room. Mom's idea. I told her I was kind of over the whole feng shui phase, which only made her more determined to show me that it works. She sprung for her deco rator/feng shui guru Justin to once again re-ignite our career and love sectors after the workmen finished with the repairs. Only this time, she told him to kick it up a notch.

It was so funny watching Justin try to explain to Martin, the Sheetrock guy, how he needed to hang a crystal heart in the wall before he sealed it back up: a little feng shui insurance policy for us. Even though Martin hadn't a clue what he was talking about, he didn't want to face Justin's wrath if he didn't get it done. Later, I heard him telling his crew, "Don't forget to hang that damn heart or you'll mess up their *fengshooley*." I almost wet my pants laughing.

It took some getting used to, but now that I look at our new and improved love corner with the red sidewall and burgundy silk drapes, I like it. Not just the look, but the *feel*. And Justin got a cream suede loveseat that he angled in the corner and accented with a faux fur throw in shades of red. He placed Brook's red leather photo album, the one memorializing our trip to Italy, on a new side table beside a vase with two bamboo stalks. He also rearranged the bookcase to display things in pairs. He said it was good to send out "couples" energy as much as possible.

When I told him about the dead rat the workmen had found in the wall, he insisted on doing a clearing. I played along as we opened all the windows, even though it was freezing outside, and burned sandalwood incense in every room. Then he pulled out a tambourine and we clapped out the bad energy in the apartment. At one point I asked if we could switch.

"I'd like to play the tambourine," I said with the excitement of a child.

He informed me with an eye roll, "We're not the Captain and Tennille, missy. This is serious business. Do you want to get rid of the dead-rat-and-leaky-toilet energy or not?" As much as I hate to attribute it to Justin and his feng shui, it does seem to be working.

Okay, back to the gala. Should I really ask Mom to come with me? I polish off what's left of my coffee and decide, what the heck; I don't want to go alone, and she'd probably love a chance to get dressed up and get out.

When she hears my voice she says, "Darling, how are you, how did the apartment turn out?"

"It looks fabulous," I tell her, admiring the room from a different angle.

"I told you Justin was the best," she says with an audible exhale.

"I thought you quit smoking."

"I did, darling, I'm doing yoga."

"Oh. Then I won't keep you. I just wanted to see if you'd like to go to this charity event with me tomorrow night. I know it's short notice, but you could take the train in, it doesn't start until eight. Brook's out of town and in light of the whole Dr. Rob debacle, I don't have a date."

"Oh darling, I'm flattered you'd think of me before you resorted to asking the *doorman*, for the love of my ass."

I wince.

She laughs. "But what the heck, second string's better than not making the team at all. I'd love to come."

"Mom, don't be silly, you know we don't have a doorman. And since when do you make sports references?"

"I don't know. It's just something I heard somewhere. So can I bring a date?"

"Mom, I'm your date." I see GG slinking up the hall toward me. "Besides, who would you bring?"

"Oh I don't know. I thought maybe Walter would like to come."

I jump to my feet and start pacing, scaring GG back down the hall. I don't know why, but the thought of him still makes me nervous. "You're kidding, right?"

"Darling, you remember how you made me promise to be honest with you from now on?"

"Dear God! It's still going on?" I sit back down before I fall. Even though I know he's alive and well, he was just much easier for me to deal with when he was buried.

"Well, yes. We've gone to dinner a few times, and breakfast—"

"Mom, please, let me stop you there before I lose mine."

"What? Aren't I entitled to date if I want?"

"Of course you can." I just can't wrap my head around the fact that my mother is *dating my dead dad*! "But why can't you just have meaningless one-night-stands like a normal person?"

"Lily, I don't see what the problem is. It's okay for you to date a gay man, but I can't date the man that gave you life?"

Here we go. I let out a long sigh while she rants on and on about the injustice of me not wanting her to have any fun. "I mean really, if you only knew what your father, James, put me through! You should be grateful that someone can bring me any joy at all at this point." I finally interrupt.

"Mom, fine, bring him." I eye the wine rack and wonder which is more of a morning wine, the pinot or the cab. "But you better find him something to wear other than holey jeans and that *Easy Rider* leather jacket."

"We'll pick you up at 7:00, dear, and don't worry, it'll be fun."

Yeah. Fun. That's what she said that time she and Dad convinced Richard and me to go whitewater rafting with them. I broke my wrist in two places, if I remember correctly.

❂   ❂   ❂

The next evening I emerge from my room at 6:30 sharp wearing a floor-length red dress reminiscent of Julia Roberts in *Pretty Woman*. It's perfect for the Snowball Gala, though with the bare shoulders and low décolletage I'll need to wear a heavy coat. Somehow, I have managed to tend to all the eleventh-hour gala details, and still have time for a manicure, a professional blowout, and even squeezed in a stress-buster shoulder massage. It worked; I do feel good. I'm loose, limber, and not at all anxious about this evening. I speak this last part aloud to myself in the mirror while I sip my second glass of pinot. Or is it the third? Anyway, here I am ready for my date with my mother and ole Walt. What a pathetic loser I am.

Oh, there's the door buzzer. *Maybe I'm getting a little buzzed myself* I think, as I skip to the door to greet the parents. After Mom drags Walt through a tour of Justin's latest work, we all sit down for a glass of wine. Seeing them together so lovey-dovey is starting to drain the good mood right out of me. I don't know why, I thought I was past all my bad feelings towards Walt. I think the fact that Richard prefers trashy Lee Ann and Rob prefers a man has ripped the scab right off of ole Walt preferring his band over me! Rejection. I'm finding it doesn't go well with wine.

Ten minutes of strained conversation later, I suggest we head downstairs for a cab. I pour myself a glass for the road. Mom frowns and asks what I'll do with the glass.

"I'll just leave it in the cab like I always do," I tell her. "That's why Brook and I buy the cheap ones. They're disposable."

Walt laughs and says he does the same, but with Dixie cups. Charming.

❂   ❂   ❂

The ballroom has been transformed into a winter wonderland, complete with fake snow and twinkling lights that look like icicles. I guess if I weren't skipping the holidays this year, this setting would get me into the spirit. Walt says he half expects the old claymation Rudolph to come sidling up any minute with his nose aglow. Mom giggles like a schoolgirl and links her arm through his. He does clean up nicely, I have to give him that. Definitely a Kurt Russell look happening there. I notice other women checking him out while we weave through the crowd to our table up front.

The stage is set up for Bon Jovi's acoustic set later. Brook's going to be so bummed she missed him. In high school, I used to tease her about doodling Brook Bon Jovi in her notebooks.

I don't see Will at our table, but I see Maddie coming toward us from a side door. She's stunning in a brown strapless dress that hugs her curves like a Formula One race car speeding down the Monaco Grand Prix. Walt's eyes light up when she flashes her hundred-watt smile our way.

"You look gorgeous," she says as she gives me a warm hug.

"So do you," I reply, thinking *what an understatement.* "Maddie, this is my mother Lauraine and her. . .*date*, Walter." Mom extends her hand, as does Walt, only quite a bit more enthusiastically.

"And speaking of mothers, how's yours doing?" I ask while scanning the room for Will.

"Oh, she's doing well, thanks to Will. He set her up with a really good orthopedic surgeon that he found through someone at the hospital."

"Great. So where is Will anyway?" I ask, trying not to notice my mother's seductive hair stroking of Walt.

"Oh, he's backstage getting some last-minute details ironed out. Where's, uh, Robert, isn't it?"

"Yeah, he couldn't make it. I'm just going to run back and see if Will needs my help with anything." I grab a glass of champagne from a passing waiter and hightail it out of there before I must explain, one more time, my mortifying island retreat. I still haven't told Will yet. I dodged the subject all week at the office. When he got back from Connecticut, all he could talk about was how great Maddie is. When he needed a subject change, how kind and beautiful and perfect she is. Did I go on about Rob like that? I'm going to take out an apology ad in the paper tomorrow because it really is annoying. Especially when you happen to be newly single.

I edge around the heavy velvet drapes separating the stage from the ballroom and spot Will backstage talking to the hotel manager. I start in his direction, trying out my best model slink, and snagging my foot in the long stage drapes. I trip, but manage to somehow hang on and not actually hit the floor. Will looks over at the sound of my champagne flute crashing to the floor and gasps. He rushes over to help, as I hang to the drape like a lemur monkey, shaking my stiletto-ed foot trying to disentangle myself. He scoops me into his arms just as I'm about to lose my grip.

"I thought I might find you hanging around back here," he says between guffaws. "But I thought it would be to coordinate with the event planner." I don't know what I planned to say. I feel dizzy. His scent envelops me. I close in on his neck and take a couple more sniffs for good measure.

"Lily, you okay?" he asks with a curious look as he puts me down.

"I'm good, yeah. I just tripped on the curtains and. . ." I think I must've wobbled a bit just then because he reaches out a hand to steady me. I didn't realize it before, but I'm starting to feel a little woozy. I try to remember the last time I ate. I think it was a bagel early this morning.

"Maybe I should get Rob, he is a doctor after all," He starts to turn away, but I grab his arm.

"No, that's not necessary. He's not here." Another of those damnable curious looks, but I continue before he can ask anything. "I came with my mother and Walt, believe it or not."

He breaks into a laugh. "I can't wait to hear the story that goes along with that, but it'll have to wait. I've got some things to check on, so I'll see you back at our table."

I nod in agreement and feel my head spin a little.

"Hey did you see Maddie, isn't she gorgeous?" he adds before hurrying away.

"Funny, that's what she said about me," I say to myself after he's gone. I wander back out to the ballroom and grab another glass of champagne on my way back to the table. Mom and Walt are dancing; Maddie and another couple chat amiably at the table. I plop into a chair and raise my glass to them. Maddie leans over to tell me how amazing it is that my mother and Walt have reconnected after all these years. "You must be thrilled to discover that your birth father is still very much alive."

Does everyone go out for popcorn during this part in the movie when said father abandons his family to tour through Europe with his hippie band? Or is it like any other Hollywood tale, where you just ignore the blaring plot holes?

"Oh, and I'm so sorry about your neurosurgeon." She reaches over and pats my hand. "Guess you might want to avoid the islands and take your next vacation in the Swiss Alps," she adds with a chuckle. All I can muster is a fake smile before I throw back the rest of my champagne. So she can find the *sorrow* in my boyfriend turning out to be gay, but she thinks my dead father's *cute*. Yeah, she's perfect all right. I'll have to remember to tell Will.

Suddenly Walt appears to whisper in my ear, "How about a dance with the prettiest girl in the room?"

"Oh, I don't think Maddie would want to dance with me right now, but I'll ask her later," I retort as I grab another glass from a passing waiter.

"Come on, don't be like that. Dance with your old man." He extends his hand in front of my face.

"I'd be happy to, but he's not here," I say, turning away. Mom gives me a stern look from across the table. Ooh, like I'm scared. I give her an eye roll and don't budge from my chair. Apparently alcohol makes me fourteen again.

"For the love of my ass, Lily, would it kill you to dance with the man?" she shouts across the table, giving everyone a reason to look at me. I never realized it before, but maybe I'm a mean drunk. I'm feeling mighty defiant and resentful as I look around the table at all the shocked faces staring at me. But I don't want to create more of a scene, especially in front of Maddie, so I swivel out of my seat and offer my hand to Walt to lead the way.

"I thought we'd moved past the whole 'hating me' thing," he says once we're dancing.

"Me too. Strange how some feelings just keep showing up like a bad penny," I manage through clenched teeth and a fake smile.

"Look, I know I was a bastard in my youth. I'm certainly not qualified to be anyone's father. So why can't you just see the situation for what it was? You were way better off without me."

At least he's moving me gracefully to the music.

"Besides the fact that you're still talking, what really annoys me is that you just don't get it," I say. We do a twirl like nothing's wrong. "You're like those inmates on death row who think they can do whatever they want, and as long as they say they're sorry and repent for their sins in the end, all is forgiven and the Pearly Gates just swing wide open for them when they're done."

"That's a little harsh, don't you think, comparing me to death row inmates?" he says with a chuckle.

"No, I don't think it is." I'm spared from having to defend my position when he swings me around again. I'm proud of myself that I don't wobble even once. Finally, the song is over and I can return to the table, a dutiful daughter. I think all the spinning on the dance floor has escalated the effects of the alcohol. I feel myself lean into Walt more than once as we make our way through the crowd.

"You okay kiddo? Maybe you should eat something to sop up some of that alcohol you've been swigging."

"Thanks, but if I want parenting advice, I have my Dad on speed dial."

I push ahead of him and arrive back at our table to find Will seated next to Maddie. She leans over and kisses him on the neck as I sit down next to Mom. She pats my knee under the table and mouths *thank you* to me. I'll deal with her later on, ambushing me like that.

When Walt saunters up, Will immediately stands to shake hands and greet him. For the love of *my* ass, why all the fuss about Walt? You'd think he actually *is* a war hero—

Oh good, here comes another cater-waiter with a tray of champagne. I pluck a glass from the passing tray and see Mom's eyebrow rise. *Yes, that's right, Mother, I'm having another.* I say this with my glass while I clink hers before taking a hefty sip. My vision's starting to get a little fuzzy, or maybe Maddie's just growing fur on her face. I wish.

I decide maybe ole Walt is right, I should find something to eat. I don't see a buffet, so I'm on my way backstage again when I feel a hand on my shoulder. It's Will, who reaches ahead and parts the long stage drapes for me to pass through.

"No swinging from the curtains this time, sunshine," he says as I giggle and stumble into him.

"I'm just looking for some crackers," I say. He gives me an amused look. I reach up and pull him closer by his tie.

"Okay, someone's had a bit too much of the bubbly." He takes his tie from my hand and eases backward. "Let's go find you a breadstick or something." He turns me around and nudges me toward the kitchen, keeping one arm around my waist. I lean into him, taking in his scent, the feel of his arm around me. That's it. I immediately turn back to face him and blurt out, "You feel like Sweater Arms!"

"What?" he asks as he still prods me along backwards. I wish the room would stop spinning so I could make eye contact. What the hell—I throw my arms around his neck and kiss him. He kisses me back for a few seconds before gently pushing me away.

"No, don't stop." I lean back in, but he backs away and takes my arms from his neck.

"Lily, you're drunk," he says gently.

"It's not that. We both know this has been brewing for a while." I try to slip my arms around his waist, but he backs away again and smiles.

"This certainly isn't the response I got when I tried to kiss you. If I recall correctly, I got a head push."

I start to laugh, then notice Will's not. "I'm sorry. I was such an idiot not to see it." I wobble into him again. "But we're like Sarry and Hally." I can't suppress the giggle this time. "I mean Sally and Sarry." I burst out laughing, nearly falling, but manage to catch his sleeve on the way down.

"Okay, that's it," he says, picking me up. "We've got to get you home."

"Yes, take me home, Will," I breathe into his neck.

"You wait here. I'll be right back." He sits me in a chair by the back door and heads into the ballroom. I imagine him carrying me to my bedroom when we get back to my apartment. Maybe he'll even put on the sweater. I feel myself start to drift off with that image when I'm suddenly scooped from my chair. I snuggle into his neck to get another whiff of his amazing cologne, but it's not there. I smell Old Spice. Wait a minute. I lean back to focus on his face, and it's Walt. I immediately start to squirm.

"What are you doing?" I demand when Will suddenly appears at my side.

"He's taking you home," says Will as he wraps my coat around my shoulders.

"But I thought you were taking me home," I whine.

"I can't leave. Walt's going to take you." He nods to Walt, who still holds me in his arms.

"But I want *you*," I say as my head rolls over onto Walt's shoulder. For some reason, I can't seem to keep my eyes open.

"Okay, I've got her from here," Walt whispers as the cold night air suddenly hits me in the face.

I open my eyes when I realize I'm propped up against a wall and Walt is rummaging through my purse. He finally pulls out my keys and unlocks my apartment door. I stumble past him before he can pick me up again and make a beeline for the couch, flinging off my heels as I go. He appears a few minutes later with a blanket and covers me up. He sits on the edge of the coffee table beside me with a jar of peanut butter and a spoon and digs in.

"Okay kiddo, open up." He waves a spoonful in front of my face.

"What are you doing?" I push it away.

"Best thing in the world for preventing a hangover. Believe me, I know. It'll also stop the room from spinning." Well, *that* would be nice, I think as I prop myself up and reluctantly take in the spoon.

"Why doesn't he want me?" I mutter while I try to swallow the big glob of peanut butter.

"You kidding me? He's crazy about you," Walt says while holding another spoonful poised to feed me. "I've known it since I met him in the coffee shop."

"No, he's got Maddie now. I can't compete with that." I let him feed me the next one.

"Oh, she's a pretty package, that's for sure. But she's all wrapping, there's nothing inside."

"What makes you say that?" I ask while swallowing hard.

"She just strikes me as a gold digger." He clangs around in the jar before pushing another spoonful toward me. I push it away. "Come on, one more. Three's the magic number with the peanut butter remedy."

"But Will doesn't have any money," I say, forcing myself to take in the last spoonful.

"Hmm, then there must be some other angle she's working. I'll get you some water." He ambles toward the kitchen while I try to think of what Maddie could want. When he returns with a bottle of water, I have to admit I feel a little bit better. My stomach has stopped flipping and the room seems to have stabilized some.

"Can I ask you something, kiddo?" he says while he takes his seat back on the coffee table.

"I guess."

"Did this James fellow love you and take care of you like you were his own?"

"He did, and he still does," I say as I take a swig of water.

"And you never had to want for anything?" He leans forward, elbows to his knees. I shake my head no as he continues, "So you'd say you had a happy upbringing?"

"The best," I reply as he studies my face for a few seconds then sits back upright.

"Then I did right by you." He slaps his knees to stand and pushes my hair away from my face. "Yeah, I definitely did right by you, kiddo." He lets the back of his hand linger on my cheek. When he starts to move, I grab it. A tear gets loose and rolls down my face. For some reason, I can't let go. I squeeze my eyes shut trying to hold back the flood that I feel building.

"Oh honey, don't cry, unless you wanna see a grown man cry too," Walt says as he slides down on his knees in front of me.

"But that's just the thing," I say breaking down. "I do!" I sit up now and face him. "I want to know that it hurt you as much as it hurt me that you chose a different path!" My face crumples into a full-on cry as Walt immediately scoops me into his arms and holds me tight, clutching me to his chest. And we cry. No, make that sob. We both sob together, gently rocking back and forth.

I don't know how long we stayed that way, but next thing I know I'm being awakened by Walt shifting me out of his lap onto the couch and placing a pillow under my head. He leans down to kiss the top of my head, and then pulls a blanket up around my chin.

"Where are you going?" I groggily ask.

"I've got to get your mother," he says putting on his coat. "Try to drink the rest of that water." He points to the bottle he left on the coffee table for me.

"Walt," I say as he crosses the room for the door, "thanks."

"No, honey, thank *you*." He gives me a wink before closing the door behind him.

I lay there motionless, trying to process the events of the night in my head. Hmm, maybe ole Walt and I have turned a corner. Oh my god! I am startled upright with an image of me kissing Will! Oh god, I feel sick. I can't believe I finally acknowledged my feelings for him, only to be shot down like an unidentified plane. How's that for karma?

I sink back into the couch, my thoughts drifting back over the last year; Dr. Rob and Herbie the crying date and the adult summer-camp episode, Walt finding his way back to Mom and me. Before I can stop myself, I'm brazenly dialing.

"Hi, it's me," I say into the phone. "I think we probably need to talk about things. Can you meet me tomorrow?" Thankfully, he agrees immediately.

∞ *Chapter* 29 ∞

W hen I roll out of bed the next morning, I'm surprised my head isn't pounding. I guess ole Walt's peanut butter trick actually does work. I throw on a sweat-shirt and a pair of flannel pajama bottoms and make my way into the kitchen. A glance at the clock is also a surprise; it's after 11:00. Wow, no wonder I'm starving. After not eating yesterday, I think I'll make pancakes.

While I arrange the ingredients across the countertop, the mortification of throwing myself at Will comes crashing down on me. What's wrong with me anyway? Since when do I have a thing for Weenie Will? I seriously ponder this while I mix and pour and griddle.

I'd have to say it goes back to the day he met Maddie. I re-member something stirring inside me that felt a lot like jealousy when she stood up to her full supermodel height and cast her spell on poor Will. Didn't Walt say something last night about her having some ulterior motive for being with him? Maybe he didn't actually say that. Perhaps it's just a subconscious need I feel to protect Will. But protect him from what?

The smell of something burning shakes me back to the pres-ent. I immediately turn off the burner and move the pan to the back of the stove when I hear a persistent knock at the door. I'm always hesitant to answer those, because the person obviously got through the front door without being buzzed in. I creep to the door with my spatula and peek through the peephole. It looks like my soon-to-be-ex husband.

It is Richard. What on earth could *he* want? I unlock the door and fling it open.

"Richard—" Before the word is out of my mouth, he scoops me into a big hug. I notice he's carrying a bakery box tied with a bow. I hope he brought donuts since my pancakes didn't work out.

"What are you doing here?" I ask when he finally releases me.

"Why? Were we supposed to meet somewhere else?" He makes himself at home, removing his coat and throwing it over the back of the couch. "You look terrific, by the way," he adds while setting the bakery box down on the coffee table.

"What are you talking about?" I ask as I finally close the door. He looks genuinely confused when he crosses toward me and puts his arms around my waist. I push him back with my spatula.

"Lily, what's going on? You called me last night and said—"

And *then*. . .it all comes flooding back. "Oh my God," I cup my hand to my mouth, "I called you last night!"

"I know," he chuckles. "That's why I'm here. I took the earliest train possible."

I break into laughter I can't help. "I drunk-dialed you!" I collapse onto the couch, still laughing.

"You didn't sound drunk," he says, his smile starting to fade.

"Well, of course I was. What did I say?" I ask as he takes a seat on the opposite end of the couch.

"You said you owed me an apology and that we probably needed to talk."

"Well, there you go." I playfully slap his leg with the spatula. "I'd have to be drunk to say something like that, now wouldn't I?"

His smile is gone, and it seems like his entire body has deflated. He shakes his head. "Wow, I was just so excited to hear from you that I didn't question why."

He crosses his ankle on top of his knee and fidgets with the back of his hair. He does that when he's embarrassed. Looking at his sad puppy-dog face makes me want to lighten the mood.

"I'm sorry you came all the way up here for the babblings of a drunken woman. What's in the box? Wouldn't happen to be glazed jelly donuts, would it?" I reach for the box as he lurches first and snatches it away.

"No, it's, uh, it's not doughnuts." He holds the box tight to his chest like a child hoarding his favorite toy.

"So it's not doughnuts. Why so possessive over the mystery pastry?" I scoot over and try to get my hands on the box; he pulls it away again. Then I slide back. "Oh no, you didn't hide my old engagement ring in an éclair, did you?" That's how his cousin proposed to his wife. It required an emergency room trip.

"Of course not. You know I wouldn't resort to such a sophomoric stunt at this stage in life." He dismisses my idea with a slight chuckle and stands. "Besides, we're still married technically." Still clutching the box, he continues, "Guess I might as well clear out of here and let you get back to whatever you were doing."

He slips one arm into his coat while still holding the box, then shifts the box to the other arm to pull the opposite sleeve on. I give him a curious frown. As he starts for the door, he says, "So, things still good with the doctor guy?"

"No, actually the doctor-guy's history," I say as I jump up and grab the box out of his hands from behind. He tries to wrestle it away and we both go down on our knees, still pulling and twisting until I lose my ground and fall over right on top of the box. Something red and white oozes out onto the carpet and onto me. I wipe a thick glob from my sweatshirt and have a little taste. I look at Richard, who gives a nod of confirmation.

"Yes, it's red velvet cake." He reaches out to help me up as I break into a smile. "I had a speech too, about how I was ready to eat nothing but red velvet cake for the rest of my life." I start to laugh, and he pulls me up to face him.

"I mean it, Lil. I've learned my lesson. I was such a fool. I'm miserable without you."

My laughter subsides as he looks me in the eye. "I promise I will never, ever do anything to hurt you again if you'll just give me another chance." His eyes start to tear as he pulls me gently into his chest. "Please, Lily, please come back to me. I love you so much."

Now here is where I obviously had some kind of delayed alcohol poisoning reaction, because the next thing I know we're kissing urgently and pulling each other's clothes off as we make our way down the hall to my room. We collapse onto my bed with a thud, sending poor GG scurrying off my pillow and under the bed. We proceed to make love frantically for the next half hour before finally flopping onto our backs to catch our breath and stare at the ceiling. When he reaches over and takes my hand in his, I feel like I need to breathe into a paper bag. What on earth have I just done? As we lay there, neither one wanting to speak first, GG jumps up on the bed and starts to pace beside Richard, emitting a strange yowl.

"What's with the kitty?" he asks without moving. I roll over on my side and prop myself up on one elbow. I notice Sweater Arms' sleeve peeking out from under Richard.

"Oh, she really likes that sweater," I nudge him as I tug on it. He lifts himself up and lets me pull it free. I toss it into the chair beside the bed and GG lunges after it.

"Was that the doctor's?" he asks while he rolls over and flings an arm around me.

"No, it's just an old one I like to sleep in sometimes."

I let him hug me for a minute, waiting for some sort of electricity to justify what just happened. Although nothing sizzles or crackles, it does feel familiar and somewhat safe.

Maybe that's reality. Maybe that Sweater Arms feeling really is just a fairy tale, and maybe it's time to grow up. Yeah, Richard betrayed me, but I know he regrets it. I suddenly picture Mom giggling like a schoolgirl on the arm of the man who betrayed her so long ago. She does seem happy now.

I pull away a little so I can look Richard in the eye. "I'm not sure what this was, exactly, but I'm—"

He puts a finger to my lips, cutting me off. "No. Don't analyze it. Just enjoy it." He leans up and kisses me softly.

"But I—"

"No. No more talking. I'm going to leave now and let you think about everything, but you know we're good together, Lil." He rolls off the bed and starts picking up his clothes from the floor. I place a pillow over my head and let out a sigh. I hear my mother's voice saying, *People do change, dear, and he is a good provider.*

Richard startles me when he sits on the side of the bed a few minutes later. He pulls the pillow off my head and hands me a picture of a sixtyish-year-old woman sitting at a desk.

"Who's this?" I ask, sitting up.

"Janet, my legal assistant. I had Lee Ann transferred to another office when we got back from Barbados last year. She ended up leaving shortly after, to stalk the real father of her child. I heard she found him and they live in North Carolina."

Again I hear Mom's voice telling me how sweet it is that he's really making an effort to turn things around. I pull the sheet up around my shoulders.

"Richard, my blood sugar level has dropped to the floor, I'm dehydrated, and I have red velvet cake in my hair. Can I please get back to you on this?"

"Of course, princess. Want me to run out and get you something to eat before I head back to DC? Or I could stay here in New York for a while if you want."

"No, that's not necessary, on either count. Just give me a few days alone to think about everything, okay?"

He breaks into an enormous grin and looks as if he might jump up and yell "yippee." It *is* kind of cute having someone want you so badly.

He grabs my face and gives me an enthusiastic kiss, then stands to leave. "Fair enough then. I am the luckiest man on earth! I think I'll tap-dance my way to the train station." He looks like a seven-year–old about to get his first bike as he leaves. When I hear the door close behind him, I jump up to find my phone. First, I need to order a pizza. Second, I must call Brook right away.

✪ ✪ ✪

"Evacuate, evacuate, find the nearest exit and get the hell out of there!" Brook shouts through my cell upon hearing about Richard.

"But don't you think it's possible he could've changed?" I say while tearing into another slice of grilled veggie pizza.

"It's possible I might be able to retire on my 401(k) someday, but certainly not probable."

"What about the fact that Justin just did a clearing in here and repaired our love corner, and then Richard shows up out of nowhere?"

"It wasn't out of nowhere, you drunk-dialed him! And I thought you were renouncing feng shui anyway." I forgot about that. She continues, "Lily, listen to me, you're just feeling vulnerable after the whole Dr. Rob thing, and then Will—which by the way I can't believe. He's had a crush on you since the sixth grade."

"Maddie apparently cured him of that," I say as I discard my fourth piece of crust into the pizza box.

"You need to get on the next plane out to California," she says. "We got a lead on a Steve Perry sighting just north of San Diego.

Why don't I pick you up in LA, and you can drive down the coast with us to check it out?"

I have to chuckle, hearing the desperation in her voice. I know she's only trying to save me from myself, but really, it doesn't seem like such a bad idea at this point to head back to my safe little life with Richard in DC. I tried the dating scene, so I don't ever have to wonder *what if.* After a few more minutes of convincing from Brook, she finally gets me to admit that a little road trip does sound fun.

I agree to look up flights as soon as I get off the phone. No need, she tells me, she's already on the travel website and is just a click away from finalizing my itinerary. Gotta love her.

◈   ◈   ◈

I read magazines for most of the flight. I check my horoscope in every women's magazine, including *InStyle* of course, as well as the *New York Times* and *LA Times.* The consensus is that I'm about to embark on a journey of everlasting love. Okay, so Richard isn't Sweater Arms. It's about time I realize there isn't any such thing as Sweater Arms. It's just a silly childhood fantasy, and I might as well get on with living my life. Besides, I asked the universe to send me my true love on that last balloon launch with Justin, and nobody showed up looking for a long lost sweater, so I'd say it's time to wake up and smell the red velvet cake.

I remember that I have a meeting for a possible donor to Will's research foundation on Monday, so I reluctantly call him upon landing. Not to worry, he says; Maddie can actually fill in—insert my eye roll here—and he thankfully didn't mention a thing about my drunken escapade the night before. Before we hang up, he says, "I'd tell you to have a Merry Christmas, but I know you're skipping holidays this year, so have fun with Brook and I'll see you when you get back."

Just as I click my phone shut, Brook spots me waiting in baggage claim. She runs to me and hugs me like she hasn't seen me in years.

"You poor thing, reduced to sex with Dick again," she says while releasing me. I give her a playful shove and am telling her to shut up when a gorgeous man with a five o'clock shadow and electric blue eyes appears at her side.

"Oh, Lily this is Seth Fidlow the cameraman," she says.

Seth's smile practically blinds me as I reach out to shake his hand. I can't help but notice that the very sexy Seth is also wearing a sweater very similar to the one that GG's no doubt lying on at this very moment in my side chair back home.

$\mathscr{C}$hapter 30

So what's the deal with Seth?" I whisper to Brook as he collects my bags from the conveyer belt. "Any hanky-panky been going on in the desert?"

"Hanky-panky? What decade have you been transported back to?" she chides.

"Seriously, there's nothing going on?" I ask while I admire Seth's rear view as he walks ahead of us.

"Nah, he's got a girlfriend," she says as we reach the Jeep Cherokee rental parked at the curb. I wonder how serious his relationship is while he heaves my suitcase into the back. "Want to ride up front?" Brook asks while holding the passenger door open.

"No, you go ahead, I should probably lie down since I'm sure you're going to analyze me." I climb into the backseat, also thinking that I can get a better view of Seth from here.

"So, ladies, I was thinking we could grab some dinner at this little place I know in Long Beach before heading down the coast." Seth says this while reaching a sweatered arm to adjust the mirror. I'm wondering how I can maneuver those arms around me later to check for electricity when he continues, "I booked two rooms in Oceanside for the night. My contact in San Diego says she knows of a house in Carlsbad that's rumored to be owned by Mr. Perry."

"Sounds good to me," I say, giving Seth a smile in the mirror. "So what's the gig again –to just ambush this poor guy with cameras and a microphone?"

"I know, pathetic, huh?" Brook says from the front seat. "But that's how these sensationalized where-are-they-now shows work. If they can't get an interview legitimately, they're not above just sneaking up on 'em."

"Well, I know how Brook ended up with this job, but how about you, Seth?"

"Oh, I usually make wildlife documentaries, but since we found out my girlfriend's pregnant, I try to secure any camera-work that comes along."

Ding ding ding. Game over, thanks for playing. Watch your step as you exit. Even if he is Sweater Arms, that's not the kind of baggage I want to be dragging with us on our everlasting journey of love.

Thankfully, Brook spares me the humiliation of laying out my life story for Seth to dissect. He's a really great guy; too bad he has a pregnant girlfriend. While he drives he tells us marvelous stories of trekking giant sea turtles through the Galapagos and filming the birth of a zebra in the Serengeti, where he also met Melissa, the pregnant girlfriend whose twenty-seven photos he carries in his wallet. It's really sweet to see someone so much in love. I wonder if Richard has a bunch of pictures of me in his wallet. I think I'll insist on it when I get back.

We finally get to the hotel, and I'm beat. I'm not *at all* up for the lecture I know is coming from Brook. Thankfully when I come out of the bathroom from brushing my teeth, Brook is sound asleep. Yay, no lecture tonight, but I do want to talk through everything with her at some point. I know she doesn't like Richard, but she does like me, and I know she only wants me to be happy.

I awaken the next morning to the sound of Seth honking the Jeep's horn: right outside our thinly-walled, cheap motel room door. Apparently the budget isn't very high for field assignments at *80's Today*. Brook sends him off to fetch coffee and bagels and promises we'll be ready in twenty minutes.

"This job sucks!" she says while she ties her hair in a bun on top of her head and heads for the shower. "But I'm trying to go with the flow of the universe until our feng shui fix kicks in," she yells through the crack in the bathroom door.

"Oh, it will," I yell back. "Look at how you skyrocketed before the big ceiling leak, and wait 'til you see what Justin did. You'll be flying to Africa with Bono in no time, covering his humanitarian work."

"I know you're right, but the *wai-ai-aiting is the hardest part.*" We both break into the old Tom Petty song when she emerges in a towel. "Speaking of feng shui," she says as I enter the bathroom to take my turn in the shower, "I was thinking when we first tried it Will was the first guy to show up for you."

"So your point is?" I shout through the shower curtain.

"Maybe he *is* the one you're meant to be with. I mean, he is everything you've been asking for."

"Not quite," I call back. "Remember, I asked for a doctor."

"No, you asked for someone in the medical field," she says when I emerge to find her scrunching gel in her dry hair to create casual waves. Hmm, she's right.

"Well, it doesn't matter now, he's happy with Maddie." I pull a sweater over my head.

"I don't know. I think he'd be much happier with you if he really thought you were serious."

I head into the room, attacking my hair with my brush. "You're very cute to try to salvage my ego, but he's just not interested anymore. I only wish I realized I had feelings for him back when he tried to kiss me."

She nearly impales her eye with a mascara wand. "What? When? You never told me that."

"I didn't want to embarrass him, so I never told you. But it was the night we went to that dance club with all the twenty-somethings."

"Right after we did the feng shui!"

Seth interrupts with a rap on the door and a "Let's go!" I gather up my stuff while she helps Seth put our bags into the Jeep. Once situated in the backseat with my sesame bagel and a vanilla latte, I can't help but wonder if she's right. Maybe Will is my feng shui love, delivered right to my door, but I've been too blind to see it. Now that I am thinking about it, Will showed up right after I threw that heart into the fountain. Brook could be right about him not thinking I'm serious. I should try a subtler approach in the sober light of day and just tell him how I feel without mauling him.

I've fully convinced myself to try again with Will by the time we pull up alongside a lovely gray beach house. Seth announces this is the place and calls the number he somehow acquired on the ride here this morning. After several minutes of conversation with someone who claims to actually be Steve Perry, Seth clicks his phone shut and announces that we're in.

"Seriously, that was *him*?" Brook asks, skeptical.

"Apparently. He said to come on up, he'd be happy to speak with us." Seth jumps out and grabs his video camera from the back as a dark-haired guy appears on the front porch and waves us in. Brook and I reluctantly exit from the other side of the Jeep.

"You think that's really him?" I ask while I follow Seth and her up the sidewalk.

"We're gonna find out in about fifteen seconds," Brook says as she swipes her lips with a lip-gloss from her pocket.

As we get closer, the smiling man sure does look a lot like him. Minus the signature long locks and tuxedo tails, and plus a few years, I'd say it is him. When he finally speaks, there's no doubt. The voice is unmistakable.

"Come on in, you caught me by surprise, so don't white-glove the place," he says, and gestures us into the house. It's decked out in modern décor with a white baby grand piano perched right in the middle of a magnificent view of the ocean. The entire back wall is floor-to-ceiling glass. A Christmas tree twinkles from the corner.

"Do you play?" I ask, stopping to plink a few keys on my way past to take a seat on a curvy white couch.

"I dabble," he says, plopping down in an overstuffed gray suede chair. "So, what is it you'd like to know?"

Brook takes it from there with a bunch of questions to start her interview. She's really quite good at making people feel at ease. After about an hour of him bringing us up to date on what he's been up to for the last couple of decades, she tells him some of the crazy rumors circulating about him. He laughs, but seems genuinely interested in the whole animal-rescue thing. Listening, I hide my smirk. I told her celebrities love animals. Thankfully she doesn't mention the ridiculous thing about him killing Sherrie and keeping her decomposing corpse in his basement. I think that one might have prompted him to dial 911, ending with him signing his autograph on the appropriate forms to restrict us from coming within five hundred feet.

I don't know where people come up with that stuff, but Mr. Perry couldn't be nicer. He shows us his memorabilia room packed full of old Journey things, and Brook and I try on one of his old tuxedo-tail jackets. He even invites us down to his basement studio to listen to some new songs he's been working on. We follow him out to his garage and through a door that leads down a stairway that seems pitch-dark after the bright sunlight outside. When I mention this, he encourages us to go ahead, telling Seth to hit the light switch on the right at the bottom. As we descend, he starts humming "Oh Sherrie" behind us.

By the time we reach what I think is the bottom step, Seth is still fumbling along the walls for the light. Steve pushes past us and ventures into the room, saying "The light is probably burned out; I'll get the switch on the other side."

Brook and I shuffle into the room, feeling our way. Suddenly the lights come on. We're momentarily blinded, but when our vision returns we focus on what's in the middle of the room—a badly decomposed woman in a white jersey sundress, the kind from the eighties that had a drop waist and hung just below the knees. She's posed sitting at a table that's set with linen and china for two. Out of nowhere, Steve steps in wearing one of his tuxedo jackets and belts out, "*Shoulda been gone . . .*"

Brook and I let out ear-piercing screams and scramble up the stairs. We get to the top, to find the door's been locked. We rattle it frantically, Steve appears at the bottom of the stairs, still singing. We both let out another scream and start kicking the door, until we hear laughter from both Seth and Steve, now halfway up the stairs behind us.

"It's okay, it's okay, it was only a joke," Seth sputters. Brook and I lean heavily against each other to keep from tumbling down the stairs.

"I'm so sorry, it was my producer's idea to promote my new CD," Steve says, then, into a walkie-talkie he's pulled out of the tux's pocket, "Hey, unlock the door, they're really scared."

We hear a latch click behind us, the door flings open and we turn to find ourselves staring face to face with none other than Brook's lost love—*the Duff!*

"Leo?" Brook and I say in sync.

"Brook?" Leo says in surprise.

Chapter 31

I'll admit that was a pretty clever promotional gimmick," I say and then grin. "Even if I'll never again listen to 'Oh Sherrie' in the dark." Laughter erupts from everyone sitting in Steve's living room.

After we get over the shock of seeing Leo and the dead Sherrie prop, we learn that Leo had indeed staged the whole "Searching for Steve" episode to promote Steve's new CD, which Leo produced.

As for Brook and Leo, it's like old-home week. Leo said he had tried to contact her many times all those years ago when he first came to the States, but Brook's father wouldn't let him talk to her. After a while, he gave up and moved on. "And shortly thereafter," he adds, "I found a token stripper wife to go along with my spandex leopard pants. Both turned out to be unfortunate mistakes."

It seems he never forgot Brook and often wondered where she was. He couldn't believe his luck in running into her now that he's single again. "In fact," he says, "I was just talking to a friend the other day about the one that got away." He shoots Brook a look. Brook just beams, listening to him talk. I can't remember the last time I've seen her so happy.

After lunch, Leo insists she ride back to LA with him so they can catch up. I ride with Seth, and we pass the time talking about our relationships. Turns out Seth's girlfriend is a big believer in feng shui, so he's familiar with the concept and can't believe that

Brook actually put a picture of the Duff on her balloon in lieu of writing a description. When I tell him about the dead rat and our bad boyfriend phase, he shakes his head and says, "Powerful stuff." He agrees that I should give this Will character another go before I turn tail and retreat back to Richard. Huh? At this point, I haven't ruled out completely the notion of returning to DC and trying to work it out with Richard, but something about the way Seth says *retreat back* worms its way into my mind.

Back in LA, Leo invites us all to stay in his guest house and attend his Christmas Eve party. Seth declines. Understandable. He misses Melissa terribly and already promised her he'd be home the minute the project wrapped. Unfortunately for Brook, now that the assignment's over, she's needed back in New York for editing. So Leo gets every phone number, street address, and email address associated with her and promises to see her soon. His limo drops us off at the airport later that day, leaving Brook on the proverbial cloud nine. He kisses her goodbye, and her smile seems permanently plastered. . .even hours later when we land in New York. She dozes in the cab, slumped against the window, and the smile is still there.

By the time we get home, Leo's called three times to tell her he misses her and will be flying into New York on Christmas day. She's still on the phone with him as we walk in, and she squeals at the sight of our new love corner. She tells Leo she'll call him back as she throws herself on the loveseat and sinks into the cushions with a sigh.

"This looks amazing," she says. "No wonder Leo came careening back into my life."

I take a seat on the couch and throw my feet up on the coffee table. "Seth and I were talking on the drive back about how amazing it was that you tore that picture of Leo out of *People* and put it on your first balloon."

"I did, didn't I? I was just doing it as a joke, who knew it'd actually work?"

"So maybe I should try it right away." I lean forward and grab a magazine from the table sporting an image of George Clooney on the cover.

"Nah, I don't think it works it that way," she says. "It was just a fluke that I actually knew this celebrity and had actually been in love with him before."

"Yeah, guess you're right. Sorry, George, we could've had a nice run." I kiss his picture on the cover of the *World's Sexiest Man* issue.

"Why don't you call Will and see how the rest of the gala went?" she asks as she gets up and heads to the kitchen. "How much money did they raise anyway?"

"I don't even know. I bolted town before I even found out." I get up to follow her.

"Then I think you should go see him first thing in the morning to find out." She gives me a wink and hands me a bottle of water. "Well, I'm beat, it's almost midnight. I think I'll climb into bed and call Leo," she giggles.

"Oh my God, you've taken over my role as the love-struck teenager," I say while I peruse the refrigerator and cabinets for something to eat. "Goodnight, Gidget."

I realize I'm not hungry, just fidgety. I'll check my emails. I head into the living room, grab my laptop and make my way to my bedroom.

"My God, GG, have you even left the chair since I saw you last?" I say to the cat while she kneads the sweater affectionately. "You have serious wool issues to work through, kitty."

I plop down on my bed and flip the computer open. Once it boots up, I sign on and open my email. Wow, at least twenty from Richard. Most are sappy greeting cards telling me how much he loves me and misses me. He sure never did anything like that before. I could probably count on one hand the number of cards he ever gave me during our marriage.

Oh, not all of them are e-cards. One is a picture, a before-and-after renovation shot of our closet at the townhouse. He's had it remodeled into a beautiful spa-like bathroom with cherry wood cabinets, creamy-granite countertops, and a steam shower big enough for two. Well, that's definitely better use of the love space there. Did I ever tell him that? I don't think I did. I wonder why he all of a sudden changed the love corner of our brown-stone. Maybe it's a sign, or the universe working its magic. So why don't I feel like Brook right now? And why do I keep wondering about Will?

Okay, it's settled. I'll see Will tomorrow and just flat-out ask if there's any chance for us. I drift off to sleep, dreaming about Italy for some unknown reason.

❂   ❂   ❂

The next morning I'm up, showered, and out of the apartment before Brook ever stirs. She was probably up late talking to Leo. I'm really happy they found each other again. I remember how in love they were that summer so long ago and how devastated Brook was when he never came for her. I don't think anyone else has measured up to him for her.

Oh God, please don't let anything screw it up this time for her, I think while I stop at *our* Starbucks and get *our* favorite lattes. I throw in a couple of pumpkin muffins and head to the hospital. Walking along, I practice what I'm going to say, but nothing sounds right. More like a used car salesman trying to sell a Pinto to a guy who already has a perfectly good Ferrari. A good therapist would ask me why I think of myself as a Pinto. Really I don't. Just compared to Maddie, I guess. Really, I'd say I'm more of a Lexus GS: sporty, sexy, but still able to carry a family of four.

I enter the office and Will immediately stands and hurries around the desk to give me a hug. Okay, good sign. He tells me that I read his mind with the latte, "I was just about to run out and get one." The *good* sign is blinking now. We make small talk about my trip to California, Steve Perry, Brook meeting Leo again—which he thinks is amazing. I ask about the fundraiser. "Oh, it went well," he says, "It's a good start to funding the new research wing."

Then, the bombshell. He's so determined to break ground by spring that he's going to fund the rest himself.

"You? Do you have that kind of money?" I ask.

"I think so," he says. "As long as I stay on budget. I guess I never mentioned I was one of the dot-comers who sold out before the bust," he says this with a wink. Oh my God, I wonder if Walt was right about Maddie's intentions. But I don't say anything, not now. He'll think that *I'm* the gold-digger.

"Will, I was wondering. . ." I stumble for the words.

"Yeah?" he asks, I must've been quiet too long.

"Um, about you and me? I know the other night I was drunk when I kissed you, but it was real. It had been brewing for a while, but then I had Rob and you had Maddie, and. . ." I notice his eyes starting to water.

His phone rings. He swipes at his eyes and answers. I hear him say "Maddie." And I see his face crumple. Is it because he hates to have to tell me he doesn't feel the same?

He hangs up abruptly and says, "Lil, I think I know where you're going with this, and I do want to talk to you about it, but I've got to go right now. I'll call you later." He gives me a quick kiss on the cheek and runs out.

No need calling, I think. I polish off my latte and throw the cup in the trash. *I get the message loud and clear. Miss Maddie Supermodel calls and you go running.*

I take a cab home. I just don't feel like walking. I call Richard from the cab and tell him I might come down for Christmas Eve. I swear I heard the man do a cartwheel in response. It's just the ego lift I need. I tell him I'll take the train down later this afternoon. He'll meet me with bells on. How original!

When I get home, Brook does her best to talk me out of it. But my mind is made up. She says she'll call Will for me. I think that's looking a bit desperate. She follows me between my bedroom and bathroom while I pack, begging me to give it some more time with Will, to trust that our love corner fixes will bring me true love. I tell her, "Maybe it has, with Richard," I just need to go find out. She grabs the sweater from the chair and throws herself in front of my bedroom door, blocking my departure.

"So what if Will's not the one," she blurts. "Sweater Arms is still out there somewhere, you can't give up now!"

GG runs from under the bed and starts yowling and circling at her feet. I chuckle and take the sweater from her and toss it on the bed for GG. She immediately leaps onto it and kneads it affectionately.

"I think GG beat me to Sweater Arms," I say while I pet the cat's head. I look at Brook. "Now move, you lunatic. I'm just going for the holiday weekend to see how things go. I'll be back on Monday."

I give her a hug, and she reluctantly lets me pass. When I'm halfway down the hall, she throws herself on the floor and hangs on to my leg. She's starting to remind me of my mother. When I stop laughing, I tell her so, and she says it's for my own good.

Only when I'm in the cab on the way to the train station do I feel myself relax. It'll be nice to see the old brownstone. I always loved that place. I should call Mom and tell her I'm going. She'll be happy to know that I'm considering giving Richard another chance. Plus, she won't badger me about coming to Philly. As I envision the chaotic scene, I wonder if she invited Walt down. Walt. The image of him and his peanut butter makes me chuckle.

I glance at my watch before leaning over the seat and blurting out a detour.

The place is all but abandoned as I wheel my pink suitcase into the dimly lit bar. Dave Matthews' "Crash Into Me" plays from the speakers. There's a lone waitress behind the bar sipping coffee and paging through a magazine. I spot Walt sitting on the edge of the bare stage, strumming guitar along with the song. I sidle up silently, jumping in when the chorus kicks in again, "*Come crash into me, and I come into you. . .*" I belt out over Walt's shoulder, startling him. He breaks into a grin when he sees that it's me.

"Hey kiddo, what are you doing here?" He motions for me to sit next to him.

"Just heading out of town for the holiday and thought I'd stop by."

"What a great gift," he says as I hop onto the edge of the stage beside him. There's an awkward silence for a few seconds before I point to his guitar and say, "You're pretty good on that."

"Ah, well, I'm no Tim Reynolds," he says with a nod toward the speakers, "But I can follow the melody."

I smile. "Maybe you could accompany me at my next gig."

"I'd be honored," he says, folding his arms across his guitar, and I see that he means it. After a few more awkward seconds he breaks in with, "Your mother invited me down to Philly for the weekend." He eyes me for a reaction.

"I'm glad," I say, breaking into a smile, and he sees that I mean it. I pat his arm then jump down to leave. "Well, I've got a train to catch."

I maneuver my pink bag in the other direction, poised to pull, and then add in a confidential hushed tone, "I'm going to see Richard."

He raises an eyebrow in surprise as he jumps down from the stage, taking hold of my pink suitcase handle. "Richard, huh?" he asks through a squint.

"You don't think it's a good idea?" I ask as we start to walk toward the door. He immediately throws up a hand in surrender.

"Honey, that's one of those questions like, *Do these pants make me look fat?*" He says the last part in a girlish tone then continues, "No comment. You know what fits you." He shakes his head, still wheeling my bag along. I have to chuckle. After a few more steps, I remember something and stop.

"Walt, do you happen to have that picture with you, the one you showed me that first day, of the three of us in the hospital together?

His face registers shock for a second before reaching around to his back pocket and producing a wallet. He pulls the picture out and hands it over, his eyes slightly moist.

"I thought I'd make a copy and put it in my family sector," I say with a wink. He wipes a sleeve to his nose and turns away, then quickly turns back and pulls me into a hug. I hug him back, the picture pressed tight against his shoulder.

❀   ❀   ❀

When I reach the train station and the cabbie unloads my luggage, I have a feeling of déjà vu. I take a deep breath and head into the station. I get my ticket and wander down to my track. It's amazing how deserted the train station is when this should be one of the busiest days of the year. I can't believe tomorrow is Christmas Eve.

I'm reading an article on the back of the guy's newspaper in front of me, about some mayor and his mistress, when suddenly, two sweatered arms embrace me from behind. I feel almost light-headed, warm and tingly. Then a sneeze shakes me from my oddly euphoric state, and I turn to see—

Will. Wearing the sweater. *The Sweater Arms Sweater*!!

"Thanks for getting cat hair all over my sweater. You know, I'm allergic," he says.

I look at him, not sure if I'm even awake, but certain I can't form words.

He reaches under the sweater, pulls something from the front of his waistband and hands it to me. A snapshot. I look at it and then back up at him. "Our school trip to Italy?"

Nodding, he points to a geeky-looking guy in the far right corner of the photo. When I take a closer look, I see a boy wearing a sweater, *THIS sweater.* My God, it's Weenie Will!

"It was my grandfather's sweater, swallowed me whole back then. Fits quite nicely now though, don't you think?" He does a model's turn.

"But what? *How?*" I stammer.

"Lily, I wanted to tell you at my office that I felt the same, but then I got a call that Maddie was arrested. I didn't want to mention it until the police were sure, but apparently she was embezzling from the research fund." My mouth drops open.

"After I confirmed it, I ran to your place to tell you, but you were already gone. Brook was looking through an old photo album and ran across this." He points to the snapshot. "She was wild, babbling like a maniac, something about this picture in her red album and that it had been in the love corner all along. I didn't know what she was talking about until she told me the whole Sweater Arms story and showed me the sweater, which of course I recognized."

He smiles. "You know, I did actually put my arms around you on that flight. You were so afraid, and when you finally fell asleep, I couldn't help myself. Figured it would be my only chance to ever hold you. Then I wrapped my sweater around you and went back to my seat. I'd forgotten about the sweater until Brook, but I'll never forget how I felt holding you."

"So it really is yours?" I manage. "No wonder GG's so crazy

about this thing."

"I'm hoping you can grow just as fond of it."

And with that, he takes me in his arms, and there it is. . .that feeling, where I belong. When he kisses me, I swear the lights in the tunnel flicker on and off.

The End

READ ON FOR AN EXCERPT OF

Feng Shui Love Child

Two months later . . .

I slide in next to Will on the buttery leather couch and fasten my seatbelt. I've never been on a private jet, and I can't believe the opulence. Rich mahogany wood cabinetry, lush carpeting, big screen TV on the wall, a bedroom, two bathrooms complete with showers. I feel like I'm in a penthouse apartment, not an airplane. Brook and Leo show up as a flight attendant sets a tray of sushi on the coffee table and takes our drink orders.

"Leo, I still can't believe you have your own plane," I say.

"Oh I don't own it, I just lease time in it," Leo says sheepishly.

"How embarrassing for you, Leo. Don't worry, we won't tell anyone," Brook teases. He pulls her into his lap for a kiss.

The captain comes out and briefs us on weather and flying time, but doesn't reveal the destination. Leo and Will arranged everything as a Valentine's Day surprise for Brook and me. They've been exceptionally good about keeping the secret. The flight attendant even informs us that she won't be turning on the air show, since no hints are allowed.

"All I have to say is, if it's a tropical island, I'm getting off now," I proclaim. Will knows my history and assures me it's most definitely not. I kiss his cheek. The flight attendant announces we're ready to close up and get airborne, and she'll need our passports now so the Captain can complete the final paperwork.

I yell to the back of the plane, "Mom! Bring your passport and come get in a seat."

"I'm coming," she replies, hurrying toward us. "I was feng shui-ing the bedroom."

"That's some crazy control panel up there," Walt exclaims as he emerges from the cockpit and takes a seat on the opposite couch next to Mom. We all hand over our passports while Walt checks his pockets as the waiting flight attendant watches.

"What did you do with your passport, Walter?" Mom asks.

"It was right here on top of the newspaper," Walt says as he looks around the coffee table, "Oh, I bet I know where it is." He heads for the bathroom. We all chuckle after him.

Will squeezes my hand and leans into my neck. "Wanna know a secret?" he whispers.

"Absolutely," I whisper back.

"We're going to Italy." He clamps his hand over my mouth before I can squeal. Italy, where it all began, though I didn't know it until eighteen years later. When my eyes relax in a smile, he removes his hand and replaces it with a kiss.

"Tell me another secret," I whisper. "What'd you write on your balloon that day in the park?"

"Why do you want to know that?"

"I'm just curious if it described me."

"That's hard to say, since it was just one word." He snuggles into my shoulder.

"Well what was the word?" I ask, suddenly concerned if it described me at all.

He continues in detail. "Picture it like a movie, and watch as the camera zooms wide with a shot of the plane." He sweeps his hand out for effect. "It thunders down the runway, and then gradually disappears into the clouds above the New York skyline. Music plays, credits roll, as the shot zooms closer and closer to the city, until the final shot. . .a partially deflated red balloon caught on the roof of a building, a small card dangling from the string with only one word—" He pauses for effect, hands framed in the air around his imaginary scene. "Lily. . ." He lets the word hang there, and then turns to me. "That's all I wrote."

Before I can even ask if that's really true, Walt comes busting out of the bathroom with his passport held high in one hand. Dear god is that what I think it is in his other hand?

"Found it in the trash," he declares triumphantly, "along with this!" He tosses the little white test stick (with the very distinct plus sign) down on the coffee table in front of us. Mom, Brook, Leo, Will and I all lean forward to get a better look at the two bright pink intersecting lines.

"So . . ." Walt prods, "Who's knocked up?"

✿   ✿   ✿

For more visit:

www.FengShuiLove.com

About the Authors

Lisa Hyatt is a corporate flight attendant whose day job is flying various celebrities and world leaders around the globe on a private business jet. Lisa has also written several screenplays and even optioned one as a television show. She currently lives in the Outer Banks.

Joni Davis is a partner with the entertainment law firm of Schroder, Fidlow and Titley, PLC. Her diverse clients include authors, artists and musicians, who are often seen scurrying out of her office with a suspicious pink heart and instructions to clear their love corner. She lives in Richmond, Virginia with her daughter and two cats.

Both women are happily involved with their own Feng Shui Loves, and have multiple success stories transforming the love lives of friends, family and casual acquaintances. They have begun writing a non-fiction guide and often participate in singles events offering private consultations. They are also hard at work on the sequel, *Feng Shui Love Child.*